SMALL COMFORT

From his cell window, Phil could see the gallows going up in the middle of the street. Halfway through the morning on the day construction began, someone erected a sign.

> On These Gallows
> Will Be Hung
> Phil Goodnight
> For the Murder of
> Sheriff Bixby.

Phil was staring at the sign, trying to fight back the fear, when he heard the front door to the building open. Turning toward the door, he saw that it was Angus Pugh.

Bixby had not been replaced, so there was no sheriff, and no one who stayed in the building to watch him. Phil appreciated the fact that he didn't have someone watching him every minute, but it did have its drawbacks. He ate and drank only if someone happened to think to check on him. It was midafternoon, and he hadn't eaten all day.

"I brung you some grub," Pugh said. "A couple of biscuits and bacon."

"Thank you," Phil said. "I see that you are wasting no time in building the gallows."

"Yeah," Pugh replied. "The boys are doing a good job with it, don't you think? Hell, it looks as good as any gallows I've ever seen."

"So much for a fair trial," Phil said.

"Oh, you mean because we are already building the gallows?" Pugh asked, almost jovially. "That doesn't mean anything. I figured we would go ahead and build them. That way, if you're found guilty, why, we won't waste no time in hangin' you. We'll just bring you right out of the court and hang you that same day. I've seen lots of men waitin' for their appointment with the hangman. They all say the same thing. It's the waitin' that gets you . . ."

BOOK YOUR PLACE ON OUR WEBSITE AND MAKE THE READING CONNECTION!

We've created a customized website just for our very special readers, where you can get the inside scoop on everything that's going on with Zebra, Pinnacle and Kensington books.

When you come online, you'll have the exciting opportunity to:

- View covers of upcoming books
- Read sample chapters
- Learn about our future publishing schedule (listed by publication month *and author*)
- Find out when your favorite authors will be visiting a city near you
- Search for and order backlist books from our online catalog
- Check out author bios and background information
- Send e-mail to your favorite authors
- Meet the Kensington staff online
- Join us in weekly chats with authors, readers and other guests
- Get writing guidelines
- AND MUCH MORE!

**Visit our website at
http://www.kensingtonbooks.com**

THE LAWMEN

Robert Vaughan

PINNACLE BOOKS
Kensington Publishing Corp.
http://www.kensingtonbooks.com

PINNACLE BOOKS are published by

Kensington Publishing Corp.
850 Third Avenue
New York, NY 10022

All Kensington Titles, Imprints, and Distributed Lines are
available at special quantity discounts for bulk purchases for
sales promotions, premiums, fund-raising, and educational
or institutional use. Special book excerpts or customized
printings can also be created to fit specific needs. For details,
write or phone the office of the Kensington special sales
manager: Kensington Publishing Corp., 850 Third Avenue,
New York, NY 10022, attn: Special Sales Department, Phone:
1-800-221-2647.

First Pinnacle Books Printing: September 2003

10 9 8 7 6 5 4 3 2 1

Printed in the United States of America

Chapter One

Risco, Texas, 1867

A sharp-eyed citizen spotted the gunfighter Dingus Malloy the moment he rode into town. The albino wasn't hard to pick out; his hair was white, his skin was without color, and his eyes were pink.

Some claimed that his eyes weren't pink but were actually red, and they said you could see the burning fires of hell when he looked at you. For many, those eyes were the last thing they ever saw, because Dingus Malloy had killed more then twenty men in gunfights.

Dingus was wearing a long, tan duster and a flat-crowned black hat. The duster was pulled back and hooked over his pistol, enabling him to get to it quickly if need be. He rode in the exact middle of the street, denying anyone the opportunity to leap out from an alley. And as he rode into town his eyes swept the top-floor windows and rooflines of every building on both sides of the street, ever-watchful of potential assassins.

By the time he was a quarter of the way down the street, word began to spread that he was here, for by now, many recognized him. Dingus stopped in front of the Cow Palace, one of the wilder saloons of the town. It featured green whiskey, crooked card games, and bad women.

Dingus took off his duster, shook the dust from it, then, very meticulously, rolled it up and stuck it in his saddle roll. Then, slapping his hands against his shirt a few times, and raising a cloud of dust by so doing, he stepped up onto the wooden porch and pushed his way in through the bat-wing doors.

A piano player was grinding away in the back of the saloon, and two of the saloon girls were leaning on the piano, singing, not for the customers, but for themselves. There were nearly a dozen customers in the saloon; three of them were at the bar, the others, at tables. One of the men at the bar was a young cowboy, and he was talking with a pretty but rather garishly made-up young woman.

"Whiskey," Dingus said. His voice sounded like an engine letting off steam.

"Yes, sir, Mr. Malloy, whatever you say," the barkeep replied nervously. "Nothing is too good for Dingus Malloy. I hope you make the Cow Palace your home away from home, as they say." Instead of turning behind the bar, where dozens of bottles sat on a shelf, their number doubled by the mirror behind, the barkeep reached down under the bar.

"Here you go, sir, our finest whiskey," he said, showing Dingus a bottle of bonded.

The young cowboy standing at the end of the bar looked up in curiosity when he heard Dingus's name called.

"Are you Dingus Malloy?" he asked.

Dingus looked at him for a moment, an expression of complete disdain in his face. He raised the glass to his lips.

"I'm pleased to meet you, Mr. Malloy," the young cowboy said. "I've heard a lot about you."

Dingus poured himself a second glass. "I want your woman," he said, without looking back toward the young cowboy.

"I . . . I beg your pardon?" the cowboy replied, not sure he understood what Dingus had said.

"I'm going to take your woman upstairs with me," Dingus said.

Frightened, the woman put her hand on the young cowboy's shoulder. "Billy, no, I don't want to go with him," she said.

Billy smiled nervously. "Well, Mr. Malloy, you heard the woman," he said. "Seems she doesn't want to go with you."

Dingus snorted what might have been a laugh. "I didn't ask her if she wanted to go with me. I said she is going. Now, you aren't too dumb to understand the difference, are you, Missy?"

The young woman shook her head. "Oh, I understand all right," she answered. "But I'm not going with you."

"Why not?" Dingus asked.

"You frighten me. You . . . You look like a maggot."

The piano player stopped the music, and everyone in the saloon gasped at the bar girl's words.

The evil smile left Dingus's face. "Cowboy," he said. "Your woman just insulted me. What are you going to do about it?"

"What do you mean, my woman?" Billy asked. "Cindy's not my woman, she's not anybody's woman. I'm just standing here talking to her."

"I asked you what you're going to do about it?"

"What do you expect me to do about it?"

"I expect you to get down on your knees and tell me you're sorry, then beg me not to kill you."

"What? Are you crazy? I'm not going to do anything like that," Billy said.

"Do it, cowboy. Or go for your gun," Dingus said.

"I'm sorry," Cindy said. "Don't take it out on him, I'm the one that did it. I'm sorry."

"Mr. Malloy, I'm sure . . ." the barkeep started, but Dingus fixed him with a terrible glare and, flinching, the bartender moved back to the far end of the bar.

Dingus pointed to the girl. "I'll deal with you later," he said. "Now, I'm talking to this cowboy. What do you say, cowboy? Are you going to get down on your knees, tell me you're sorry, and beg for forgiveness?"

"Billy, do it," the girl pleaded. "Please do it! Can't you see that he's crazy? He'll kill you if you don't do it."

"Better listen to your woman . . . Billy," Dingus said, setting the name apart.

"No, by God, I'm not going to do it," Billy said. "Look, mister, I don't know if you are touched in the head or not. But I fought four long years of war and came back empty handed. Now I'll be damned if I'm going to get on my knees in front of the likes of you. Why the hell should I apologize to you because Cindy said you look like a maggot? You do look like a maggot, you pasty-faced son of a bitch."

"Billy, please!" Cindy said. Then to Dingus, "I'll go with you."

"You'll go with me, all right. After I deal with your boyfriend here."

"Mr. Malloy, please!" Cindy said.

"Better step aside, Cindy," Billy said resignedly.

The evil smile returned. "I'll tell you what I'll do," he said. "Just to make it fair, I'm going to let you draw first."

Not only the piano player's music, but all conversation in the saloon stopped. The loudest sound to be heard was the tick-tock of the grandfather clock that stood against the back wall.

From somewhere outside, someone laughed, the high-pitched trill of laughter incongruous with the events playing out inside. A heavy wagon rolled down the street in front of the saloon, the driver calling and whistling to his team. It was as if there were two different worlds, the reality of outside, and the bizarre world in here.

"I'm going to count to three, cowboy," Dingus said. "You can draw anytime you want, but when I get to three, you had better draw because I'm going to. One," he started.

One of the customers glanced up at the clock, making a mental note of the time, 2:38 in the afternoon.

"Two."

"I'll be waiting for you in hell!" Billy shouted. He made a grab for his gun, but it was only halfway out of his holster when Dingus's gun boomed, filling the room with its fire and thunder. A heavy discharge of smoke rolled up, forming an acrid, blue-white cloud over the scene.

Billy let the gun fall back into his holster, then looked down at the hole his chest, almost in surprise. He put his hand over the wound, fell back against the bar, then slid down to the sitting position. He pulled his hand away and looked down into his cupped palm. It was filled with blood.

"Billy!" Cindy shouted.

Billy looked up at Dingus, his eyes questioning

how a day, so innocently started, could end like this. Then his eyes glazed over as life left his body.

"Upstairs," Dingus said to Cindy.

"What?" Cindy sobbed. "No, are you crazy? You think I would go upstairs with you now, after this? After you murdered . . ."

Dingus held up his finger and wagged it back and forth. "I didn't murder him," he said. "If you recall, he drew first."

"After you forced him into it," Cindy said.

"None of this would have happened if you had gone upstairs with me when I asked. Now I'm going to ask again." Dingus was still holding the pistol in his hand, a tiny wisp of smoke still oozing from the end of the barrel. He raised the pistol, pointed it toward the bartender, then pulled the hammer back. It made a deadly sounding double click as it engaged the sear and rotated the cylinder, putting a fresh load under the firing pin. "Because if you don't, I'm going to kill this man, too."

"Mr. Malloy, no, what are you doing?" the bartender asked in sudden fear.

"Tell her to go upstairs with me," Dingus said.

"Cindy, for God's sake, go with him!" the bartender pleaded.

"All right, all right, I'll go," Cindy said, tears streaming down her face.

Sheriff John Carmack was pouring himself a cup of coffee when he heard the shot. As he stepped out of his office, he saw Malcolm Peabody hurrying up the boardwalk toward him.

"What happened, Malcolm?"

"Dingus Malloy just shot Billy Cole," the editor and publisher of the *Risco Avenger* said.

"Where?"

"At the Cow Palace," Malcolm said.

John left the boardwalk and crossed Franklin Street, walking briskly toward the saloon. "How is Billy?"

"Dead," Malcolm said.

"Dingus still there?" John pulled his pistol and checked his loads.

"As far as I know, he is."

When John pushed his way into the saloon, he saw two men leaning over Billy. Billy was sitting up, leaning against the bar. Both hands were down by his side, and one of his hands was bloody, as was the front of his shirt. His eyes were open and glazed, and his mouth was half open.

"He's upstairs, Sheriff," the bartender said, glancing toward the head of the stairs.

From upstairs, John could hear the muffled sound of a woman's voice.

"No," she said. "Please no."

"What room?"

"Cindy's room is number three, Sheriff," one of the other girls said. "Second door on the right."

Nodding, John went up the stairs, taking them two at a time. When he reached the room he tried the door, but it was locked. He banged on the door.

"Dingus, this is Sheriff Carmack. Come out of there!" he called.

Something told John to step to one side, and it was lucky for him he did so, because three gunshots rang out and three bullets, heart high, blasted through the door.

John got an idea.

"Uhn!" he shouted, then he kicked the wall on the opposite side of the room. He waited and, as he knew it would, the door opened. Dingus stepped out into the hallway, the smoking gun still in his hand.

"Drop the gun, Dingus," John said.

Dingus swung his gun toward John and fired. The bullet whizzed by John's ear, so close that he could feel the concussion of its passing. John fired back, hitting Dingus in the chest. The splash of red was a vivid contrast to the white of his skin. Dingus backpedaled a few steps, raised his gun to fire again but, instead, tumbled over the banister. He fell, crashing to the floor below.

John, with his gun still drawn, ran down the stairs, keeping his eyes on Dingus's prostrate body. Hurrying to him, he hooked his boot under Dingus, then flipped him over.

Dingus was dead.

"John," the newspaper publisher said. "I don't care if you are on duty. I'm going to buy you a drink."

The others in the saloon cheered and applauded.

"I saw the way you ran up those stairs," Malcolm said. "You should be more careful about such things. You don't need to be leaving Sue a widow and Clemmie without a father."

"Yeah," John said as he tossed down his drink. "I don't mind telling you that thought did cross my mind."

Chapter Two

Four Years Later

Risco, Texas, was on the spur of the Chisholm Trail, and cattlemen who were driving their steers to market often halted their herds nearby, using the town to buy supplies and to give the cowboys a break from the trail. As a result, Risco had many saloons and gaming houses, attracting not only the cowhands, but gamblers, drifters, and soiled doves. Prostitution was legalized, and a red-light district called the Reservation was established just on the other side of the tracks of the Risco and Northwestern Railroad.

Frequent gunplay among the cowboys had earned the town the sobriquet of Six-Shooter Junction, and it took courage and skill to police not only the town, but the county.

Earlier in the afternoon, Porter Robison had halted a herd of steers just outside of town. Robison was trail boss for the Bar-W ranch, and had been on the drive for two weeks. It had been a difficult drive so far, with weather, accidents, and other impediments to their progress causing them to average less than half the distance of a normal drive.

Robison, who had been a Sergeant Major for Colonel Ralph Wilson, came back from the war to work for the owner of the Bar-W. Robison walked over to the chuck wagon where Tucker Andrews was rolling out biscuits for the evening meal.

"Mind if I pour myself a cup of coffee?" Robison asked.

Tucker chuckled. "You're the trail boss, Mr. Robison. I reckon you can do just about anything you want."

Robison chuckled and shook his head. "Oh, no. I learned a long time ago that around the chuck wagon, the cook is king."

"I knew there was something about you I liked," Tucker said. "Never have been able to figure out just what it was before now."

Robison laughed again as he poured himself a cup of coffee.

"How many will there be to supper, do you think?" Tucker asked.

"Prob'ly no more'n five or six," Robison answered. "I let all the rest of 'em go into town to blow off a little steam."

"Better hope that's all they blow off," Tucker said. "'Specially the Kincaid twins. Seems like this drive has been snakebit from the get-go and whatever trouble there's been, those boys have been right in the middle of it."

"You got that right," Robison said as he took a drink. "For two cents I'd pay both of 'em off right now and send 'em back."

"What in Sam Hill put it in Colonel Wilson's

mind to hire 'em on for this trip, anyway?" Tucker asked.

"Colonel Wilson owed Major Kincaid a favor."

"Must've been a big favor."

"I reckon it was big enough. Kincaid saved the Colonel's life during the war."

"Yeah, now that you mention it, I do remember hearin' something about that. At Saylor Creek, wasn't it?"

"Yes."

"Well, Major Kincaid is a fine gentleman. The question is, how'd he turn out two no-accounts like Travis and Troy?"

"Damned if I know," Robison answered. "Unless someone else done a little plantin' in his garden," he added with a laugh.

Tucker laughed with him.

At that moment Travis and Troy Kincaid walked up. Nineteen years old, the twins looked so much alike that it was almost impossible to tell them apart. But it wasn't just their looks that made them alike—they shared the same arrogance and the same irritable disposition.

"How 'bout somethin' to eat, ole man?" Travis asked.

"You goin' to be here for supper?" Tucker replied. "I thought you two would be goin' into town."

"We are," Troy said. "But we figured we'd take our supper now, give us a head start on town."

Tucker shook his head. "If you are going to take supper here, you'll take it when I serve it, with the rest of the hands."

"You got some of them biscuits rolled out already, wouldn't be no trouble for you to put a few into bakin' now."

"You heard the cook," Robison said. "If you are going to take supper, you'll take it with everyone else."

"Come on, Troy," Travis said. "Like as not anything we can get in town will be better than the swill this belly robber serves, anyway."

"Yeah, I know," Travis replied. "I just didn't want to waste drinkin' money on food."

Grumbling, the two walked over to the remuda, cut out their horses, and began saddling them.

"Mr. Robison, I been trailin' a long time, startin' back before the war," Tucker said. He pointed to the twins. "And I've seen cowboys like them before. You mark my words, they're goin' to cause some serious trouble some time durin' this drive."

Porter took the last swallow of his coffee, then tossed away the dregs. "I wish I could disagree with you," he said.

Sheriff Charley Dawson was sitting at his desk, and looked up when his son, Greg, came into the office.

"Did you pass the test?" Charley asked.

"With flying colors," Greg answered, proudly. Greg was a student at West Texas Normal, located in Risco.

Charley smiled. "I knew you would, son. I never had any doubt," he said.

"Ha!" Greg said as he walked over to the little pot-bellied stove to pour himself a cup of coffee from the blued pot. "You seemed awfully worried about it yesterday."

"Because you weren't worrying about it," Charley said.

"I don't have to worry. You worry enough for both of us."

"It's just that I want you to have a good education," Charley said. "I want you to be able to make something of yourself, rather than wind up like me, sheriffing sometimes, hiring out as a security guard other times."

Greg laughed. "It seems to work well for you and Mr. Carmack. When John Carmack is sheriff, you're chief of security for the Risco Manufacturing Company. When you're sheriff, Mr. Carmack is chief of security. You two just keep changing jobs."

"I can't help it if the county is so dumb they keep voting him into office."

"Maybe they just can't make up their mind between two good men. Every other election they seem to vote you in."

"Two good men?"

"Pop, Mr. Carmack is a good man. I've heard you say that yourself."

"He's a pompous ass," Charley grumbled.

"He sure has a pretty daughter."

Charley leaned back in his chair and looked at his son. "You're not sniffing around her, are you?"

"Sniffing around her?"

"You know what I'm talking about."

"Well, I'm taking her to the cotillion, if that's what you're talking about," Greg replied.

"Son, during the war I commanded troops younger than you are now, so I expect you're a man, full grown, and can make your own decisions. But I'd hope you'd have more respect for me than to get mixed up with the Carmack girl."

"She's not the Carmack girl. She has a name," Greg said. "It's Clementine."

"I know Clemmie has a name," Charley said. "And to be honest, I can't fault her for being born to John Carmack. I know she's a pretty thing—"

"Prettiest girl in Tywappity County," Greg interrupted.

"And as far as I know, she's a good girl," Charley continued. "But there are other things to consider."

"Like the fact that her father is John Carmack?"

"Yes," Charley said.

"Don't you think her father is telling her the same thing about me?"

"Well, if he is, that's one of the few things John Carmack has done in his life that I agree with," Charley said.

The Bar-W herd was not the only trail drive camped just outside of town. The Double-D was there as well. In addition, there was a company of riders coming back through Risco after having delivered their herd to Ft. Worth. As a result, the area known as the Reservation was very busy.

Madam Lillian's House of Pleasure was the largest and most elaborate of all the houses. As could be expected, it was also the fullest.

Madam Lillian prided herself on providing not only girls of particular beauty and charm, but also of culture. She boasted that every one of her girls came from fine old Southern families, but were forced into the business because their fathers, all of whom had been colonels or generals during the war, had returned to plantations that were destitute, driven to ruin by the savagery of the Yankees and the cruelty of war.

In fact, Madam Lillian was the only one with such a background. Lillian Culpepper's father, a

brigadier general in the Fifth Georgia, was acci-
dentally killed by one of his own men while in-
specting the picket-line. After the war, taxes and
the loss of the labor force resulted in the banks
foreclosing on Pine Hill Plantation. Widowed and
forced out of her home, Lillian's mother died of a
broken heart.

Eighteen-year-old Lillian Culpepper had no recourse but to fall back on her beauty and sexuality,
but she couldn't bring herself to enter such an oc-
cupation in her own home state, so she went West,
protected on her journey by the only former slave
who had stayed loyal to her, six-foot, six-inch Monroe
Pratt.

Settling in Risco, Lillian opened Madam Lillian's
House of Pleasure. She selected only the most attractive and best-mannered girls. Most of them
came from sharecropping or shopkeeping families, drifting into the profession as a means of bet-
tering their lot. Lillian trained them before she
put them on the line.

As a result of Madam Lillian's tutelage, the girls
were valued for more than just their sexual attrib-
utes, and could charge nearly twice as much as any
of the soiled doves in the other houses. In addition, Madam Lillian always provided a free spread
of food and drinks. Her house also had a well-
appointed parlor where the cowboys could relax
for a few minutes of what Madam Lillian called
genteel conversation.

At the moment, Travis and Troy were in the parlor, sitting on the sofa with one of the girls. As a
joke, Travis had grabbed one of her breasts, while
at the same time, Troy grabbed the other.

"Don't!" the girl said, slapping their hands away.

"What do you mean, don't?" Travis said. "You're

here, trying to sell your wares, aren't you? Do you expect a man to buy without knowing what he is buying?

Something about the demeanor of the twins had alerted Lillian from the moment they came into the establishment, and when they grabbed the girl, she was there.

"What I expect," Lillian said. "No, what I demand, is that you behave as gentlemen when you are in our home."

"Your home?" Troy said. He laughed out loud. "This is a whorehouse, and all these women are whores. Where do you get off telling us we have to be gentlemen around whores?"

"I'm afraid I'm going to have to ask you to leave now," Lillian said.

"Leave?" Travis said. He shook his head. "Woman, we got two weeks of trail dust on us. We ain't leavin' 'til we decide to leave."

"Monroe, would you please escort these two . . . gentlemen . . . outside?" Lillian asked.

"Yes, ma'am," Monroe said. Monroe who had been with Lillian since she was born, was a powerful man, with a barrel chest and strong arms. He walked over to Travis and Troy. "You heard Miz Lillian," he said. "She wants you to go, so I 'specs you better do that."

"The hell I will," Travis said. "Ain't no nigger bastard goin' to tell me when to leave."

Monroe reached down to pinch the nerve between their neck and shoulder, doing it to each of them. The result was a numbing pain, so paralyzing that neither one of them could move their arms to pull out their pistols.

Both of them cried out.

"This way, gentlemen," Monroe said, walking them toward the front door.

Still cringing under Monroe's powerful gasp, Travis and Troy had no choice but to go with him. One of the other visitors to the establishment opened the front door and, to the laughter of all, Monroe pushed both out onto the front porch.

"I don't expect Miss Lillian will want to see you two anytime soon," he said, brushing his hands together as if he had just taken out a load of trash.

Monroe turned to walk back to his piano and, as he did so, he was applauded by the others. He acknowledged their applause with a broad grin.

Suddenly two shots rang out, and the smile left Monroe's face, to be replaced by an expression of pain and surprise. He turned toward the door.

Travis and Troy were standing there, each of them holding a smoking gun.

"We'll teach you to put your hands on us, you black son of a bitch!" Troy shouted.

Each of them fired a second time and Monroe pitched back.

Amazingly, Travis and Troy holstered their pistols, then came back into the room, grinning broadly.

"All right, we've got that out of the way," Travis said. He looked over toward the girl that he and Troy had been sitting with. "I'm going to take that one," he said. "You'd best get your own."

"Are you crazy?" Lillian said, horrorstruck by what they had all just witnessed. "You just murdered Monroe."

"Well, he was a nigger," Travis said. "I don't imagine anyone's goin' to cry any tears over him."

"That's where you are wrong. Monroe was a good

man. A much better man than either of you," Lillian said.

Travis laughed, then turned to his brother. "You got your girl picked out yet?"

"I'm still lookin'," Troy answered.

At that moment, Sheriff Charley Dawson stepped through the front door.

"I heard shooting, Miss Lillian," he said. "Anything . . ." That was as far as he got before he saw Monroe lying dead on the floor. "What happened here?" he asked, his voice tight.

"These two galoots shot 'im," one of the other men said. He pointed to Travis and Troy.

"Is that right, Miss Lillian?" Charley asked.

By now, Lillian was crying, and she wiped her eyes and nodded. "They never gave poor Monroe a chance. They shot him in the back."

"In the back?" Charley asked, looking at Monroe, who was lying face-up.

"That's right, Sheriff," one of the other cowboys said. "They shot him in the back, then when he turned around, they shot again in the front."

Charley looked at Travis and Troy. "Better give me your guns, boys," he said. "I'm going to have take you in."

"For shootin' a nigger? Come on, you have to be kiddin'," Travis said.

"Unbuckle your gunbelts," Charley said.

In nonverbal communication that could only be shared between twins, Travis and Troy went for their guns at the same time.

"Look out, Sheriff!" someone shouted, and everyone in the house dived for cover.

Charley didn't need the warning. He had perceived the danger the moment it started, and his reaction was as quick as thought. By the time Travis and Troy cleared their holsters, their grin of triumph changed to an expression of shock as they realized Charley already had his gun in his hand. He fired twice, the shots coming so close together that it sounded almost as if one, sustained roar. Both bullets found their marks, and both bullets were deadly.

"Anybody know them?" Charley asked, gun still in hand, as he stood there, looking down at the two bodies.

"Yes, sir, we know 'em," one of the cowboys said. "They're twins, Travis and Troy Kincaid. But don't none of us ever know which one is which."

"Who is we?" Charley asked, looking at the speaker. He had not yet holstered his pistol, not sure as to whether or not the two men's friends would try and avenge their death.

"Me'n Frank," the speaker said, pointing to one of the other cowboys. "The four of us ride with the Bar-W. We're just on the outside of town."

"Friends of yours?" Charley asked. "What I mean is, I'm not going to have any trouble from you, am I?"

"Hell, Sheriff," Frank said. "Them boys ain't nobody's friend. You ask me, you done Mr. Robison and the whole company a favor by shootin' their sorry asses."

"Are their horses outside?"

"Yes, sir."

"Get 'em on their horses and get 'em back to your trailboss."

"What you want Mr. Robison to do with 'em?"

"Bury 'em out on the prairie or take 'em back with him, I don't care which," Charley said. "Just as long as they are out of my town."

"Come on, Timmy, give me a hand here," Frank said.

"We'll help you boys," one of the other cowboys said, and Frank, Timmy, and two other cowboys carried Travis and Troy outside.

Charley watched until they were outside, then he turned to Lillian. Lillian, who was being comforted by two of her girls, was standing over Monroe's body, weeping almost uncontrollably.

"Miss Lillian, I'm sorry about your man," Charley said. "I know he was a good man."

"Nobody has any idea how good a man he really was," Lillian sobbed. "He's been with my family since I was born. I should have left him in Georgia. To think that I brought him out here to this. I'll never forgive myself."

"Don't be blaming yourself, Miss Lillian. Wasn't anything you did."

"I'm trying to tell myself that," Lillian said.

"Listen, if there's anything I can do for you, let me know."

"I can't think of anything," Lillian replied. "Somebody's going to have to tell Sally. And I'm afraid I'm the only one who can do that."

"That would be his wife?"

Lillian nodded. "They just got married last year. She does for Mrs. Allen."

"Yes, ma'am, I know her," Charley said. He touched the brim of his hat. "Give her my condolences too, will you?"

"I will," Lillian said. "You're a good man, Sheriff. I'm not one for violence, but I confess to being glad to see that those two got what they deserved."

Charley stepped out onto the front porch. He grabbed hold of the porch post and took several slow, deep breaths, trying to come back down from the edge. He saw Frank and Timmy riding off, each one of them leading a horse. Travis was belly-down on one of the horses, Troy on the other.

He watched until they cleared the edge of town. Then, his nerves back to normal, he walked back across town toward his office.

He wouldn't eat supper tonight. Sometimes killing was a part of this job and he could do it when he had to. But it did put him off his feed.

Chapter Three

One Year Later

It was election day, not only in Risco, Texas, but all across the nation, and at one end of Franklin Street a stump speaker extolled the virtues of Ulysses S. Grant, Republican candidate for re-election to President. At the other end of the street supporters were gathered to hear a speech in favor of Horace Greeley. Greeley was also a Republican who chose to run against Grant in the general election and, because the Democrats had been unable to come up with a candidate, they threw their support behind Greeley.

In honor of the occasion, red, white, and blue bunting decorated the porch overhangs and hung from the false fronts of the buildings that lined either side of the street. Every pillar and fence sported election bills, extolling the virtues of this candidate or that. Despite the interest in the Presidential election, the greatest interest was in the contest for sheriff of Tywappity County.

For the last several years, Tywappity County had been blessed, not with one, but two good men in the sheriff's office: Charley Dawson and John Carmack.

The problem was that the two men were bitter political enemies. Charley Dawson was the current sheriff, opposed in this election by John Carmack. John had been the sheriff before Charley, and Charley had been the sheriff before John.

Both men had loyal followings, and both men had, while sheriff, performed their jobs admirably, even heroically. In fact, the suggestion had been made, not entirely in jest, that Tywappity County might be better served if the two men would agree on a co-sheriff arrangement. Obviously, neither Charley nor John was in favor of anything like that.

Both men had served in the war. In his dispatches from Shiloh, General Beauregard had cited Charley Dawson for bravery. John Carmack was singled out for special praise from General Longstreet for his action during the battle of Gettysburg. Although neither man had anything good to say about the other, both were honest enough to admit that their opponent was free of any scandal or dishonesty.

As soon as the polls closed, the saloons opened their doors, and Charley and John retired to their respective political headquarters—Charley at the Golden Spur, which anchored the west end of the street, and John at the Silver Dollar, anchoring the east end of Franklin. All the politicking was over, and now all they could do was await the results to see who would be the next sheriff.

About five miles outside of town, just as they reached the Wahite River, Angus Pugh held up his hand, calling the riders with him to a halt.

"We'll water our horses here in the Wahite," he said, leading his own horse down to drink.

Angus was one of those restless men who had not been able to return to the plow in the peace that came after the Civil War. A rider with Quantrill, he now followed the outlaw trail.

Pugh was about five feet eight inches tall, bandy-legged and rawboned with hair the color of old rope. Although he could still see out of both eyes, the orbit of his left eye was disfigured by a scar that started in the eyebrow, hooked around his eye, then, like a puffy, purple lightening flash, slashed down his cheek to end at his lower lip.

The scar was the result of an encounter with the saber of a Kansas Jayhawker. Pugh held his horse's reins while the animal drank. One of the other riders began relieving himself nearby.

"Damn, Arnie," Pugh growled. "You think these horses are going to want to drink in the river after you get through pissin' in it?"

Arnie shook himself off, then rebuttoned his trousers.

"I didn't piss in the river," he said. "All I done was water me a few lilies."

"Hey, Pugh, how much farther is this here town you're talkin' about?"

"Risco? It's only about five more miles or so."

"And they got money in the bank?"

"What are you talkin' about?" Purgh replied, gruffly. "They prob'ly got as much money in that bank as there is in any bank this side of Houston. Cattle sellers and cattle buyers come through there all the time. The bank needs to keep a lot of money on hand for them. And right now it's there, just a'waitin' for us."

"You ain't forgettin' about Charley Dawson, are

you?" one of the other riders asked. This was Miller, generally conceded by the others to be second in charge after Angus Pugh.

"Who's Charley Dawson?" Arnie asked.

"He's the sheriff of Tywappity County," Miller answered. "And he's one rough-as-a-cob son of a bitch, I tell you. I once seen him shoot down two cowboys at the same time."

"Damn, I wouldn't want that son of a bitch on my trail."

"Well, maybe Dawson is the sheriff and maybe he ain't," Pugh said. "Don't forget, today is votin' day. Ole Dawson may have been turned out."

"Yeah, but if Dawson ain't the sheriff, then that means John Carmack is," Miller said. "And folks are still tellin' how he took down Dingus Malloy in a face-to-face shootout."

"I'll be damned. I heard that some sheriff had shot ole Dingus," Arnie said. "But I never learnt who it was. I'il say this, whoever done it had to be somethin', 'cause Dingus was the best man with a gun there ever was."

"Second best," Miller corrected. "John Carmack proved that he was better."

"So, what you're sayin' is, we'd be better off if Dawson is still the sheriff?" Arnie asked.

"I ain't saying nothin' of the sort," Miller replied. "Choosin' betwixt Dawson and Carmack is sort'a like tryin' to decide on whether you want to face up to a grizzly bear or a mountain lion."

"Angus, I hope you got some kind of a plan," Arnie said. "'Cause if you don't, I ain't goin' no farther. I ain't lookin' to go up against anybody like them two men Miller just described."

"Yeah, I got me a plan," Pugh answered. "The thing is, between now and midnight tonight, they don't nobody really know which one of 'em is sheriff. So, like as not they'll get to arguin' amongst themselves while we're ridin' out of town with the money, high, free, and handsome."

"How much money you think there is?"

"What with the cattlemen's money and all?" Pugh scratched his crotch before he sat back down on his saddle. "I'd say anywhere from ten to fifteen thousand dollars, easy," he said.

"Whoo. I'm goin' take my share of the money down to San Antone," one of the others said. "I know me a Mex girl down there that I am to spend ever' penny on."

"Ugly as you are, Cleetus, you'll need a lot of money just to get any girl to look at you, Mex or not."

The others laughed.

"Yeah, well, before we can spend it, we gotta get it," Pugh reminded them. "Mount up. I want to be in position by nightfall."

Shortly after nightfall, when the first vote tallies started coming in, a very large blackboard was erected on the courthouse steps. Dozens of lanterns were brought out and the bubble of light thus created, was the brightest spot in town. The names of all the candidates for every office were listed, followed by several squares, each square representing a precinct. As the numbers came in from each poll, clerks from the courthouse filled in the squares.

A crowd collected on the street in front of the blackboard, and as the results were placed in each box, those gathered would react with cheers or groans, depending upon what effect the latest entry had on the candidates of their choice.

* * *

At half-past eight, while the results were still being tallied, Greg Dawson, the son of the current sheriff, knocked on the door of the parsonage of the First Church of Risco (Nondenominational). Emma Flowers, a middle-aged, overweight woman with a pleasant smile, opened the door. Emma was the parson's wife, and she smiled when she saw Greg standing at the door, holding a bouquet of daisies.

"Good evening, Greg," she greeted.

"Evening, Mrs. Flowers. Uh, is Clemmie—"

"She's in the backyard, sitting in the gazebo," Emma interrupted.

"Thank you, Mrs. Flowers," Greg said. "Oh, uh, nobody saw her come here, did they?" he asked, anxiously.

"I don't think so," Mrs. Flowers said. "I take it you were just as careful?"

"Yes, ma'am. If word got back to my father, or hers, what we are about to do, it would cause all sorts of trouble."

"It's a shame folks can't let other folks live their own lives," Mrs. Flowers said. "Well, perhaps you had better come in before someone sees you."

Greg stepped inside and, seeing Parson Flowers, nodded at him.

"Good evening, Parson."

"Evenin', Greg."

"Is everything ready?" Greg asked.

"Doesn't take a lot to get ready, son. All I need is a couple legally entitled to get married. And of course, agreement from the man and the woman that they want to get married. So that would be up to you and Clementine."

"Clemmie hasn't changed her mind, has she?" Greg asked anxiously.

The parson chuckled. "Well now, you'll have to ask her that question yourself," he said.

"Surely she hasn't changed her mind," Greg said, as he hurried toward the back door.

"Owen, you are awful," Emma said. "Making that young man nervous like that."

"Oh, Emma, what's the use of marryin' folks if you can't have a little fun now and then?" the parson replied with a laugh.

When Greg stepped outside, he saw Clementine Carmack sitting in the gazebo with her hands folded in her lap. Greg didn't think he had ever seen anything more beautiful than the picture Clemmie made, there in the parson's garden, the moon making a halo of her hair. Seeing him, Clemmie smiled, got up, and came to him.

They embraced and kissed halfway between the gazebo and the back porch.

"You haven't changed your mind, have you?"

"What?"

"You do still want to get married?" Greg asked, anxiously.

"Yes, of course," Clemmie answered. "More than ever. Why would you ask such a thing? You . . . You aren't having second thoughts, are you?"

"No, not at all," Greg said. "It's just . . ." Greg paused in midsentence, then continued. "It's just that, I can hardly believe my luck. Why someone like you would be willing to settle for someone like me is beyond my understanding."

She kissed him again. "Don't be silly," she said. The smile left her face. "But, I do wish—"

"I know," Greg said, interrupting her. "I wish we could have our parents' blessing as well. But under the circumstances, our fathers being such bitter rivals and all, I don't think that's going to happen."

"I don't either," Clemmie agreed. "And you were right to pick today to get married. They will both be so tied up with the election that we will be the last thing on their minds."

"We'll be on the train out of here before they miss us," Greg said.

"We'll have to let them know," Clemmie said. "But not until we are somewhere beyond their reach."

"Did you write the letter to your parents?" Greg asked.

"Yes."

"I did too. After the train has safely left, Parson Flowers can deliver the letters for us. Then, when we reach Memphis, we can send them a telegram, telling them that we are all right."

"I do hope we are doing the right thing," Clemmie said.

"We are absolutely doing the right thing," Greg said, taking her in his arms.

Suddenly there were a lot of loud shouts, whistles, and gunshots coming from the west end of the town. The Silver Dollar was at the west end. Greg looked in the direction of the noise, then smiled as he looked back at Clemmie. "Looks like your pa just won," he said.

"I'm sorry," Clemmie said.

Greg laughed. "No, don't be sorry. With any luck, all the well-wishers will keep him occupied for a while so he won't have time to worry about where you are."

The parson stuck his head out the back door. "You folks ready to get this done?"

"Yes, sir," Greg said.

* * *

Back in the Golden Spur, Dewey Gimlin pulled out his gold pocket watch and looked at it. "It lacks twenty minutes of nine," he said.

His announcement wasn't necessary. There was a large Regulator Clock standing against the back wall of the saloon, and its hands registered the same time Dewey had just announced. But announcing the time called attention to the watch Dewey carried with such pride.

He closed the case, then put the watch back in his vest pocket, its position noted by the gold chain that stretched across his chest. Dewey had the deserved reputation as being the sharpest dresser in town.

Almost immediately after Dewey announced the time, Doc Isbell came in, carrying a tablet.

"All the votes are in?" Charley asked.

The current sheriff was sitting at a table in the corner of the Golden Spur Saloon. There were at least two dozen of his most faithful, awaiting the final results with him. All looked anxiously toward Doc Isbell.

" 'Fraid so, Sheriff," Doc Isbell answered. Doc Isbell, in addition to being the town's only doctor and one of Charley's closest friends, was also his campaign manager. He had just come back from the courthouse.

"You don't have to tell me. I can hear 'em all celebratin' down there," Charley said. "I mean, hell, a deaf man can hear 'em, shoutin', caterwaulin', shootin' their guns off.

"I'm sorry," Doc Isbell said.

"How bad did he beat me?"

"Six votes."

"Six votes?" Charley replied. "Ha! As I recall, I beat him by nine votes last time."

"You did indeed."

Dewey Gimlin stood at the batwing doors, looking down the street toward the Silver Dollar. Dewey was a professional gambler, but his unlikely friendship with the law came from the fact that he was an honest gambler.

"Look at them down there," Dewey said. "They are running around like a bunch of chickens with their heads cut off."

"Hell, you'd have to be without a head to vote for John Carmack," one of the others said. "I tell you the truth, Tywappity County's in trouble now."

Charley walked over to the bar, poured himself a drink, and tossed it down. It was his first one tonight.

"Oh, it's not all that bad, Slim," Charley said. "It's not like John has never been sheriff. At least he'll know where to find the outhouse once he takes over."

The others laughed.

Charley poured himself one more drink, then tossed it down and wiped his mouth with the back of his hand. "I reckon I'd better go down there and congratulate him," he said.

"I'll go with you," Doc Isbell said. "Though I'd rather take a beating."

Chapter Four

In the parsonage, which was located almost exactly in the center of town, and right across the street from the depot, the son of the defeated, outgoing sheriff, and the daughter of the just elected, incoming sheriff were standing side by side. Clemmie clutched the bouquet of daisies Greg had brought her. Parson Flowers was in front of them, while Mrs. Flowers, the witness, stood just to one side, beaming proudly as the wedding progressed.

"I require and charge you both as ye will answer at the dreadful day of judgment when the secrets of all hearts shall be disclosed, that if either of you know any impediment, why ye may not be lawfully joined together in matrimony, ye do now confess it. For be ye well assured, that if any persons are joined together otherwise than as God's word doth allow, their marriage is not lawful."

* * *

Malcolm Peabody saw Sheriff Dawson and Doc Isbell coming up Center Street toward the Silver Dollar.

"Gentlemen!" he shouted. "Gentlemen!" he called again, louder this time to be heard above the celebration. "Guess who's coming to concede the election?"

"Ain't no concedin' to it," Marcus Smith said. "John's done beat him, fair and square."

The others in the saloon laughed and cheered.

"Now, fellas, we can be magnanimous in victory," John said.

"Magnanimous," the newspaper editor said. "Now, I ask you gentlemen, who wouldn't be proud of a sheriff who has such a command of vocabulary?"

The *Risco Avenger* had not only backed John, Malcolm had been John's campaign manager. When it was pointed out to him that he was also running ads for Charley Dawson, Malcolm reminded them that a free press demanded the right of expression for those with opposing points of view.

"It would be undemocratic not to run Sheriff Dawson's ads," Malcolm said.

"To say nothing of the fact that he would lose the advertising revenue," Drury Gilmore added.

Charley Dawson stopped just outside the batwing doors, took a deep breath as if he were about to plunge into an icy stream, then stepped inside. Doc Isbell came into the saloon with him.

"Hey, Dawson, what you doin' wearin' that badge?" one of the patrons shouted. "You ain't the sheriff no more."

"I'm the sheriff until midnight, Vernon," Charley replied. "Which still gives me time to lock your ass up for drunkenness."

"The hell you say," Vernon replied. "I ain't drunk!"

"You must be drunk. Otherwise you've just insulted a peace officer, in which case the jail term would be sixty days. Drunk, it's just overnight. I could overlook the whole thing if you were drunk, but if you did such a thing while sober—"

"You got no—"

"Vernon, if you don't shut up, I'll put you in jail myself," John said, interrupting Vernon.

Some of the others laughed nervously, but most grew quiet to witness the confrontation between the outgoing and the incoming sheriffs.

"Well, John, it looks like the people have spoken," Charley said.

"It looks that way," John said. "I make it six votes. What was your count?"

"Six," Charley said. "Listen, if you need any help takin' over, I'll come in in the morning to show you the ropes."

"Thanks, but I don't believe that will be necessary. I've been here before."

"Yeah, I know."

Even as the two sheriffs were conducting their meeting, unknown to them, their son and daughter were getting married.

"Wilt thou have this woman to be thy wedded wife, to live together after God's ordinance in the holy estate of matrimony? Wilt thou love her, comfort her, honor and keep her in sickness and in health; and forsaking all others, keep thee only unto her so long as ye both shall live?" Parson Flowers asked.

"I will," Greg answered.

The pastor looked at Clemmie.

"And Clementine, wilt thou have this man to be thy wedded husband, to live together after God's holy ordinance in the holy estate of matrimony? Wilt thou obey him, and serve him, love, honor and keep him in sickness and in health; and, forsaking all others, keep thee only unto him, so long as ye both shall live?"

"I will," Clemmie said.

Pastor Flowers joined their right hands together, then said, "Those whom God hath joined together, let *no* man put asunder."

The pastor emphasized the word "no" by way of telling Greg and Clemmie that, at this point, despite the disapproval of their parents, their marriage was now in God's hands. Neither Charley Dawson nor John Carmack had anything to say about it.

"For as much as Greg Dawson and Clementine Carmack have consented together in holy wedlock, and have witnessed the same before God and this company, and thereto have given and pledged their troth each to the other, and have declared the same by declaration and joining of hands; I pronounce that they are man and wife."

Greg and Clemmie continued to look at each other.

Pastor Flowers cleared his throat. "It is customary at this point for the bride and groom to kiss," he said.

Greg's smile grew broader as he pulled Clemmie to him for a deep and loving kiss.

"Well, Mr. and Mrs. Dawson," Emma Flowers gushed, "let me be the first to congratulate you. Where do you go from here?"

"I have a job waiting for me at the Memphis cotton exchange," Greg said.

"It will be a shame to lose such nice young people as the two of you are," Pastor Flowers said.

"Yes, sir, well, if our parents—" Greg started.

"Oh, heavens, son, you don't have to explain anything to us," Parson Flowers said. "Emma and I have seen this feud go on for some time now. And it is a shame because they are both such good men."

"Maybe some day, when their politicking is over, they will come to understand and appreciate each other," Greg said.

"I just hope they do so before it is too late for them to enjoy their grandchildren," Emma said.

"Oh, my, it's much too early to be talking about grandchildren," Clemmie said, blushing. "We have some settling in to do before we start thinking about a family."

Emma laughed. "Honey, you are married now," she said. "I think you will find that having children is more a thing of the Lord's schedule than yours."

The clock struck nine.

"We'd better hurry if we want to catch the train," Greg said, taking Clemmie by the arm.

Parson Flowers took both their hands in his. "God go with you, God keep you, God make his countenance to shine upon you."

"Thank you, Parson, for everything," Greg said as he and Clemmie left the parsonage. They walked quickly down to the depot, hearing not only the whistle, but the puffing of the engine as the Midnight Flyer approached from the west.

It was nine-fifteen. With all the results in and posted, the crowd had left the courthouse, adjourning to the nearest saloon or parlor to celebrate or commiserate with each other over the outcome of the election. The lanterns had all been extinguished, the bubble of light was no more, and the town was dark.

Angus Pugh and his riders waited just on the outside of Risco. The sounds of the town drifted out to them. Here and there, gunshots were fired into the air in celebration.

A dog barked.

From a house on the near edge of town, a baby cried.

From the nearest saloon there was a high-pitched woman's squeal, followed by the deep-throated laughter of several men. From the saloon at the far end of town came the tinkling of piano keys.

About one mile away from the town, and travelling east, was the puffing steam of the train that, moments before, had left from the Risco Depot.

Pugh held his hand up. "All right, boys," he said. "Ride easy now, and let's go on down into town."

There were six of them, and they moved into town in three columns of twos, much as they did in the days when Pugh rode with Quantrill. The clopping sound of their hoofbeats echoed back hollowly from the buildings that fronted Franklin Street.

Two shots rang out, and the men reached for their guns, but relaxed when they heard the shots were followed by laughter.

"This is perfect," Pugh said. "They'll be shooting off guns all night long."

They rode to the bank, then dismounted.

"You four, move across the street, into the shadows, out of sight, and keep an eye open," Pugh ordered. "Miller, you come with me. Bring the powder."

Miller took a small keg of gunpowder down from his horse, then followed Pugh around to the alley.

There, Pugh fired his pistol into the door lock. Immediately afterward, they both laughed loudly, mimicking the celebration of the town.

After shooting, they looked around, ready to react if anyone checked up on the gunshot, but no one did.

"This is going to be like taking candy from a baby," Pugh said, with a cynical laugh. He pushed the door open and they went inside.

"Hard to see," Miller said. "We ought to light a lantern."

"Lantern's too bright," Pugh said. "I've got a candle."

Pulling a candle from his pocket, Pugh lit it. Then they used the golden glow to pick their way through the bank and to the vault in back.

From the Silver Dollar, Malcolm saw a dim light from within the bank.

"Is Percival working tonight?" he asked.

"Percival? No, I just seen Percival. He ain't workin' tonight," someone replied.

"Well, does he have anyone working in the bank?" Malcolm asked.

"On election night? Hell, not even ole Percival would make a body work on election night."

John had been talking with some of the others, but something about Malcolm's questioning caught his interest, and he walked over to the front window.

"Why are you asking all these questions, Malcolm? What are you getting at?" John asked.

"I'm not sure," Malcolm answered.

"You're not sure?"

"Well, I thought I saw a light inside the bank a

moment ago. But I don't see it now. It's probably nothing."

"Yeah, probably," John said, though he continued to look toward the bank. "Maybe, just to be on the safe side, it should be checked out."

"You're the sheriff now," one of the other men said. "You could check it."

"No, I'm not the sheriff," John replied, shaking his head. "I won't be sheriff until midnight. Go get Dawson, Malcolm."

"All right," Malcolm replied, starting out the door.

"No," John said, reaching out to grab Malcolm's shoulder. "Go out the back door, and use the alley. And tell Dawson to use the alley coming back."

John continued to look out the window and after a few moments, his diligence paid off. He spotted four men, standing in the shadows across the street from the bank, just before Malcolm returned with Charley Dawson.

"What is it?" Charley asked, coming up to the front window of the saloon.

John pointed through the window. "There's a very dim light in the bank," he said. "And across the street, in the shadows, there are four men, minding six saddled horses."

"Yeah, I see them," Charley said. "Damn if it doesn't look like someone is robbing the bank."

"Yeah, that's what I'm thinking too," John agreed. "No doubt they figured they could sneak in and out in the middle of the election, and nobody would notice it."

"How do you want to handle it?" Charley asked.

John shook his head. "I'm with you, but it's your call," he said. "You're still sheriff until midnight."

"All right," Charley said. "Hold up your right hand."

John did so.

"You're deputized," Charley said. "Now, what do you say we go out back, and come up from behind the bank?"

John pulled his pistol, checked the load in his cylinder, then nodded. "Ready when you are," he said.

By now everyone in the saloon knew that something was up and the music, laughter, and boisterous conversation stopped. It was quiet enough to hear a pin drop.

"Hold it! What's that?" Pugh asked, holding up his hand.

"What's what? I don't hear anything," Miller replied.

"Yeah, that's just it," Pugh said. "Why don't we hear anything? What happened to all the noise?"

Miller looked around. "Damn, you're right," he said.

"I don't like this. Something is wrong. How much longer?"

"Couple of minutes," Miller answered. "I've got to get the powder down into the hinges."

"What would happen if you just set off the whole keg, right here?"

"It would blow the wall out, and maybe bring the whole bank down," Miller said. "But it probably wouldn't do anything to the vault."

"Well, hurry up."

* * *

When Charley and John reached the back of the bank, they saw that the door had been broken open. Charley stepped into the building; then John came in right behind him. From here, they could see a small patch of orange light shining from somewhere up front.

"They're at the vault," Charley said, quietly.

They moved through the door that separated Percival's office from the front of the bank; then Charley motioned for John to move to the left of the front room, while he came up along the right side.

Crouching down to be behind the teller counter, Charley moved up to the end, where he saw two men near the vault.

"Hold it right there!" Charley called loudly.

Seeing that they were caught, Pugh held his candle toward the powder keg.

"Drop your gun or I'll set this off," he said.

"Are you crazy? If you set that off, you'll kill yourself."

"And you," Pugh said. "Put your gun down, now!"

Suddenly a gun boomed in the darkness behind Charley. He felt and heard the bullet whiz by his ear. Then he saw the candle flame snuffed out.

"Son of a bitch!" Pugh shouted.

Miller drew his gun and fired toward Charley. Charley returned fire and he heard Miller groan, then drop.

"Don't shoot, don't shoot!" Pugh shouted. "I give up."

"Charley, the other robbers are out front!" John called.

Charley took one quick step toward Pugh and brought his gun down over Pugh's head. As Pugh went down, Charley turned toward the front, following John through the door.

John shouted for the four men across the street to stop, but they answered with gunfire. Because of the sudden outbreak of noise and light, the outlaws' mounts began twisting and rearing. As a result of the nervous horses, the would-be robbers were not only unable to flee, their gunfire wasn't very accurate.

On the other hand, the gunfire from Charley and John was deadly accurate, and within seconds, three of the four were down. The fourth threw away his gun and started screaming.

"I give up! I give up! Don't shoot! I give up!"

"Get down from that horse, Mister," Charley called. "John, you watch him. I'm going back inside to check on the other one."

"I've got him covered," John said.

Inside, Pugh was just now getting to his feet, but he was so groggy that it was all he could do to stand. Charley grabbed him by the shoulder and pushed him outside.

With the shooting ended, both saloons emptied into the street because everyone wanted to see what was going on. They cheered both sheriffs as the two prisoners were marched down to the jail.

Abner Prufrock, the town mortician, checked out the three bodies lying in the street.

"There's another body inside," Charley informed him as he passed by.

Charley and John took their two prisoners down to the jail. After locking them in the cell in back, they came back out front where they were surprised to see two women waiting for them. The women were Charley's wife, Sue, and John's wife, Ann.

"Ann, what are you doing here?" John asked.

"I came with Sue."

"What are you doing here, Sue?" Charley asked. "You know I don't like for you to come down to the jail."

"I know," Sue said. "But I thought you might be interested in this."

"And I thought you might be interested in this," Ann said.

The women were holding out white envelopes.

Charley shook his head in confusion. "What? What is that?"

"This is a letter from Greg," Sue said.

"And this is from Clemmie," Ann added.

The confusion on the faces of the two sheriffs didn't clear up.

"They are married," Ann said.

"What?" John shouted. "Clemmie married that scoundrel?"

"I'll have you know my son isn't a scoundrel," Charley said. "Though he is obviously not a man given to wise decisions. Where is he now? I would like to talk to him."

Sue shook her head. "You can't."

"What do you mean, I can't?"

"They left town," Ann said.

"Clemmie left town? She would never do something like that on her own. That has to be Greg's influence."

"Well, of course it is Greg's influence," Ann said. "And that is as it should be. Greg is now Clemmie's husband."

"Married? She married him? Without so much as a farewell?"

"Yes, they are married," Sue said. "And if you," she looked at Charley, "if both of you hadn't been such stubborn mules, we would be planning a wedding now, a happy event, instead of worrying and wondering about where they are and what they are doing."

"Ann, did you know about this?" John asked.

"No. But I agree with Sue. If you two hadn't been so pig headed, this would never have happened."

Ann began crying, and Sue put her arms around her to comfort her.

"Well, look, I mean, I didn't expect anything like this," Charley said. "I never thought—"

"That's just the problem with you, Charley," Sue said. "That's the problem with both of you. You didn't think."

Chapter Five

Texas State Penitentiary, Twenty Years Later

During his twenty years in prison, Angus Pugh's hair changed from black to gray. His skin, which was once weathered and leather tough, was now wrinkled, and scars of dozens of prison battles competed with the still-prominent scar he had received during the Civil War.

Summoned to the prison administrative building, he was escorted into the warden's office. He was now standing in front of the warden's desk, but so far the warden had made no effort to acknowledge his presence. Completely ignoring Pugh, the warden was intently studying the file folder before him.

Pugh shifted his feet, but the warden didn't look up.

Pugh sighed, audibly, but the warden still didn't look up.

Pugh had been in this office many times during his twenty-year incarceration, almost every time to answer for some offense. He had been a difficult prisoner, never doing anything serious enough to warrant an extension of his sentence, but often earning time in the hole, as the other prisoners called the solitary-confinement cell.

The nameplate on the warden's desk read T.J. Fitzgerald. That nameplate had changed four times since Pugh was brought through the front gates, in handcuffs, so long ago. But it wasn't only the wardens who had changed. There had been other drastic changes since Pugh's arrival, the most notable being electricity.

A few years ago, incandescent bulbs had replaced the gas fixtures for light. The electric lights were more for the guards' benefit than the prisoners', because they eliminated the dark areas where, before, prisoners could find some escape from watchful eyes.

Sitting on a shelf on the wall of the warden's office was an electric fan. It whirred quietly as it sent a breeze of air across the warden's desk. Pugh watched as the current of air caused the edges of the papers to flutter. It was very hot in South Texas in the summer, and the fans that cooled the warden and hummed in the guards' break room were the envy of all the prisoners, who sweated out their time in the nearly airless cells.

There was also a telephone on the warden's desk, and it stood, importantly, to one side. It was said that, with this phone, the warden could talk directly to the governor, and, on the days prisoners were to be executed, a telephone was connected right next to the gallows, allowing for the possibility of a last-minute reprieve.

When Cleo Wright had been hanged last year,

Pugh had a little fun with him. "Don't be waitin'
on no governor's reprieve," Pugh told him. " 'cause
I plan to personally cut the wire to the telephone
so he can't call."

As Cleo Wright climbed the steps to the gallows,
he began weeping and screaming, pleading with
the warden to check the telephone line to make
sure it hadn't been cut. Later, when Pugh learned
that normally stoic Wright had broken down on
the gallows, he laughed uproariously over the success of his joke.

Now, as Pugh waited, he cleared his throat and,
again, shifted his feet impatiently.

"I know you are there, Mr. Pugh," Warden Fitzgerald said. The warden was not yet forty. He had
been too young to vote when Pugh was brought to
prison. Finally, he looked up.

"I have been going over your file very carefully,
Mr. Pugh," Warden Fitzgerald said. "And though I
have tried, I can't find any reason to keep you any
longer. You will be released tomorrow morning at
nine o'clock."

"Well, now, it breaks my heart that I'm going to
have to be leaving such good company," Pugh said,
sarcastically.

The warden made no note of Pugh's comment.
"As usual, upon your release, you will be given twenty
dollars, a pair of pants, and a new shirt," he said.

"Twenty dollars?" Pugh whistled. "Damn, that
means I earned a dollar a year. Hell, if I could stay
for another nine hundred and eighty years, I'd
have a thousand dollars." He laughed mockingly.

"Believe me, Pugh, if I could find some way to
keep you for another one thousand years, I would
do so," the warden said.

"Yeah, well, there ain't no way you can do that though, is there, Sonny?" Pugh said.

"How old are you, Mr. Pugh?"

"I'm fifty-nine," Pugh replied. He pointed to the file in front of the warden. "But of course, you know that, seein' as you got my entire life right there in front of you."

The warden picked up the file. "I do have your entire life here, don't I?" he said. "That's a sad commentary, don't you think? Life is a gift from God, Mr. Pugh. When you go before the final judgment, you are going to have to explain to the Almighty how you have used that gift."

"Don't be givin' me any of your religious bullshit, Warden. I ain't exactly what you would call a religious man."

"No, I suppose not," the warden said. "But one would think that, with age, would come a little mellowing of the spirit. As nearly as I can tell, you have the same emptiness of soul that got you in here in the first place."

"Am I going to have to listen to your bullshit until nine tomorrow morning?" Pugh asked impatiently.

"No, Mr. Pugh, that's all for now."

"For now?"

The warden pushed a button on his desk. That rang a buzzer in the outer office. "Yes, for now, Mr. Pugh. I'm sure you will be back soon. That is, if you aren't killed first."

A uniformed guard appeared in the office.

"Yes, sir?" the guard said.

"Mr. O'Malley, would you please escort Mr. Pugh back to his cell?"

"Do you mean the transition cell, Warden?" O'Malley asked.

"No, I mean his cell," Warden Fitzgerald said, pointedly.

"Yes, sir."

On the night before release, most prisoners were housed in a different cell, called the transition cell. It was away from the other inmates, and marginally better than their permanent cells.

Pugh laughed as he was escorted out of the office. "Do your damndest, you little pissant," he called back over his shoulder to the warden. "Tomorrow at nine, I'll be out of here."

Blodgett, Texas

Lucy Goodnight stood on the depot platform, barely able to contain her excitement. Behind her, the train that had brought them from Memphis sat like some living thing, venting steam and popping and snapping as bearings and wheel boxes cooled.

Lucy and Phil, her husband of but two weeks, were in Blodgett to start their married life together. Phil, a recent graduate of Mississippi State University, had been hired as manager of the Cattlemen's Bank of Blodgett. It was a responsible position with good enough income to enable them to think about buying or building a house.

The depot was teeming with people: those who, like the Goodnights, had just stepped down from the train, and others who were just leaving. There were also people greeting arrivals and others bidding goodbye to the departing passengers. In addition, there were several vendors working the crowd, from confection salesmen to newsboys.

It was to one of the latter that Phil had gone,

and Lucy saw him working his way back through the crowd, carrying a copy of the *Blodgett Standard*.

"The first thing we have to do is get a feel for our new town," Phil said, smiling broadly as he held up the paper. "And the best way to do that is to read the latest news."

"What do you find interesting?" Lucy asked.

"Well, I see that Governor Hogg is cracking down on railroads and banks."

"Oh, that's not good, is it?" Lucy asked. "I mean, with you just taking over this bank and all?"

"On the contrary. It's very good," Phil said. "How do you think I got this job? I think the bank's directors were concerned over the crackdown, and wanted to make certain everything was up to snuff." He looked at Lucy's sketch pad. "Did you finish?" he asked.

Lucy showed him the picture she had drawn. It was of the inside of the train car, and it depicted the conductor talking to two people in the front seat.

"That's very good," Phil said, looking at her drawing. "You know, when we get settled in, you should take up painting full-time. I'm sure you could sell some of your work."

"Oh, I don't think I'm that good," Lucy said.

"You underestimate yourself. Your drawings are as good as any I've ever seen."

"Board!" the conductor yelled from behind them. Immediately following the conductor's call, the engineer gave two whistles. Air pressure hissed and popped as the brakes were released, and there was a loud puff of steam being vented to the actuating cylinders. The piston rods turned the driving wheels, and the cars rattled as the train took up slack in all the couplings. The train began rolling out of the station.

"Bye!" people shouted from the open windows of the slowly rolling cars.

"Bye, don't forget to write!" came from those on the platform who were now walking alongside the moving train, prolonging the departure as long as possible.

The train gathered momentum and, within a few moments, it had pulled completely away from the depot. With the train's departure, those who had gathered on the platform began to drift away.

"I was told the bank would have someone here to meet us," Phil said, looking around anxiously.

"Phil, are there any houses for sale in the paper?" Lucy asked.

"I don't know, but we can look for those when we get to our hotel room," Phil said. He looked back at the front page. "Oh, here is something you'll find interesting."

"What's that?"

"Former Sheriffs Charley Dawson and John Carmack, both retired, had a fistfight in the town park of Risco last week."

"What? Let me see that," Lucy gasped, reaching for the paper.

Laughing, Phil held the paper just out of her reach. "Now, now, you don't want to read about your illustrious grandfathers making complete fools of themselves, do you?" he asked.

Lucy's face relaxed when she realized that Phil was teasing.

"You!" she said, hitting him on the chest.

Phil continued to laugh. "Well, after everything you have told me about your grandfathers, I wouldn't be surprised to read such an article. And, truth to tell, you probably wouldn't either."

"I don't really know them," Lucy said. "I haven't seen either one of them since I was eleven, when I went to Grandma Dawson's funeral. They still don't get along with each other, so Mom and Dad have sort of stayed away from them. As a result, they have never really been a part of my life. But they are the best lawmen in the history of Texas," she added proudly.

"So you say."

"So everyone says," Lucy insisted. "Over the years, Mom and Dad have collected dozens of articles about them."

"I just read you an article about them," Phil teased.

"No, not like that one. I mean real articles. Oh, Phil, can we go see them soon? I mean, now that we are in Texas? I'd like to get reacquainted with them. And I'd like you to meet them as well."

"Sure," Phil said. "As soon as I can legitimately ask for some time off, we'll go see them. I confess to some interest in meeting these hero grandfathers of yours."

"Mr. Goodnight?" a thin, middle-aged, bespectacled man asked. He was holding his hat in his hand, and his manner was almost obsequious.

"Yes, I'm Phil Goodnight."

"I'm Mr. Watson, sir. Josh Watson?"

It took a second for Watson's name to register, but Phil was able to make the connection. Along with his letter of employment, had come a list of names of the board of directors and the employees of the bank. Josh Watson was one of the employees. In fact, he was the chief teller and, until Phil was hired, Watson had also acted as bank manager.

Phil smiled broadly, then extended his hand. "Mr. Watson, of course, you are the chief teller," he said. "I'm very pleased to meet you," he said. "I'm told that you have filled a very responsible position admirably, and I congratulate you for that."

Watson took his hand, smiling in satisfaction at having his name recognized.

"Thank you for your kinds words, sir. I've brought a carriage to collect you and your missus. Where is your luggage?" Watson said.

"That's very kind of you, Mr. Watson," Phil said. "The luggage is just over here."

Turning, Watson snapped his fingers, and an old black man, his hair gray and his back bent with years, shuffled slowly toward the luggage.

"That's not necessary, I can get it," Phil said, feeling guilty at having one so old do heavy lifting on his behalf.

"Nonsense, Mr. Goodnight," Watson said. "Mason can handle it. Don't let his age fool you."

Despite his age and the slowness of his gait, Mason collected all the luggage and carried it, seemingly without any additional strain, over to an open landau carriage. The springs of the carriage sagged under the weight of the bags. Once the luggage was loaded, Mason climbed into the driver's seat and held the reins while Phil and Lucy got into the backseat, facing forward. Watson climbed into the front seat, facing backward, then turned and spoke over his shoulder to the driver.

"The Dunn Hotel, Mason."

"Yessuh," Mason replied, slapping the reins against the backs of the team.

Chapter Six

That evening, the Board of Directors for the Cattlemen's Bank of Blodgett held a welcoming dinner for Phil and Lucy Goodnight. The Dunn Hotel had a private dining room for just such events, and the board and the hotel pulled out all the stops in making the town's new bank manager welcome.

The hotel's finest china, silver, and crystal glistened under the electric lights. Two overhead fans twirled, providing a cooling current of air to keep the guests comfortable. A menu was at each setting, and Lucy picked one up.

Cream of Celery Soup
Roast Beef Baked Fish
Franconia Potatoes Yorkshire Pudding
Macaroni with Cheese Tomato and Lettuce Salad
Strawberries and Cream
Wine
Café Noir

After the meal, Frank Martel, who was Chairman of the Board of Directors for the bank, tapped on his glass to get everyone's attention.

"Mr. Goodnight, would you come forward, please?" he asked.

Phil dabbed at his mouth with the napkin, put it aside, and after getting his hand squeezed by his wife, stepped up to Mr. Martel.

"I can't give you the keys to the kingdom, but I can give you keys to the bank," Martel quipped. There was a smattering of polite laughter. "Here, too, is the combination to the vault. I'm sure you appreciate the awesome responsibility of being responsible for . . . Mr. Watson, how much cash is in our vault at the present time?" Martel asked, interrupting his own welcoming speech.

"As of close of business today, we had 43,615 dollars and seventy-three cents cash on hand," Watson said officiously. There were a few whistles in the room.

Martel chuckled. "Let that be your first lesson, Mr. Goodnight. If you wish to know something about the bank, ask Mr. Watson. I'm sure you can understand why we seriously considered promoting Watson to the job of bank manager but, after some discussion, we decided to go for youth and education. That's why we chose you."

"I will try to be worthy of your choice," Phil replied. He looked toward Watson. "And I look forward to working closely with Mr. Watson."

Watson nodded.

"And now, in conclusion," Martel said, "the town of Blodgett, and the directors, employees, and customers of the bank welcome you, and wish you much luck in your new position."

"Thank you very much. I'll serve you to the best

of my ability," Phil replied, accepting the keys and the sheet of paper bearing the vault's combination.

"And now, if you would, we will adjourn to the ballroom where we can have punch and all of you will have an opportunity to meet Mr. Goodnight." Martel looked down the table toward Lucy. "And the even more pleasant opportunity to meet his lovely wife."

The applause was spontaneous and enthusiastic.

11:30 P.M.

Phil Goodnight stood in the open window of his hotel room, looking out over the town. It was very late, and though the street was quiet and deserted, he could hear the sounds of pianos coming from the town's saloons, although, commingled as they were, they produced more cacophony than music.

"Phil, aren't you going to come back to bed?" Lucy asked.

"I'm too excited to sleep," Phil said.

"Well, who said anything about sleeping?" Lucy asked, and something in the tone of her voice caused Phil to look toward her. She was holding the bedsheet in front of her in such a way that provided some modesty, while still revealing that she had not put her nightgown back on.

"Darling, I don't have the . . . uh . . . stamina to do that again," he said with a self-effacing laugh.

"Well, we could snuggle," Lucy suggested.

"That's what you said last time, and look where it led."

"I know," Lucy said with a conspiratorial smile. "You said you didn't have the stamina then, either."

She lowered the sheet enough to reveal one of her small but perfectly formed breasts.

"It's not fair," Phil said.

"Who said I had to be fair?"

"No, not you. I mean that it isn't fair that I can't do right now, what I want very badly to do. Look, maybe if I walk around town for a few minutes."

"Walk around town? In the middle of the night?"

"Well, I would like to get a feel for the town," Phil said. "And this is the best time to do it, without people telling me this and that." He smiled. "And, maybe when I come back . . ." He let the sentence hang, but the expression on his face got his point across.

"When you come back, I'll be asleep," Lucy said, pouting.

Phil walked over to the bed, leaned over, and kissed her. "I can always wake you up," he said.

"I wouldn't count on that. You know that I sleep pretty soundly."

Reaching toward her, Phil let his fingers slide across the smooth globe of her breast, then rest on the little hard button of the nipple.

"Like I said, I can wake you up," he repeated. He squeezed her breast and kissed her more deeply.

"Uhmm, go, hurry, walk around town," she said. "You talk about not being fair. What you are doing to me now isn't fair."

Phil laughed as he let himself out the door.

As Phil walked down the boardwalk of Blodgett, he examined the town that was to be his new home. Born and raised in Memphis, towns as small as Blodgett were still rather strange to him. He found himself wondering how he was going to be to live in a place this small. He took a mental inventory of the types of stores as he walked down the street: a book and stationery store, a cigar store, a boot and leather shop, a dry-goods store, a general store, and the bank.

He stopped to look at the bank for a moment. It was one of the more substantial buildings in town—brick, with a marble façade, including Corinthian columns in bas-relief. It was actually a very attractive building and he was going to be proud to—

There was someone inside the bank! Through the windows, he could see the soft, golden glow of a dim light moving around.

Curious as to what it might be, Phil crossed the street and tried the front door. Finding it locked, he took out his keys, and locating the correct one, opened the door and stepped inside. He took one step in, then felt a blow to the back of his head. He went down.

"Who is it?" Angus Pugh asked.

"His name is Phil Goodnight. He's to be the new bank manager."

"The hell you say," Pugh said. He walked over, put his boot under the body, and, using his foot, rolled him over onto his back. "He sure is young."

"Hell, Pugh, you're just old," one of the others said, laughing.

"Is he dead?" one of the others asked.

Pugh dropped to one knee beside him, then felt of his neck. "No, he ain't dead. But he's going to have one hell of a headache when he wakes up."

"What's he doing here this time of night? It's nearly midnight."

"I don't know," Pugh said. "But," he stopped in midsentence. "Wait a minute. It might be a good break for us that he is here."

"Why's that?"

"Think about it," Pugh said. "He's the new manager, ain't he?"

"Yes."

"And he knows how to get into the vault, don't he?"

"So do we, Pugh. We already got the combination, remember?"

"That ain't the point. If we take him with us, folks are goin' to naturally think he's the one that stole the money. They won't even be lookin' for us. But if they do figure it out and come lookin' for us, why, we'll have ourselves a bargainin' chip."

"Damn, Pugh, that's pretty smart."

"Yeah, well, when you sit around in prison for twenty years, you got a lot of time to think about things. And the more you think about things, the smarter you get."

When Lucy awakened the next morning, she yawned and stretched deliciously.

"Good morning, darling," she said. Then, reaching over to touch him, she discovered that he wasn't in bed.

She sat up, then realized with some embarrassment that she was still nude. Quickly, she put on her dressing gown, then walked over to the door to the bathroom and knocked lightly.

"Phil? Phil, are you in there?" she called.

Not getting an answer, she opened the door and looked inside. The bathroom was empty.

She smiled, figuring that Phil must be out looking around the town again. *He really is anxious to get to work.*

"Whatever you are doing, Phil, I hope you don't forget to come get me for breakfast," she said quietly. "I hate to admit it, after that huge meal we had last night, but I'm getting a little hungry."

Half an hour later, Lucy was dressed and waiting. Moving a chair over near the window, she was looking out upon the street scene. She was hoping to be able to see Phil as he returned, but she was also enjoying all the morning activity.

Directly across the street from her, a storekeeper was sweeping the boardwalk in front of his establishment. She could hear the hammering of a carpenter as he worked, hanging a sign, and she watched two loaded freight wagons rolling slowly down the street. The drivers were sitting, bent over on the high board seat, their long whips tucked into holders. As the freight wagons left, a stagecoach arrived in town, the six team horses pulling at a rapid trot down the street. The driver pulled the coach to a stop in front of the hotel, hauling back on the reins and pushing the wheel brake with his foot.

From her position, she could look directly down on top of the stage, and she saw several parcels securely covered by tarpaulins. Two drummers, carrying their samples kits, got out of the stage, and a young woman and her child got in.

Lucy felt a warmth for the woman and her child as well as a longing to have a child of her own some day. If it was a boy, she would name him Phillip Gregory, after her husband and father. If it was a girl, she would name it—hmm, what would be a good name for a girl?

Suddenly the door burst open, and three men came rushing in.

"Oh!" Lucy shouted in alarm. Jumping up from the chair, she looked at the intruders in fear. But her fear subsided somewhat when she saw that one of the men was Frank Martel, the Chairman of the Board of Directors for the bank. That was when she also noticed that the other two men were wearing badges.

"Mr. Martel? What are you doing here?" she asked. "Why did you break into our room like this?"

"Where is he?" Martel asked angrily.

"I beg your pardon?"

"Where is that thieving son of a bitch you are married to?"

"I don't know what you are talking about," Lucy said. "What is going on here?"

"You, look in there," Martel directed one of the men. He pointed to the bathroom. "And you look under the bed."

The two deputies hurried to do his bidding.

"He's not in here," the one who looked in the bathroom said.

"He's not here, either," the other deputy replied.

"Where is he?"

"Where is who?"

"Phil Goodnight," Martel said, gruffly. "Where is he?"

"Well, I'm not exactly sure."

"You're not sure?"

"No, he was gone when I woke up this morning. I assumed he was taking a walk around the town. Mr. Martell, what is this? What is going on?"

"You know damn well what is going on," Martel replied. "That thieving, no-account, low-assed bastard you are married to robbed the bank last night!"

Chapter Seven

Risco

It was a quiet summer afternoon, and the Golden Spur was nearly empty. Don Norton was behind the bar, polishing glasses. Dewey Gimlin was sitting at a felt-covered table, dealing poker hands, turning them up to look at them, shuffling the deck, and redealing them.

Kayla Manning was at the same table as Dewey, selecting the hand she thought would be the winning one on each of his deals.

"That one," she said, pointing.

Dewey turned all of the hands over. Kayla's selection was wrong.

"I wouldn't make a very good gambler. I'm not very good at this," Kayla said. "I'm only right about one-fourth of the time."

Dewey chuckled. "That's the way it's supposed to be if the dealer is honest," he said.

Although Dewey's once coal-black hair was now brindled gray, he was still an impeccable dresser, and most women considered him the most handsome man in town. None of the women had any aspirations about marrying Dewey, though. Dewey thought that, for a professional gambler, a wife would be excess baggage.

Kayla considered Dewey a good friend, but had no romantic interest in him. Like Dewey's profession, Kayla's was one that had no room for marriage—she was a prostitute.

Kayla had never told anyone exactly how old she was, though most believed she was in her early- to mid-thirties. She was blond and pretty, and, despite her profession and the amount of makeup her profession dictated that she use, had a look of innocence about her.

Kayla had come to Risco six years ago as part of The Prairie Players, a performing troupe of actors, singers, and dancers. But when the director of The Prairie Players left on the night after the first performance, taking with him all the house receipts, Kayla and the others in the troupe were stranded.

The others left, but Kayla remained and was now as much a part of Risco as any of its citizens. She was a soiled dove, but preferred to ply her avocation in the Golden Spur saloon rather than in one of the houses on the Reservation. An arrangement with Don Norton, who was not only the bartender but the owner of The Golden Spur, allowed her to do that.

At the back of the bar, Doc Isbell sat at a table with Charley Dawson. Doc Isbell was still practicing medicine, but he had taken on his son as partner a few years ago. Unlike Doc Isbell, who had learned his medicine first as an apprentice, then on the battlefield as an army surgeon during the Civil

War, his son was a graduate of medical school. Doc was a man who knew his limitations and he appreciated and learned from his son, and let Young Doc, as his son was called, handle some of the more difficult cases.

Charley Dawson was eating a lunch of ham and eggs. It was the exact same thing he had eaten for breakfast. It was eight years since Sue had died, and though Charley still lived in the same house and cooked his own meals from time to time, he took many, if not most, of his meals right here in the Golden Spur.

"I hear Sheriff Turley is putting on two new deputies," Doc Isbell said.

"How many does that make?" Charley asked. He wiped up yellow yolk with a piece of biscuit.

"That makes eight," Doc said. "Imagine that, eight deputies. And you never had more than what? Four?"

"Three," Charley answered. "I never had more than three. John Carmack had four, and would've had more if the county had let him. And it should have. Old John needed all the help he could get. It was all he could do to hold down the job."

Doc chuckled. "You don't need to be politicking with me, Charley. I always supported you, remember? But the days of you and John Carmack changing office every two years are over. Looks like young Sheriff Turley is there to stay."

"Yes, well, Mitchell Turley's a good man."

"Should be. You trained him when he was your deputy," Isbell said.

"Yeah, but I had to retrain him every time after he got through deputying for Carmack."

Doc laughed again. "Seems to me like John used

to say the same thing. In fact, about the only thing you and John ever agreed on is both of you endorsed Turley for sheriff when you two retired."

"Well, that's the only thing he ever got right," Charley insisted.

At that moment, someone stepped through the front door. For a moment, the brightness of the outside light made the visitor visible only in silhouette. The silhouette stayed there for a moment, apparently studying the inside of the saloon, though as the face wasn't visible, no one could be sure.

"Something I can help you with?" Don asked from behind the bar.

When the door closed, they could see that the visitor was a young woman. She was very pretty, with big, blue, wide-set eyes; high cheekbones; a thin nose; and full lips. She walked over to the bar.

"I wonder if I might have a drink of water," she asked.

"Water? Yes, ma'am," Don said. Quickly, he filled one of his recently polished glasses with water and handed it to her.

"Thank you," the woman said. She drank thirstily, then put the glass down.

"Would you like another?" Don asked.

"No, thank you," the young woman answered. Looking around the room, she saw the two men at the back and, with a smile, walked back to the table. "You would be Sheriff Charley Dawson?" she asked.

"Well, I'm Charley Dawson. I'm not the sheriff anymore," Charley answered. "I haven't been for a long time. Is there something I can do for you, Miss?"

The woman's smile broadened. "You don't recognize me, do you?"

Charley shook his head. "No, ma'am, I surely don't," he said. "I know I'm getting old, but it's not likely I would forget meeting someone as pretty as you are."

"I don't blame you for not recognizing me. You haven't seen me in eight years. I was eleven, then."

"Eight years?" Charley paused for a moment then, very quietly, he said, "Lucy?"

"Hello, grandpa," Lucy said.

"God in Heaven, it is you!" Charley said. Quickly, he got up from the table, then hurried around to greet her. Charley and Lucy embraced heartily.

"Folks!" Charley called to the others in the saloon. "I want you to meet my granddaughter, Lucy Dawson."

"Goodnight," Lucy said.

"I beg your pardon?" Charley asked, confused by her strange reply.

"My name is Lucy Goodnight," Lucy said. "I'm married, Grandpa."

"The hell you say. Well, congratulations! All right, folks, I want you to meet Lucy Goodnight. But, married or not, she is still my granddaughter."

Kayla, Dewey, and Don all came over to join Doc Isbell in greeting the young visitor.

"What brings you to Risco after all these years? Is your father with you?" Charley asked, hopefully.

"No," Lucy answered.

"Ah, your husband then? You brought your husband to meet me. Good for you."

"No, Grandpa, Phil isn't with me either."

"Then what—"

"Grandpa, I want you to come with me to talk to Grandpa Carmack. I have something I need to ask of you. And I need to ask it of both of you."

"Honey, whatever it is you want, I'll do it for you.

You know that," Charley said. "You don't need John Carmack."

"I think I do," Lucy said.

Charley stroked his chin. "Yes, well, maybe you don't realize this, but your grandpa Carmack and I aren't exactly what you would call good friends."

Lucy laughed. "Oh, heavens, Grandpa, I know all about the differences between you and Grandpa Carmack all these years," Lucy said. "How could I not know? But I need both of you right now. And I was hoping that the two of you could put your feud behind you, at least long enough to help me."

"Honey, suppose I told you I would do that. Even if I did agree to a truce with your Grandpa Carmack, you'd still have John to worry about. He's the one you are going to have to convince."

"If Grandpa Carmack is willing to call a truce, would you be willing to?"

"Honey, you don't know all the things that man has done over the years. I'm not sure you know what you are asking."

"Oh, for heaven's sake, Charley," Kayla said. "Give your granddaughter a chance. All she is asking is for you to be human for a change."

"Listen to Kayla," Dewey said. "She's got a point. It's not like Lucy is asking you to put a burr under your saddle and right a bull."

"You, my friends, are turning on me now?" Charley asked. "You know what John Carmack is like. Doc, you tell them. You've known John as long as anyone in town."

"Yes, I know what he's like," Doc Isbell said. "He is exactly like you. The reason you two never got along is because you are so much alike. You're like the same poles of a magnet."

"I can't believe this," Charley said, shaking his head. "I can't believe you are all turning on me like this."

"Would you please try to get along with him, just for this one thing?" Lucy asked. "It's very important."

"What is it? What is so important that John and I have to get along?"

"I'll tell you later," Lucy said. "First, I need you to promise me that you will try to get along with Grandpa Carmack."

Charley ran his hand through his gray hair. "All right, all right," he said. "I'll give it a chance. But I'm telling you, John is the one you are going to have to convince. Now, what is it you need from us?"

"I'm staying at the Hotel Barron. I would like for you to have supper with me tonight. I'll tell you then."

"Have supper with you?" Charley smiled broadly. "Of course I'll have supper with you."

"And Grandpa Carmack," Lucy added.

"Whoowee, now that is something I would purely like to see," Don Norton said. "Charley Dawson and John Carmack sitting down to supper at the same table."

"Has John already agreed to come?"

"I haven't asked him yet."

"He won't do it."

"Will you?"

"Yes, I'll be there. But I can tell you right now, if John Carmack gets wind of the fact that I'm going to be there, he won't be."

"You leave that up to me," Lucy said.

"Have you seen your Grandmother Carmack yet?"

"Not yet. First, I had to get this arranged between you and Grandpa Carmack. I'm going to see her this afternoon."

"You do that. Ann Carmack is a good woman. A mighty good woman. How in the world John Carmack ever wound up with her is beyond me."

Lucy kissed her grandfather on the cheek. "I'll see you at six," she said.

"What do you mean, you are staying at the Hotel Barron?" John asked after he learned the identity of the beautiful young woman who had come to the Silver Dollar to see him. "You'll do no such thing. You'll stay with Ann and me. We have plenty of room for you."

"So does Grandpa Dawson," Lucy said. "He's staying in that big house all by himself."

"You're . . . you're not going to stay with him, are you?" John asked, the hurt of the thought clearly in his voice.

"No, Grandpa, I'm not going to stay with him."

"Good," John said with a sigh of relief.

"And I'm not going to stay with you and Grandma either. Can't you see the hurt that would cause for Grandpa Dawson?"

"She's right, you know," Malcolm Peabody said. Malcolm was still publishing the *Risco Avenger*, and the newspaper was now a twice-a-week publication. "You and Charley have no business putting this lovely young lady in the middle of the ridiculous feud you two have carried on for all these years."

"Malcolm, whose side are you on, anyway?" John asked. "I thought you were my friend."

The newspaper editor smiled. "Well, right now I'm on your granddaughter's side." He put his arm around Lucy. "You know, darlin', you are the spittin' image of your mama when she was your age," he said. "Tell me, how are she and your papa getting along?"

"They're doing just fine, Mr. Peabody. Papa is vice president of the Memphis Cotton Exchange now. And Mama is president of the Memphis Garden Club."

"Vice president of the Cotton Exchange. My, my," Malcolm said. He looked, pointedly, at John. "Well, now, that sounds pretty good for a boy who was never going to amount to anything."

"I never said Greg wouldn't amount to anything," John defended himself. "I have nothing against the boy, never have. And his mother was a saint. It's just his no-account father I have trouble with."

"Would that be the same no-account father who received a solid-gold badge from Governor Hogg for a lifetime of service as a peace officer?" Malcolm asked. "You do know what solid-gold badge I'm talking about, don't you? If memory serves, you got one of your own at the same presentation."

"All right, all right, you've made your point," John said. "Though I must say the fact that Dawson got the award also sort of lessened its value for me."

The others laughed because they knew how important the award had been for John. He kept the gold badge prominently displayed in his home.

"Grandpa, I would like for you to have dinner with me at the hotel restaurant tonight," Lucy said.

"Of course, darlin', I'd love to," John said.

"And with Grandpa Dawson," Lucy added.

"Wait a minute. You want me to have dinner at the hotel with you *and* Charley Dawson?"

"Yes. Please, Grandpa. It is very important."

John looked at Lucy. "Tell me, Lucy. Has Charley Dawson agreed to this?"

"Yes, sir," Lucy said.

"And he knows I'm going to be there?"

"He knew I was going to ask you."

"And he said yes?"

"Yes."

"I'm surprised the old goat would agree to be even in the same room with me, let alone share a dinner table. Well, thanks, but no thanks. I don't want one minute of my time with you to be corrupted by the fact that Charley Dawson will be there too."

Lucy sighed. "Then I guess Grandpa Dawson was right."

"Right? Right about what?"

"About you. He said you wouldn't be there," Lucy said.

"Well, I hate to admit that he is right about anything, but he is right about that. I won't be there."

"Wait a minute, John. Can't you see through this?" Malcolm asked.

"See though what?"

"Charley Dawson is counting on your not being there. That way he can have your granddaughter all to himself," Malcolm said.

"By damn, you might be right," John said. He thought for a moment, then nodded. "You are right. Why, that conniving, manipulating . . ." He stopped in midsentence and looked at Lucy. "Well, you can just tell Mr. Dawson for me that his plan is not going to work."

"Right, it's not going to work," Malcolm said, nodding his head and winking at Lucy, who was now catching on to the tactic Malcolm was using.

"Damn right it's not going to work. Because I am going to be there," John said, resolutely.

"Oh, good, good," Lucy said, clapping her hands together in joy. "That's more than good, it's wonderful."

Chapter Eight

Risco was abuzz. Word had spread from one end of the town to the other that Charley Dawson and John Carmack were going to have dinner with their granddaughter. Not only that, they were all going to sit together, at the same table, in full view of the public, in the dining room of the Barron Hotel.

As a result of this astounding news, dinner reservations for the hotel dining room were so heavy for that evening that the restaurant had to close out its reservation book by four that afternoon, and the kitchen found it necessary to put on extra help to handle the increased demand.

In addition to the sold-out dining room, as it approached six o'clock, the hotel lobby, which opened onto the restaurant, began filling up. Residents of the town who never came to the hotel began dropping in just to "read the out-of-town newspapers," or to sit in one of the overstuffed chairs.

"What is this? What's going on?" an arriving hotel guest asked as he was signing the registration book. He looked around at the crowded lobby. "Is there some event that I am not aware of? Why are there so many people here?"

"Well, I reckon they just came in here to get warm," the clerk replied.

"Get warm? What are you talking about? It isn't cold at all. In fact, quite the opposite, it's rather warm outside."

"Oh, it isn't cold yet," the clerk said. "But word has it that Charley Dawson and John Carmack are going to sit down at the same dinner table tonight."

The hotel guest shook his head. "I'm sorry, I don't know those people, so I don't understand the significance."

"For the last thirty years, folks have been saying that it would be a cold day in hell before those two got together," the clerk said, laughing uproariously at his own joke.

One of the nearby townspeople heard the clerk's remark and thought it was funny enough to tell someone else, so that ripples of laughter moved through the room as the joke was passed from one little conversational cluster to the other.

As the hour of six approached, even the sidewalks of the town began to fill. This was because husbands, who ordinarily would never honor their wives' request to go for a walk, suddenly decided that on this particular evening a nice stroll around town was just what they needed. As husbands and their wives walked arm-in-arm, their meanderings just happened to take them by the big front window of the hotel restaurant.

Malcolm had just left the newspaper office and was locking the front door, as Sheriff Turley, who was out making the rounds, happened by.

"Is it true?" Sheriff Turley asked. "Are Charley

and John actually having a friendly get-together tonight?"

"It must be true," Malcolm said, laughing. "I can't think of anything else that would have you making rounds when you've got deputies to do it for you."

"Well, it doesn't hurt for a sheriff to keep his hand in things," Turley said.

"Uh-huh," Malcolm said. He tried the door and, satisfied that it was locked, dropped the keys in his pocket.

"I never thought I'd live to see the day those two would get together," Turley said. "I wonder what brought it about?"

"Their granddaughter pulled it off," Malcolm explained.

"You don't say? Well, as they say, 'and a child shall lead them.' "

Malcolm chuckled. "I wouldn't exactly call Miss Lucy a child. She's a woman, full grown. And believe me, she's pretty enough to make a train follow her down five miles of dirt road."

"Well, I'll be interested to see how this all turns out," Sheriff Turley said. He touched the brim of his hat, then walked on down the street, greeting the others.

When Lucy came into the dining room at about five minutes until six, she was carrying her sketch pad with her. As she looked around the room, she was quite surprised by the size of the crowd. Extra tables had been brought in, and every table was filled with diners.

Lucy was, though she didn't realize it at the moment, the center of attention, and the buzz of conversation that flew around the room at that moment was about her. She stood for a moment in the wide opening that connected the restaurant to the hotel lobby. Looking out over the crowded dining room, she didn't see an empty table. Sighing, she stepped back into the hotel lobby. She was sure there must be another restaurant in town, suitable for her meeting with her grandfathers. Perhaps she should wait out front and when her grandfathers arrived, have them suggest another place to her. As she turned to leave, she heard someone call her by name.

"Mrs. Goodnight," the maitre d' said, hurrying over to her. "No, no, you mustn't leave."

"I'm sorry," Lucy apologized. "I had no idea you would be so crowded. Perhaps I should have made a reservation."

"Oh, but you *do* have a reservation," the maitre d' replied.

"How can that be? I haven't made a reservation," Lucy said.

"It's all taken care of," the maitre d' said. "This way, please."

Puzzled by his comment, she followed the maitre d' into the dining room.

"I hope it is a nice table, I'm having dinner with my grandfathers and I—"

"Here is your table," the maitre d' said, interrupting her and stopping in front of table that sat up on a little riser in front of the window. The table was beautifully appointed—in fact, more beautifully appointed than any other table here. And it took but one quick glance to realize that not only was it a good table, it was the best table in the entire restaurant.

"I hope this will be satisfactory," the maitre d' said.

"Oh. Oh my, yes. This will be wonderful, thank you," she said. "There will be two more joining me."

"Yes, Sheriffs Dawson and Carmack," the maitre d' said.

"Ah, I see now," Lucy said, smiling in understanding. "One of my grandfathers made the reservation, didn't he? Which one? No, don't tell me. I think, under the circumstances, I'd rather not know."

"Neither of them did," the maitre d' replied. "Your reservation was arranged by the restaurant. And, might I add, the cost of your dinner tonight is all taken care of."

"What? Why would that be?"

"Perhaps you have noticed how busy we are tonight?" the maitre d' asked.

"Yes, I have."

The maitre d' smiled. "That's all because of you. It is only fitting that we show our appreciation in some way, and taking care of your meal tonight is our way of showing that appreciation."

"I don't understand. How is it because of me?"

"Young lady, you have done something no one has ever been able to do. You have brought together the two best sheriffs Texas has ever had," the maitre d' said. "And that is something everybody in town wanted to see."

"Oh, my, I had no idea."

The maitre d' pointed to Lucy's sketch pad. "Would you like me to put that somewhere out of the way for you?"

"No thank you," Lucy replied. "I will keep it."

"Very well, Miss. Bon appetit," said the maitre d' as he walked away.

Almost immediately thereafter, a waiter brought

Lucy a glass of water and, as she drank it, she happened to glance outside. When she did so, the strangest thing happened. It was almost as if everyone outside were standing still, and began to move only when she glanced toward them.

"Hello, Lucy."

Turning, Lucy saw her grandfather Dawson.

"Hello, Grandpa," Lucy said, smiling broadly. "Thanks for coming." She stood up and gave him a hug, which he returned, somewhat awkwardly.

"I wouldn't miss it for the world," Charley said. "But I see that John isn't here."

Lucy started to respond, when she saw John just coming into the dining room.

"Sure he is," she said, brightly. "There he comes now."

"Hrmmph. Well, I am surprised."

Lucy greeted John with the same enthusiastic hug she had given Charley. Then the three of them sat down, Charley on the right side of the table and John on the left side. The chair nearest the window was empty. Lucy's chair had its back to the dining room, leaving her facing the window and able to look out onto the street. She folded the napkin and put it on her lap.

"I'm so glad the two of you could come," she said.

"There was no way I was going to let him have you all to himself tonight," John said.

"I should've figured you'd show up just to spite me," Charley said. "So it turns out that your being here has nothing to do with just wanting to spend some time with your granddaughter."

"Yeah, you'd like it if I weren't here, wouldn't you?" John said.

"It would make the company more pleasant," Charley replied.

"Grandpa, Grandpa," Lucy said, looking first at one, then the other. "Can't we please call a truce? Just for a little while? For me?"

"You're right," Charley said, reaching over to pat her on the hand. "This isn't your fight. We've got no business hauling you into it."

"I agree," John said. "There aren't many things Charley Dawson and I agree on, but I agree with him on this. I'm sorry, darlin', we had no right carrying on like we were."

Glancing out the window, Lucy got the same, distinct impression she had gotten a few minutes earlier. Everyone was stopped until she looked up. Then they began moving.

"That's strange," she said.

"What is strange?" Charley asked.

"Those people out there," Lucy replied. Turning quickly, she saw that nearly everyone in the dining room was looking at her, though all looked away when she glanced toward them. Had only one or two done so, she might not have noticed, but practically the entire dining room turned their heads at the same time.

"In here too," Lucy continued. "Do you get the idea that people are sort of . . ." She let the question hang.

"Sort of what?" John asked.

"Staring at us," Lucy said.

To Lucy's surprise, both Charley and John laughed.

"What is it? What is so funny?"

"They *are* staring at us," Charley said.

"They are? But why? I don't understand."

"This meeting between Charley and me has been the talk of the town all day," John said. He took in the dining room with a sweep of his hand. "You think the restaurant is this crowded every night?"

"Well, the maitre d' said something about it, but I wasn't really sure what he was talking about," Lucy answered.

"Well, believe me, on a normal night, there wouldn't be one-tenth as many people as are here right now."

"Same thing with the hotel lobby," Charley said. "Most of the time, that place is as deserted as a tomb."

"And there haven't been this many people out on the street since the Fourth of July Parade," John added.

"And they are looking at us?" Lucy asked.

Charley nodded. "That they are, honey. That they are."

"What on earth do they hope to see?" Lucy asked.

"Oh, I expect they'd like to see Charley and me shoot it out," John said.

"Oh, good heavens!" Lucy gasped. "I hope I haven't caused . . . something like that!"

Again, Charley and John laughed.

"You don't have to worry about anything like that," Charley said. "I've never figured John to be worth the price of a bullet."

"And I've always thought a lifetime of being a burr under his saddle was better than shooting him any day," John added.

"Well," Lucy said. "I'm glad we are going to disappoint them."

"Believe me, darlin', they aren't disappointed," John said. "Seeing Charley and me at the same table is like going to see the elephant."

"What is it, Lucy?" Charley asked. "Why have you come here like this? And you are by yourself? You told me you are married. Where is your husband? Why isn't he with you?"

"He is the reason I am here," Lucy replied. Although she had been laughing and smiling but a moment earlier, her eyes suddenly filled with tears.

"What is it, darlin'? That son of a bitch hasn't left you, has he?" John asked.

"No!" Lucy replied quickly. "Phil is wonderful! It's nothing like that!"

"John, you are a dumb ass, upsetting her like that," Charley said. Then, more gently, he asked Lucy, "What is it, honey? What has you upset?"

"He's gone, Grandpa. He disappeared."

"Disappeared? You mean he left?"

"Yes. No. I mean, I don't know. I don't know what has happened to him. Oh, I don't know where to start."

"Maybe you should start at the beginning," John suggested as he handed his handkerchief to Lucy.

Lucy began by telling how she had known Phil since they were both young. She told about Phil going to Mississippi State University and how proud and happy they were when he got a job as bank manager for the First National Bank of Blodgett.

"They held a welcome ceremony for us," she said. "Oh, it was so lovely. They gave us a wonderful dinner, and then they gave Phil the keys to the bank."

"Who is they?" John asked.

"They," Lucy said, waving her hand dismissively. "You know, the board of directors, the townspeople. They," she said.

"All right, they gave you a welcome banquet. Then, what happened after that?"

"We went back to our hotel room," Lucy said. As she recalled just what exactly did happen when they returned to the hotel room, she felt herself blushing. She cleared her throat, then took a swallow of water, trying to make the awkward moment, and the heat of her blushing, pass.

"Then, he decided to take a walk around Blodgett," Lucy said.

"What time was that?"

"About eleven thirty or so that night," Lucy said. "Maybe almost midnight."

"What in the world was he doing walking around town at midnight?" Charley asked.

"I don't know. He said he was too excited to sleep. He said he wanted to get the feel of the town. Neither of us had ever been there before."

"What time did he come back to your hotel room?" Charley asked.

"Well, that's just it, I don't know. I went to sleep shortly after he left, and when I woke up the next morning, he wasn't there. At first, I assumed that he had come back in the middle of the night, saw that I was asleep, and didn't want to wake me. Then I thought perhaps he got up early the next morning to have yet another look around town."

"You said, at first you thought that," John said. "You don't think that anymore?"

Lucy didn't answer verbally, but shook her head no as she dabbed at the tears in her eyes.

"What do you think?" Charley asked.

"It turns out that, during the night, the bank was robbed," Lucy said. "I think that, somehow, Phil must have stumbled onto the robbers. And they took him."

"Took him? Not killed him, but took him?" John said.

"Killed him? Oh! Oh, Grandpa, I never thought of that! I mean I just assumed that they took him. Do you think they might have killed him?"

"John, don't you ever think before you speak?" Charley demanded. Then to Lucy. "I don't think they killed him. If they were going to kill him they would have killed him right there at the bank, rather than be bothered with taking him along with them."

"So then, you think the chances are good that he is still alive?" Lucy asked.

Charley nodded. "I reckon if he was alive when he left the bank, that means they wanted him alive for a reason. And that being the case, then he should still be alive."

"Charley is right," John said. "Your husband is probably still alive unless he is the type who might try something foolish."

"Foolish? What do you mean, foolish?"

"Foolish. You know, like go after the bank robbers with his bare hands, or something like that," John explained.

Despite herself, Lucy laughed.

"What is it?" John asked. "What are you laughing at?"

"You don't know Phil very well," she said.

"Darlin', I don't know him at all."

"Well, would you like to see a picture of him?"

"Yes," John answered.

Lucy reached down beside her chair and picked up her sketch pad. "I made this drawing of him today."

The drawing was richly detailed, showing a young man with keen, intelligent-looking eyes, a thin nose, rather full lips, and a strong chin.

"You made this drawing?" Charley asked in surprise.

"Yes."

"What a wonderful drawing," John said. "I had no idea you were such a good artist."

"Thank you," Lucy said. She stared at the picture for a moment. "He is a handsome man, don't you think? Oh, and Grandpa, you don't have to worry about Phil doing anything like going after the bank robbers with his bare hands. Or even with a gun, for that matter. Phil is a very sensible person. Why, he would never think of taking any kind of a risk." She smiled brightly. "That's what makes him such a good banker."

"Then the chances are very good that he is still alive," Charley suggested, and John agreed.

"Good, because that's why I came to you two for help."

"You came to us for help? What kind of help?"

"Those men, whoever robbed the bank, took him with them. I have no idea why they did so. But I want you to find him and bring him back to me."

"Wait a minute, you want us to go look for your husband?" Charley asked.

Lucy nodded. "For as long as I can remember, Mom and Dad have told me what wonderful lawmen you two were. And I believe them because I've seen all the stories in the newspapers and I've heard others talk. And if you are that good by yourselves, think how good you would be working together!" She looked at each of them with a bright smile. "That's why I want you to find Phil for me."

"Oh, darlin', you don't really want us to do that," John said. "We're both a couple of broken-down old has-beens. We're way too old for anything like that. Besides, you say it happened in Blodgett?"

"Yes," Lucy said, nodding her head.

"Then you ought to let the sheriff over there at Blodgett go after him. Have you asked him?"

"I don't want him to go after Phil," Lucy said resolutely.

"Why not?"

"Because," Lucy said. She looked both her grandfathers in their eyes, first Charley, then John. "The sheriff over there thinks Phil did it."

Chapter Nine

Blodgett, Three Days Earlier

When Phil regained consciousness, he was belly-down over a horse. For a moment, he was aware only of intense unease, a pain in the back of his head, and the discomfort of his position. His hands and feet were tied together by a rope that passed under the horse.

Where was he? What was he doing here? And, for that matter, where *was* here?

Looking around to the degree he could, he saw that there were at least six riders.

"Hey!" he shouted. "Hey, what is this? What's going on?"

"Angus, he's awake," someone said. "Can I cut 'im down now?"

"You takin' him to raise, Muley?" Angus replied.

"No, but there ain't no sense in makin' 'im stay like that anymore," Muley said. "How 'bout you let me cut 'im down?"

"All right, let's hold up for a moment," Angus said.

The riders stopped, and Phil started wriggling around, trying to get himself free.

"Take it easy, Mister. I'm goin' to cut you down," one of the riders said, and a hand with a knife appeared in front of Phil. The knife cut through the ropes.

"All right, slide down."

Gratefully, Phil slid off the horse. He stood alongside the horse for a moment, then suddenly got very nauseous. He threw up.

"Whoa, son of a bitch, look at that!" one of the other men said, laughing. "Hey, Angus, he's pukin' his guts out back here."

One of the riders was considerably older than the others, and he slid down from his own horse and looked at Phil.

"You all right, boy? Or, are you going to be pukin' some more?" he asked.

Phil spat a few times. "Could I have some water?" he asked.

"Yeah, sure. Muley, give him some of your water," the older rider said.

"I got water and whiskey," Muley said. "Which would you rather have?"

"Damn, Muley, I believe you have taken him to raise," one of the other riders said. "Offerin' him some of your whiskey."

"I'd rather have water, please," Phil said.

Muley took his canteen down from the saddle and handed it to him. Phil drank deeply, then wiped his mouth with the back of his hand.

"Thanks. Muley, is it?" he said, handing the canteen back.

"Yes. Well, my real name is Gary Slater, but folks call me Muley," Muley said, sticking his hand out. "What's yours?"

"Goodnight. Phil Goodnight," Phil said.

"Hey, Muley, you plannin' on puttin' his name on your dance card?" one of the other riders asked, and the others laughed.

"It don't hurt to be nice to someone, Weasel," Muley replied. "You should try it sometime."

"Can you ride, Goodnight?" Angus asked.

"I'd rather not. I'm not what anyone would call a very good horseman," Phil replied.

"Well, here's the way I look at it," Angus said. "You can either ride sittin' up, or we can tie you belly-down across the saddle the way you was ridin'."

"No, I'll ride," Phil said.

"Get up on the horse, then."

With some effort, and a little help from Muley, Phil managed to climb onto the saddle.

"Well, now, you look like you was born to ride," Angus said.

"May I ask who you are?" Phil inquired.

"The name is Pugh. Angus Pugh."

"Mr. Pugh, what happened? Where am I, and how did I get here?"

"You don't remember anything?" Pugh asked.

Phil shook his head. "The last thing I remember is being in the hotel with . . . my wife!" he suddenly said. "Where is Lucy?"

"Lucy?" Pugh shook his head. "I don't know anything about anyone named Lucy. When you helped us rob the bank, she wasn't with you," Pugh said.

"What are you talking about? I haven't robbed any bank."

Pugh laughed. "How about that, boys? Our banker friend here says he didn't help us rob the bank."

"Of course I didn't help you rob the bank! I'm the bank manager."

"You mean you was the bank manager," Pugh said.

"Were," Phil corrected.

"What?"

"Never mind. What makes you think I helped you rob the bank?"

"Look in the saddlebag, Phil."

"Where do you get off calling me by my first name? I don't know you. I don't know any of you."

Pugh laughed. "What do you think, boys? Our partner doesn't even want us to call him by his first name."

"And don't call me your partner. I am not your partner!" Phil said emphatically.

"Look in the saddlebag, *Mr.* Goodnight," Pugh said, emphasizing the word "mister."

Phil opened the saddlebag and looked inside. He saw several bound stacks of bills.

"What? What is this?" he asked, taking one of the stacks.

"That's your share of the money," Pugh said.

Phil shook his head. "You're crazy. You are all crazy."

Pugh laughed again, and the others laughed with him. "He's a funny man, don't you think, boys? Yes, sir, Mr. Phil Goodnight is a very funny man."

"You say I'm your partner?" Phil asked.

"That's right."

"Then, if I'm your partner, why was I tied over a horse?"

"You had a little accident at the bank and got yourself knocked silly," Angus said. "That was the only way we could get you out of there. We couldn't very well leave you for the sheriff now, could we?"

"The sheriff," Phil said. "That's it. I'll turn myself in to the sheriff." He started to turn his horse away.

"Weasel, you want to stop our partner there?" Angus said, and a rider near Phil reached out to grab the harness of Phil's horse.

"I thought you said I was your partner," Phil said. "If that's true, shouldn't I be able to leave if I want to?"

"Yes, well, see, that's the thing. You are already getting nervous, so, like I was telling you, it's best that we all stay together for awhile. I don't think any of the boys would like it if you tried to ride out on us now. The way you are acting, you might try and turn yourself in to the law. And if you did that, why, you could bring the law down on all of us."

"What if I leave anyway?" Phil asked.

Pugh brought his pistol up, pointed it at Phil, and cocked it.

Phil gasped, and threw both his hands up in front of him.

"Like I said," Pugh told him in a low, even voice. "I don't think any of us would like for you to ride away just now. In fact, I don't think I would let you."

"Good Lord, you aren't going to shoot me, are you?" Phil asked in a frightened voice.

"I won't shoot if you give us your word you won't try and run away," Pugh said.

Phil looked around him. Never in his life had he been in country as desolate as this. He saw nothing but wide-open prarie land, rolling hills, and a few scrub trees. He had absolutely no idea where he was.

"All right, I give you my word that I'm not going anywhere," he said with a sigh. "I wouldn't know where to go, anyway."

When they made camp that night, Pugh produced a set of handcuffs and a pair of leg irons, which he used to secure Phil.

"I'm sorry about this, partner," he said. "But I wouldn't to think that you would run away from us while everyone was sleeping."

"I'm not your partner, and you know I'm not your partner. You are trying to take advantage of the fact that I have amnesia, but it isn't going to work."

"Amnesia? What is amnesia? I've never heard of that."

"It means a temporary loss of memory," Phil said. "When you can't remember something that just happened to you."

Angus smiled. "Oh, you mean like when you get so dead drunk that the next day you can't remember a thing?"

"Yes, something like that. Though in the case of amnesia it is often caused by a blow to the head."

"Yeah, well, you took a blow on your head all right," Angus said.

"I know I did," Phil said. "And it's all coming back to me now. I was walking around the town when I saw a light through the bank windows. When I went inside to investigate, someone hit me on the head. That blow to the head is what caused the amnesia."

Pugh smiled, and looked at the others. "Well, boys, looks like our fun is over. Mr. Goodnight here has got all his memory back."

"As long as he remembers that, that money in his saddlebag ain't his'n," Weasel said, and the others laughed.

"Oh, I think he's smart enough to know that," Pugh said.

"Why did you bring me with you?" Phil asked. "Why didn't you just leave me there? If I was knocked out, I couldn't have stopped you. Besides that, I never even saw you, so there is no way I would've been able to identify you."

"Oh, we thought you might come in handy," Pugh said. "You see, this way the folks back in Blodgett will have someone to pin the robbery on."

"What do you mean, someone to pin the robbery on?"

"Well, you figure it out, smart boy," Pugh said. "We didn't use no dynamite to blow up the vault. We just used the combination and opened it as sweet as you please. You had the keys to the bank and the combination to the vault on you. So, when they find that the safe wasn't blowed open, what do you think the people back there are going to believe?"

"Oh, my God!" Phil said. "They are going to think I had a hand in this!"

Pugh chuckled. "That's about the size of it."

Salcedo, Texas

It wasn't much of a town. Hot, dry, dusty, and out in the middle of nowhere, it sat in the desert, baking like a cow plop in the hot sun. It was small and fly-blown, an ugly little spot in the middle of sagebrush and shimmering heat waves.

As they approached the town, a rabbit popped in front of them, ran for several feet along the trail, then darted under a dusty mesquite tree. The air blowing up from the south felt as if it were coming from a blast furnace.

They passed a sign that announced the town.

You are Entering
SALCEDO
Population Unknown
The Law Ain't Welcome
If You Got No Business Here,
Get Out, or Get Shot

As they rode, Phil surveyed the town. It had only one street, with a few leaning shacks constructed from rough-hewn lumber, the unpainted wood turning gray and splitting. There was no railroad serving the town, so no signs of the outside world greeted them. It was a self-contained little community, inbred and festering.

Phil examined the buildings. There was a rooming house, a livery stable with a smithy's shop to one side, and a general store that said: "Drugs, Meats, Good," on its high false front. Next door was a smaller building, with crudely formed letters in red paint, spelling out the word "Saloon."

As they passed the saloon, a woman passed through the front door. Phil glanced at her, then gasped in surprise. The top of the woman's dress was scooped all the way below her breasts! For all intents and purposes, the woman was naked from the waist up!

"Hello, Angus," the woman said. "Good to see you back. Will you be comin' to see me?"

"I'll be right there, Mabel, soon as I take care of a little business," Pugh said.

"I'll have a beer waitin' for you," Mabel said. She went back into the saloon.

Looking around, Pugh saw the expression on

Phil's face, and he laughed. "Well now, what's the matter with you, Mr. Goodnight? You ain't goin' to tell me you ain't ever seen a woman's titties before, are you?"

"But she . . ." Phil said, pointing back toward the saloon, "she was outside, in the open."

"Yeah, well, that's the way we do things here," Pugh said. "Things is a little more open and free here in Salcedo. Right, boys?"

"Yeah, we ain't exactly, what you call, fancy-dress people," Muley said.

"In fact, sometimes, we don't dress a'tall," Weasel added, and the others laughed.

They stopped in front of a brick building.

"You know what this is, Mr. Goodnight?" Pugh asked.

"I'm afraid I don't."

"Why, this here is a bank," Pugh explained. "In fact, it's our bank. And right now we're going to make a deposit, which is funny when you think about it, 'cause most of the time I'm takin' money out of banks, rather than putting money in. Get down, come on in, and let me show you around. You bein' a banker and all, I'd like to see what you think."

"I must tell you, Mr. Pugh. These past few days have been the most bizarre experience of my entire life," Phil replied as he got down from the horse. "I just hope Lucy is all right."

"Bizarre? Now, that's another word I don't understand," Angus said. "You sure do know a heap of big words," he teased.

Phil rubbed his backside. They had been riding for three days. He had never ridden a horse that long before, and his backside was rubbed raw.

"Your ass hurtin', is it?" Muley asked. "Well, you won't be ridin' no more, so I reckon it'll get better after a bit."

Phil went into the bank with the others. The inside of the building looked remarkably like any bank he had ever seen, complete with a tellers' cage and a table with blank deposit and withdrawal slips. There was a calendar on one wall that looked much like the calendars Phil had seen on the walls of many other banks.

"Mr. Pugh," one of the tellers said, smiling at him from behind the tellers' cage. "I trust it you had a successful business trip."

"That I did, Mr. Collins, that I did," Pugh said. He emptied his saddlebag on the table where the deposit slips were. The others emptied their saddlebags on the table as well. Phil noticed that one of the men had brought in the saddlebag from the horse he had been riding.

"I would say that you were successful," Collins said.

"We've got us a pretty big deposit to make."

"I'll take care of the paperwork," the banker said. "How shall I record it? Another cattle deal?"

"Cattle deal, yes," Angus said. "We sold a herd."

"Hey!" Phil said. He pointed to the money. "That money didn't come from a cattle deal. I'll have you know that money came from a bank. My bank."

The banker looked at Phil for a long moment, and Phil thought he saw a glimmer of understanding in the banker's eyes. Suddenly, the banker laughed, then turned back to Angus. "What are cattle selling for now? I'll need to make an estimate on the number of head."

"Didn't you hear what I said?" Phil asked. "This isn't . . ." He stopped in midsentence. It was now clear to him that this banker knew the money was stolen. He was part of the operation.

At that moment, the door to the bank opened and another man came in. He was wearing a sheriff's badge.

"Sheriff, thank God!" Phil said. "These men—"

"So, how did it go, Angus?" the sheriff asked, interrupting Phil in midsentence.

Angus reached over to the pile of money and selected a stack of bills. He tossed it to the sheriff.

"Here you go, Bixby. Don't say I never paid my taxes," Angus said.

Everyone, including the sheriff and the banker, laughed.

"My God, what sort of place is this, where the banker and the law are in league with bank robbers?"

" 'In league with,' " Pugh said. "I tell you what, this here little feller ain't much of a rider, but he sure can talk pretty. 'In league with.' "

Everyone in the bank laughed.

"What are we going to do with him?" Sheriff Bixby asked, nodding toward Phil.

"I don't know yet," Angus replied. "I tell you what, just take him down there and stick him in your jail until I figure out what to do with him."

"What? You are putting me in jail? On what charge?" Phil asked.

"What charge? Why, we ain't going to charge you nothin', Mr. Goodnight," Pugh said. "We're goin' to let you stay in our fine jail for free."

Again, everyone in the bank laughed.

Chapter Ten

Risco

On the morning after the dinner with their grand-daughter, John and Charley were waiting in the sheriff's office when Sheriff Mitchell Turley showed up for work.

"It's damn near eight o'clock," John said irritably. He pointed to the clock on the wall.

"John, Charley, good morning," Turley said.

"When I was sheriffing, I was always here by seven," John said. "Hell, even Charley was."

"I have deputies," Turley said. "We have shifts. The daytime shift starts at eight." He stared with curiosity at the two men who were such known enemies that they rarely appeared together. "You two had dinner together last night, and now you are together in my office this morning. Truly this must be the fulfillment of some scripture in Revelations that I don't know about. Is this a signal that the world is coming to an end?" He chuckled at his own joke.

"We want you to deputize us," Charley said.

Turley stared at them in surprise. "You want to be my deputies? Both of you?"

"Yeah, something like that," Charley said.

Turley laughed again. "Lord, lord, the world *is* coming to an end," he said. He walked over to the blue pot sitting on top of the stove, picked up a cloth to protect him from the hot handle, and poured himself a cup of coffee. "Would you like some?" he offered.

Neither John nor Charley answered. Instead, they just stared at him.

Turley took a swallow of his coffee, then studied the two former sheriffs over the rim of his cup.

"Wait a minute," he said, lowering the cup and looking at them with an expression of wonder on his face. "You men are serious, aren't you? You actually want me to make you my deputies?"

"We don't just want you to do it, Mitch, we expect you to do it," Charley said.

"In fact, we demand it," John said.

"Yeah," Charley agreed.

"Whoa, now, you two fellas hold on just a damn minute here," Turley said, holding his hand out in front of him. "Just where do you two get off, demanding that I make you deputies?"

"You wouldn't be where you are today if it weren't for us," Charley said. "And you know it."

"All right, you're right, I do owe you a lot. Both of you," Turley agreed.

"I'm glad you see it that way."

"But I'm not going to deputize you."

"Why not?"

"Well, for one thing, I don't have the money in my budget."

"Oh for crying out loud, Mitch, did you hear either one of us ask for money?" John asked.

"Well, no, but—"

"We just need the badges and the authority, that's all," Charley said.

"In fact, we don't even need the badges. We've got our own," John said, showing Turley the solid-gold badge he had been given by the governor. Charley had one just like it. "We just need the authority," he added.

"You're too old," Turley said.

"I'm sixty-four," John said. "And Charley is a year younger."

"It's been ten years since you were sheriff, John," Turley said. "And, Charley, it's been eight years since you were sheriff. You two gave it up after your last term because you said you were too old. Have you suddenly grown younger?"

"We're older. We're not dead," Charley said. "Now, are you going to deputize us or not?"

"What is so all-fired important about being deputized?"

"Last night, we promised our granddaughter that we would find her husband for her," John said.

Turley chuckled. "Is that what the big meeting was about? Everyone has been wondering about it. What happened to him? Did he run out on her? Hell, you don't need my authority to find him. Just go look for him."

"It's not that simple," Charley explained. "He was a banker over in Blodgett. The bank was robbed, and the robbers took him with them."

The smile left Turley's face. "Over in Blodgett, you say?"

"Yes," John answered.

"Would this fella's name be Goodnight? Phil Goodnight?"

"Yes," Charley replied. "Have you heard something?" he asked anxiously. "Has he been found?"

"The robbers took him with them because he was in cahoots with them," Turley said.

"How do you know?" Charley asked.

"It come out over the telegraph wires nearly as soon as it happened," Turley said. "And last night, I got some dodgers on him. I just haven't had time to put them out yet."

Turley walked over to a table and picked up a couple of wanted posters. Bringing them back, he handed one to each of the old sheriffs.

WANTED
For Bank Robbery
Phillip R. Goodnight
$5,000 Reward
Contact Sheriff Bill Dobson
Blodgett, Texas

"What makes Dobson so sure that Phil had anything to do with this?" Charley asked, as he looked at the reward poster Turley gave him.

"I don't know, but he must be pretty certain. You don't put a reward this big on someone if you don't have some pretty damning evidence."

Lucy was in the parlor of John Carmack's house having tea with her grandmother when John and Charley returned from the sheriff's office. Badges were conspicuous on the vests of both men.

"Sheriff Turley deputized you," Sue said. "I knew he would."

"Yeah, he did," John said. He looked at Lucy. "Darlin', are you sure you want Charley and me to go looking for Phil?"

"What? Yes, of course I'm sure," Lucy replied. "Why would you even ask?"

John looked over at Charley, and Charley pulled the dodger from his shirt pocket. "They've got wanted bills out on him," Charley said.

"I told you, the sheriff over at Blodgett thinks he did it."

"What we're getting at, honey, is what if he did do it?" Charley said.

Lucy's eyes filled with tears, and one of them spilled over and began rolling down her cheek. She shook her head. "If you knew Phil the way I know him, you would never ask such a question," she said. "He didn't do it, Grandpa. Please find him and bring him back safely so he can clear his name."

Blodgett, Texas

John and Charley dismounted in front of the sheriff's office, then raised a cloud of dust as they patted themselves down to get rid of the trail dust. Then they tied their horses off, stepped up onto the sagging wood porch, and went inside.

A deputy sitting behind the desk was on the telephone. He held up his finger, as if asking the two visitors to give him a minute, until he finished the conversation.

"No, ma'am, there is no mention of a broken window on any of our reports. I'm not saying the window wasn't broken last night, Mrs. Withers, I'm just saying that none of our deputies noticed it during their rounds. Yes, ma'am, I'll tell Sheriff

Dobson about it as soon as he comes in. Good-bye."

The deputy hung up the phone. "I swear, it had to be easier before telephones were invented," he said. "Then if anyone had a complaint, they had to come down to the office to file it. That got rid of a lot of the minor stuff. Now it is too easy for them to just make a telephone call."

"It's not anything I ever had to deal with," John said.

"Me, either," Charley added.

The deputy rubbed his hands together, as if putting a window between the telephone conversation and the business at hand. "Now, what can I do for you, gentlemen?" he asked.

"We'd like to talk to Sheriff Dobson," John said.

"He's not here right now."

"Where is he?"

"I'm not sure. What is this about?"

"It's about law business," Charley said.

"Law business? Well, maybe you didn't notice, but this is a sheriff's office and I'm the deputy. That makes this the place to come to do law business."

"If you don't mind, we'd prefer to talk directly to the sheriff," Charley said.

"Yes, well, the sheriff is a busy man. I'm not sure he would have time to talk to you."

"I believe he would talk to us," John said, patting the badge on his vest.

"Look, I don't know who you are or what you are doing in my office," the deputy said. "But you don't just come in here wearing a shiny, brass badge and expecting the sheriff to talk to you. Now, if you've got any real business, you can tell me. As far as you are concerned, I'm all the lawman you need."

"Those badges aren't brass, Bobby. They are gold," another voice said.

Recognizing the sheriff's voice, John and Charley turned toward the door.

"Hello, Bill, long time no see," John said.

Sheriff Bill Dobson chuckled and shook his head. "Lord, lord, who would've ever thought the two of you would show up in my office? And, together, no less."

"You know these two men, Sheriff?" the deputy asked. He stood up so quickly that he knocked his chair over, then, grabbing for it, he knocked over the telephone and a stack of in-baskets.

"Oh, for God's sake, Bobby, sit down before you fall down," Sheriff Dobson said. "You are as clumsy as a bull in a china shop."

Bobby sat back down quickly, but forgetting that he had turned over the chair, went all the way to the floor.

"Excuse me, I'm sorry," Bobby mumbled as he hopped back up and repositioned his chair.

"Come on into my office," Dobson invited, taking the two men into another room off the main lobby. "Would you like some coffee?"

"Sure, thanks," Charley said.

"Thank you," John said.

"Bobby, bring three cups of coffee in," Dobson called through the door. "Have a seat," Dobson invited.

John and Charley sat opposite Dobson's desk and were just settled when the deputy brought in three cups of coffee. He handed them out, then stood by.

"Thank you, Bobby. That'll be all," Dobson said.

"I thought maybe . . . you know . . . in case you needed me I would—"

"That will be all, Bobby, thank you," Dobson said. "And shut the door on your way out," he added.

"Yes, sir," Bobby mumbled.

Dobson waited until the door was shut. Then he sighed and shook his head. "Bobby Gilmore is the mayor's nephew," he explained. "Now, to what do I owe the honor of a visit from two of the greatest peace officers Texas has ever produced?"

"We're looking for Phil Goodnight," John said.

"Ha! Aren't we all?" Dobson replied. "Though I must say, I can't see the two of you as bounty hunters."

"We're not looking for him for the reward," Charley said.

"You're not? Then, why are you looking for him?"

"Mr. Goodnight is married to our granddaughter," John explained.

"The hell you say."

John and Charley nodded.

"Well, fellas, I'm sorry to hear that," Dobson said. "It's a shame when men with your reputations have a relative go bad on them. Even if he is only a relative by marriage."

"What makes you so certain Phil Goodnight went bad?" John asked.

"Well, I don't know how people look at it over in Tywappity County, but here in Robison County, if you rob a bank that means you've gone bad."

"What I mean is, what makes you so certain that Phil robbed the bank?"

"The evidence against him is overwhelming and conclusive," Dobson explained.

"Share it with us," John suggested.

Dobson looked at the two old sheriffs for a moment, then he sighed and stroked his chin. "All right. To begin with, the bank wasn't broken into, but was entered through an unlocked door. Phil Goodnight had the keys to the bank.

"Next, the vault door was standing open. It wasn't blasted open; it was opened by combination. Phil Goodnight had the combination."

Dobson leaned back in his chair and crossed his arms across his chest. It was obvious that he was about to hit them with his most damning piece of evidence.

"And, finally, we found a sheet of paper with the combination lying on the floor of the bank right next to the open vault."

"Is that all you have?" John asked.

"Believe me, in any court in the country, that is enough," Dobson assured them.

"If Phil Goodnight knew the combination, why would he have to have it written on a piece of paper? It sounds to me like this would point more toward someone else doing it, someone who would need the combination written for them," John suggested.

"Ordinarily, I would agree with you," Sheriff Dobson said. "But not in this case. You see, Phil Goodnight had just arrived in Blodgett on the very day the bank was robbed, so like as not, he hadn't had time to learn the combination. And, to further implicate him, Mr. Martel identified the paper that was found in the bank that night as the same sheet of paper he had been given Phil Goodnight on that very evening when the bank threw a big welcome dinner."

"Phil Goodnight was going to be the bank manager, wasn't he?" Charley asked.

Dobson nodded. "Yes, he was. And everyone rolled the red carpet out for him. To be honest, I think that's why everyone is so angry with him now. I mean, it's bad enough to have the bank robbed, but they feel like he turned on the town, after we went all out to welcome him and his pretty young wife."

"Doesn't it seem odd to you that someone with that good of a job, who has just married and just moved to town, would throw everything away his first night here?" Charley asked, continuing his own reasoning.

Dobson nodded. "Yeah, it does somewhat. I'll admit that. But on the other hand, if robbing the bank is what he had in mind all along, why would he wait? When you think about it, the first night he is here is as good as the one thousandth night."

"You're convinced that he did it?" John asked.

"I'm totally convinced," Dobson answered. "Like I said, the evidence is just too strong."

"That piece of paper could have been planted there," John suggested.

"That's pretty unlikely, isn't it? In order to plant the paper, they would have had to steal it from Goodnight."

"Still, it could've been planted, and you don't have any eyewitnesses who can actually put him in the bank that night, do you?" John asked.

"No, we don't have any eyewitnesses who can tell us where he was." Dobson paused, then smiled triumphantly. "But we do have an eyewitness to where he wasn't. He wasn't in his hotel room where he was supposed to be."

Dobson paused, hoping one of them would ask who the eyewitness was. When they didn't ask, he volunteered the information.

"That eyewitness is unimpeachable. You see, it is his wife, your own granddaughter."

"That just tells you where he wasn't, not where he was," Charley said.

"Look, if he didn't do it, why did he run away?"

"Maybe he didn't have any choice. Maybe the real robbers took him away," John suggested.

"I wish I could believe that. Especially now that I know his connection to you two. But I have to go with where the evidence leads me."

"Well, if you don't mind, we are going to start our own investigation," John said.

"No, I don't mind at all. In fact, if there is anything I can do to help you, please let me know."

"We appreciate it," Charley said, putting his now-empty cup on the desk and standing up. John got up from his chair as well.

"We'll let you know if we need you," John added.

Dobson hurried around the desk, then opened the door for them. "Listen," he said. "Look around all you want but—and this is awkward for me, especially given your history and all—I don't want you to forget who is the law in this town."

"We will be ever-mindful," Charley said.

Bidding Dobson goodbye, John and Charley left the office and started down the street toward the nearest saloon.

Dobson stood at the door and watched them for a moment.

"What did those two old geezers want?" Bobby asked. "Can you imagine someone actually making them deputies?"

Dobson turned toward him, glaring at him. "Deputies?" he said. "Let me tell you something, Sonny. If you put all the deputies in the state of Texas together, they wouldn't make a pimple on the ass of

either one of those men. That was John Carmack
and Charley Dawson."

"Carmack and Dawson? I've heard of them,"
Bobby said.

"I should hope you have."

"What are they doing in Blodgett?"

"They are looking for Phil Goodnight."

"They are? I'll be damned! Who would have ever
thought that something that happened in little old
Blodgett would be important enough to attract
people like that? Are they still sheriffs somewhere?
I thought they were retired. Actually, I thought
they were dead. I mean, they are real famous people that you just hear of, like Sam Houston, and
Stephen Austin. Like Robert E. Lee and George
Washington. They aren't somebody you would
ever expect to meet."

"You've got them in the right company, all right,"
Dobson said. "But as you can see they are defi-
nitely not dead."

"Why are they looking for Phil Goodnight?"

"They are after Goodnight because . . . get this . . .
he is married to their granddaughter."

"I'll be damned!" Bobby said.

Chapter Eleven

There was a piano in the saloon, but nobody was playing it. The saloon was dimly lighted by half a dozen incandescent light bulbs hanging from the ceiling by long wires, their yellow glow barely pushing back the shadows. Three overhead fans were turning, the action causing the cloud of tobacco smoke to swirl and spread across the room.

A card game was in progress at one table; at another part of the room, two tables had been pulled together, and several men were sitting there, drinking beer and talking. A couple of cowboys stood at the bar, staring into their mugs. A bar girl was at the far end of the bar, and she looked up with interest when John and Charley came in, but looked back down again when she saw that they were probably too old to invest any time or money in what she had to offer.

John and Charley bought two beers, then carried them over to the table where the men were talking.

"Mind if we join you?" Charley asked.

"No, not at all. Pull up a chair."

Travelers from town to town were nearly always welcome in any group of talkers because they were able to introduce new stories to the conversation. That was exactly what John and Charley were counting on, and it worked because within a few minutes, without their pushing it, the conversation swung around to the recent bank robbery.

"Have any of you fellas been over to the bank recently? Josh Watson is bank manager now. The board just made it official."

"Really? Ha! I'll bet he is struttin' around like he's king of the walk," one of the others said.

"Yeah, well, best thing that ever happened to him was having the bank get robbed."

"Wait," John said. "This man, Watson, is bank manager, but the best thing that ever happened to him was getting the bank robbed?"

"You better believe it."

"How so?"

"You tell 'im, Smitty. Your brother-in-law is on the board of directors for the bank, ain't he?"

"Yes," Smitty answered. "Here's the way it has all come down," he said, leaning forward to rest his arms on the table, enjoying his moment at the center of attention. "Whenever Governor Hogg got this new law passed about regulating banks and all, the board figured they needed a bank manager. So they hired Phil Goodnight."

"Which was wrong," one of the others said. "Josh Watson was the chief teller. If they needed a manager, they should'a just give him the job."

"Well, they did talk about it," Smitty said. "But they figured that, what with all the new regulations and all, they probably needed someone with a lot more education than Watson has."

"I don't suppose this Watson fella appreciated that much," John said.

"Whoowee!" one of the others said. "He didn't appreciate it at all. My cousin was in the bank right after Watson was told. He said he never knew that little fella could cuss that good."

The others laughed.

"But you say he's the bank manager now?"

"Oh, yes. After Goodnight robbed the bank of over forty thousand dollars, why, they just naturally promoted Watson," Smitty said.

"I heard tell Watson wouldn't take the job until they made it official and promised him that it wasn't just a temporary job," one of the others said.

"That's true," Smitty said.

"Well, hell, I don't blame Watson," one of the others said. "I mean, they didn't do him right. Besides which, he was the one who found the paper with the vault combination."

"And that's how come we know Phil Goodnight is the one that robbed the bank," another said.

"Yes, well, I'm not all that sure Goodnight did it," Smitty said. "I mean, why would he? Being bank manager is a well-paying job, and it's not like he was going to have to be doing physical labor."

"You got that right. Ain't nobody ever worked in a bank doing physical labor," another said, and they all laughed.

"Nobody thinks Goodnight did it alone, do they?" Charley asked.

"Oh, hell no. Why, that Eastern dude couldn't pull off something like that by his own self. Besides which, there were seven horses that rode out of town that night."

"Including Dan Norton's mare that was stolen from right out front," Smitty added.

After finishing their beers, John and Charley walked over to the bank. It wasn't hard to pick out Josh Watson. He was in the process of berating one of the tellers when they went in.

"Mr. Watson?" John asked.

Watson's face underwent an instant change, from officious to obsequious. "Yes, I am the bank manager," said. "May I help you?"

"We would like to talk to you about the bank robbery," John said.

"And you would be?"

"I'm John Carmack, and this is Charley Dawson."

"We are special agents for the governor," Charley said, showing his badge.

Watson's eyes widened when he saw the badge. "Oh my, that's gold, isn't it?"

"Yes. Like I said, we are special agents for the governor."

"Well, uh, come into my office," Watson offered.

John and Charley followed Watson into the small office at the back of the bank and, at his invitation, sat in chairs across the desk from him.

"Now, gentlemen, what can I do for you?"

"Do you believe, as everyone else seems to, that Phil Goodnight robbed the bank?" John asked.

"Oh, yes. I have no doubt about that. You see, I found a paper—"

"With the combination to the safe, yes, we heard that," John said.

"And you are the one who found it?" Charley asked.

"Yes, I came to the bank early the next morning, discovered the front door was unlocked, the vault was standing open, all the money was missing, and that's when I saw the paper on the floor."

"But there were others with him, weren't there? The report we heard was that several riders rode out that day," John asked.

"That would seem to be the case."

"Do you have any idea who any of them might be?"

"Oh, heavens, no. I don't associate with such people," Watson said.

"Tell me something, Mr. Watson. If Goodnight had the combination to the safe, why didn't he just come in here alone, in the middle of the night, take the money, and then leave on the midnight train with his wife? Why did he leave her at the hotel?"

"Who can explain the criminal mind?" Watson replied.

"You don't mind if we talk to the other employees of the bank, do you?"

"No, of course not. Be my guest," Watson invited.

One by one, John and Charley talked to the other employees, most of who had nothing to add, since the investigation was active by the time they came to work that day.

It wasn't until they spoke to Troy Jackson, the black man who was sweeping the floor, that they got any fresh information. Jackson was nervous about being interviewed by two lawmen.

"I didn't have nothin' to do with robbin' the bank," he said.

"No one is accusing you of that," Charley said, trying to put his mind at ease. "But you did come in that morning, didn't you?"

"Yes, suh, I was waitin' out front of the bank for when Mr. Watson come. I'm supposed to sweep the floor so it be clean before all the customers come."

"So you were here when he put the key in the door and saw that it was unlocked?"

"No, suh."

"No? I thought you said you were here when he arrived."

"Oh, yes, suh, I be here all right. But Mr. Watson, he didn't need no key. He just reach down and turn the door knob and the door just come open pretty as you please."

"You mean he tried the door knob before he put the key in the door?"

"Yes, suh."

"Then what happened?"

"When we come inside, Mr. Watson take one look around and he say, 'Troy, go get the sheriff. This here bank done been robbed.' "

"Did you go for the sheriff?"

"Yes, suh. Well, first, Mr. Watson, he tell me to come around behind the counter and he showed me a piece of paper on the floor. Then he say I'm to tell the sheriff that I seen that paper first thing when I come in."

"Did you tell that to the sheriff?"

"Yes, suh. I say just that."

"What did you do then?"

"Mr. Watson tell me, don't do no sweepin' 'til the sheriff done lookin' around."

"That was smart. What did you do then?"

"I also do the sweepin' for the land office. That's just across the alley from the bank. So that's what I done. I just let myself out the back door so's not to get in the way of the sheriff and the law."

"Did Mr. Watson come unlock the back door for you?"

Jackson thought for a moment, then he shook

his head. "No, sir. Now that I recollect on it, the back door done be unlocked."

John and Charley looked at each other. "Did you see Mr. Watson unlock it?" John asked.

"No, suh. Mr. Watson, he didn't unlock that door."

"You are sure of that?"

"Yes, suh, I be real sure of that."

"Sheriff, was there any mention of the back door of the bank being unlocked?" Charley asked Sheriff Dobson after he and John returned to the sheriff's office.

"No," Dobson said. "Was it unlocked?"

"Troy Jackson says it was. He said he went out that door in order to go to work over at the land office."

"I'll be damned," Dobson said. "No, that never came up."

"Don't you think that might be significant?" Charley asked.

Dobson thought for a moment, then shook his head. "I don't see how."

"If Phil Goodnight robbed the bank, why would he feel it necessary to unlock both doors?" John asked.

"I don't know."

"Here's another thing. According to Troy Jackson, Watson didn't even try to unlock the front door. He just opened it," John said.

"He didn't have to unlock it. That's the whole point," Dobson said.

"No, Sheriff. The point is, he didn't even *try*. That can only mean that he already knew it was unlocked," Charley said.

"Watson has keys to the bank, doesn't he?" John asked.

"Yes, of course he does."

"And he knows the combination to the safe?"

"What are you suggesting? That Watson robbed the bank?" Sheriff Dobson laughed. "That's a little far-fetched, isn't it?"

"Don't you think it is a possibility?" Charley asked.

"No."

"Why not?"

"Well, for one thing, he is still here. Goodnight is the one who is gone."

"If there were others involved in the bank robbery, they could've taken Goodnight with them," Charley said.

"But why would they do that?"

"What if Goodnight was walking around town and saw something going on in the bank? Then, when he investigated, he stumbled onto the robbery in progress," John suggested.

"By taking him with them, it would throw suspicion on him and get him out of town so he wouldn't be here to defend himself when he was accused," Charley said.

"And it would also keep him from testifying against someone he might have recognized in the bank," John concluded.

"Ha! How would he recognize anyone? He only arrived in town that very day. He didn't know anyone."

"According to my granddaughter, he was met at the depot by Josh Watson," Charley said.

"So?"

"If he saw Josh Watson robbing the bank, he would recognize him," John said.

"You two are serious about this, aren't you? You

really think Josh Watson had something to do with it."

"We do," John said.

"But he's been right here at this bank for over ten years," Dobson said. "He's had the keys to the bank and the combination to the vault all that time. If he was going to do something like this, why didn't he do it long before now? I mean, he was almost the manager of the bank, when you stop to think about it."

"Almost," John said cryptically.

"Before Phil Goodnight came along," Charley added.

"And now that Phil Goodnight is gone, Josh Watson is the bank manager," John said.

"Rather convenient for him, don't you think?"

The expression of incredulity left Sheriff Dobson's face, to be replaced by one of sudden comprehension.

"Son of a bitch," he said, reaching for his hat. "You two may just be on to something."

Chapter Twelve

Salcedo

By standing on his bunk and looking through the small, barred window of his cell, Phil could see out over almost the whole town. During the long afternoon, he examined Salcedo through that window, watching it go about its normal business. He recognized, almost immediately, that there was something different about the town, and after a while it came to him.

Unlike other towns, there were no signs of normal, domestic life here. The only women he saw were soiled doves, and they moved up and down the street freely, garishly made up and outlandishly dressed. Some, like the woman he had seen in front of the saloon when they first arrived, were practically undressed. He saw more than one bare breast over the course of the afternoon as the women paraded without shame or censure.

The town that had seemed sleepy, almost deserted during the day, seemed to come alive at night.

From his jail cell, Phil could hear the sounds of revelry. There was only one saloon, but it was more than loud enough to make up for the fact that it stood alone.

And the sounds were different—not only louder, but more out of control. There was no music, but there were screams, shouts, raucous laughter, and gunfire. Phil didn't know whether the not infrequent gunshots were fired in anger or were part of the overall boisterous condition that prevailed.

If the sheriff was as crooked as Angus Pugh—and from the obvious payoff Phil had witnessed, he was sure that was the case—then he knew he could expect no help from that quarter. His only chance would be if he could find some citizen of the town who had enough moral and ethical character to help him. But from his overall perception of the town, he had come to the conclusion that no such person existed.

Phil sat on his bunk, contemplating his situation. He thought about his wife, and he wondered where Lucy was right now. What was she doing? He knew she would be worried, and he felt sick at heart, not only for his own condition, but for the agony he knew she must be experiencing.

He wished he had some way of getting in touch with her, but he knew that wasn't possible. He had seen no poles or wires, which meant there was no telephone or even telegraph service. He knew there was no railroad, and he was pretty sure there was no stagecoach operation either. Just how did these people communicate with the outside world?

Inexplicably, he smiled. The truth was, he decided, Lucy was probably handling this situation better than he. It had been his observation that she was made of pretty strong stuff, no doubt something she had inherited from her illustrious grandfathers.

Sighing, Phil stood up and walked over to the cell door. Standing there, he happened to glance over to the wall nearby, and that's when he saw the key to his jail cell. It was hanging by a little loop of rawhide, from a peg in a board that was nailed to the wall. That board was right next to the jail cell.

That's it! He thought. *If I can get that key, it's my way out of here!*

There was nobody in the jail watching him. Sheriff Bixby, if indeed he was a sheriff, had merely locked him in the cell and left him. There were no deputies, at least, none that he had seen so far. Bixby had shown up around midday with a bowl of beans and a cup of water, but Phil hadn't seen him since then.

Phil looked at the key, estimating how far it was from the cell. Once he had a good idea as to what he needed to do, he started thinking of a way to do it.

The saloon in Salcedo had no name.

"Hell, it don't need no name," Ed Meeker advised the others. "I mean, bein' as it's the only one in town, all folks need to know about it is that it is a saloon."

Ed Meeker owned the saloon. He had never owned a saloon before, but he had managed a few of them, and though he had no particular criminal past, he had been fired on at least two previous occasions for stealing from his employer.

"Folks can trust me now," he liked to say. "I ain't likely to steal from myself now, am I?"

Despite a past record of cheating his employers,

Ed had never been prosecuted; thus, he had no criminal record. That being the case, he wasn't above trading with outlaws and profiting from the misdeeds of others.

Like the other merchants in town, Ed's profit was considerably greater than it would have been under normal conditions. That's because these enterprising entrepreneurs were, literally, the only game in town. Outlaws would pay Meeker's inflated price for rotgut whiskey or they didn't drink. These same outlaws also paid more for boots, dry goods, groceries, restaurant fare, guns, bullets, or any and all other goods they might want or need.

Salcedo was a robbers' roost, a haven for men on the run. Fully three-fourths of the residents of the town were outlaws, and the remaining population made their living by serving the outlaws. None were of sterling reputation.

Although a few residents had wives, the wives generally stayed off the streets and out of the businesses. As a result, the only women visible were the soiled doves, and they purposely made themselves visible in order to entice business. Most of the soiled doves of Salcedo, while still relatively young, were already showing the effects of their life on the line. In the normal towns of cities of Texas, referred to by the residents of Salcedo as "out there," the girls' early dissipation affected their earning potential. This was especially true when they had to compete with the younger, fresher girls who were just entering the profession.

Although there were no elections and no traditional city government, Salcedo wasn't without some structure. Differences of opinion could be settled by fists, knives, or guns. But once a final settlement had been made between two adversaries, it was over. If one of the parties was killed in the course of the "solution to the problem," that person's relatives or friends had no further recourse. Vengeance and prolonged feuds weakened the cohesion of the town, which had to be able to bury all personal grievances to stand together against encroachment from "out there." This was especially true if the encroachment from out there was an unwanted visit from lawmen.

Angus Pugh was the agreed-upon mayor of the town. His self-appointment was accepted without challenge by the other residents of Salcedo. Although Pugh had spent twenty years in prison, the criminal activity of his younger years, his robberies and shootings and even his activities while riding with Quantril were legendary.

And since leaving prison, despite his age, Pugh showed that he still had what it took to thrive in the world of the lawless. His successful robbery of the Bank of Blodgett proved that.

"He would'a never pulled it off if he hadn't had that little pipsqueak of a banker to help him," one of the patrons of the saloon said.

"You mean the fella he brought back with him? The one he put in jail?"

"No. The one that helped him is still back in Blodgett, still runnin' the bank. He done the whole thing for five thousand dollars. Let Pugh and the others into the bank, opened the vault, everything. I mean, it ain't like Pugh shot his way in to get the money or anything."

"Yeah? Well, to my way of thinkin', it just goes to show how smart ole Pugh is, to be able to talk someone on the inside into helpin' him like that."

"Hell, it was his cousin. How hard would it be to talk your cousin into doin' something like that?"

The subject of the conversation, currently unaware that he was being talked about, was sitting at what had become his private table in the back of the saloon. He was enjoying a meal of fried ham and potatoes and was flanked on either side by a couple of the working girls.

Pugh was not a particularly randy person; in fact, more often than not he was impotent, though that secret was so well guarded by the women who had encountered his impotence that they didn't even discuss it with each other.

There were two reasons they didn't discuss it. One reason for keeping quiet was their fear of what he might do to them if it got out that they were talking about such a personal problem. However, that fear had never been planted in them by any kind of threat, actual or implied. The second reason they guarded his privacy was financial. Despite the fact that Pugh rarely took advantage of whatever sexual pleasures the girls could offer, he was always very generous with them for sharing their time with him. The girls understood that, and didn't want to do anything to jeopardize that beneficence.

And, despite Pugh's decreased libido, he truly did enjoy the company of women.

"Hey, Angus, what you reckon we ought to do with our prisoner?" Muley asked, calling over from the bar.

"I figure we'll keep him in jail for a while, then let 'im out and give him a job in our bank," Pugh said. "I mean, hell, if he was good enough for the Bank of Blodgett, then he ought to be good enough for us."

Muley and the others laughed.

* * *

Back in the jail cell, Phil was making progress. Removing the laces from his shoes, he tied them together, then tied a bolt he had taken from the bars to the end of that double length of string. Holding onto one end of the string, he started swinging the bolt up toward the key, trying to catch onto it.

Several times he almost got it, but barely missed. Once, he nearly succeeded in knocking the key off the hook, but in such a way that would have sent it even farther away. He held his breath as the key ring swung back and forth a few times, then hung on still once more.

On the next try, he succeeded in knocking the key to the floor, fortunately immediately below the peg so that it wouldn't be out of reach.

"Yes!" he said when the bolt fell exactly where he wanted it to fall.

Now, carefully, Phil tossed the bolt out, just beyond the key. Pulling very carefully on the string, he managed to hook onto the key with the bolt and start sliding it toward him. Then, as soon as the key was within arm's lenth, he grabbed it, stood up, put it in the keyhole, and turned. There was a satisfying click as he turned, and when he pushed on the cell door, it swung open.

Phil was halfway across the floor when the front door suddenly opened and the sheriff came in, carrying another bowl of beans.

"I got more vittles here," the sheriff said, then, seeing Phil standing outside of the cell, he dropped the beans and reached for his gun.

"No!" Phil shouted. Without thinking, he picked up the chair and brought it crashing down on the sheriff's head before the sheriff's gun cleared leather. The sheriff went down.

Without waiting to check on the sheriff's condition, Phil darted outside. There was only one saddled horse in view on the entire street. It was tied to a hitching rack right next door to the jailhouse, and Phil ran to it. Untying the horse, he swung into the saddle, then jerked the reins around and urged the horse down the street.

It was dark, and Phil didn't know where he was going; he just knew he wanted out of here. Because of that, he urged the horse into a gallop. But the horse, not used to this rider and unwilling to gallop in the dark, suddenly balked, and when he did so, Phil was thrown over the horse's head.

It was Phil's bad luck that he was thrown right in front of the saloon, and before he could even get up, the saloon was emptying of people who, attracted by the sound of a galloping horse, had come out to see what was going on. One of those who came outside was Muley.

"Well now," Muley said, smiling broadly. "Looky what we have here."

Shaken, Phil got up from the street and dusted himself off. Looking around, he saw that nearly a dozen people were around him, including Angus Pugh, Muley, and Weasel, the only three he knew by name.

"Tully," Pugh said. "Go down and tell Bixby we've got his man."

"All right," one of the men said, starting up the street toward the sheriff's office.

"Hey, Mort," Muley called out to Tully. "Tell 'im we took him inside to buy him a drink. Here in Salcedo, anyone who can break out of jail deserves a drink. That's all right, ain't it, Angus?"

Pugh nodded, but said nothing.

"Damn right, let's all have a drink!" someone else said and, laughing, they dragged a frustrated and still-frightened Phil inside, treating him almost as much as a hero as someone who was their captive.

"Belly up to the bar, gents!" Muley called to the others when he went inside. "This here Eastern dude has just broken outta jail, and I aim for us to all have a drink to him before we put him back."

Phil had a glass of whiskey thrust into his hand, and, though it had a sour, unpleasant smell, he figured that, at this moment, a drink, any drink, was just what he needed. He tossed it down and nearly gagged as it burned all the way down his throat.

"Was that kerosene?" he asked.

"Well, there was just a little of it that the bartender puts in for taste," Muley said. "Hell, without that, you couldn't even drink this stuff." He refilled Phil's glass. "Have another."

"No, thank you very much," Phil said. "But one drink is sufficient."

"Mister, when someone offers you a drink, it ain't polite to turn him down," Weasel said. "Now, Muley offered you a drink."

"He don't have to drink another'n iffen he don't want to," Muley said. "He done drunk one."

"He drunk the one you offered him. Now I'm offerin' him one," Weasel said. "Have another." There was an edge to his voice.

"Very well, if you insist," Phil said. Lifting the glass to his lips, he made another face, then managed, somehow, to toss it down.

"How about another?" Weasel said, reaching for the bottle to pour it. Muley reached down and clamped his hand around Weasel's wrist.

"He don't need another'n," Muley said.

"You goin' soft on us, Muley?" Weasel asked.

Muley smiled. "No," he said. "I just don't like to see good whiskey go to waste."

"Good whiskey?" someone said. "You call Ed Meeker's horse piss good whiskey?" He laughed loudly, and everyone else in the saloon laughed with him. The laughter broke the tension, and Weasel walked away from the bar.

"Thanks," Phil said.

"Well, iffen you don't like whiskey, no sense in makin' you drink it," Muley said. "You may as well enjoy your visit with us until Bixby gets here to bring you back."

At that moment Mort Tully came back into the saloon.

"Step up to the bar and have a drink, Mort," Muley said. "Did you tell Bixby that Goodnight was down here?"

"I didn't tell 'im nothin'," Tully replied. He poured himself a drink, staring directly at Goodnight all the while. "To tell you the truth, I wouldn't a'thought this little pissant had it in him."

Muley laughed. "To escape? Me neither. That's why we're all drinkin' to him."

"Nah, I ain't talkin' about him escapin'," Tully said. "To escape, all you got to do is run, and any-one can do that. No, what I'm talkin' about is, I didn't think this little feller had it in him to kill Bixby."

"What?" Weasel asked. "Are you sayin' Goodnight killed Sheriff Bixby?"

"That's what I'm sayin'. He smashed Bixby's head in with a chair, he did. Ole Bixby's layin' down there on the floor, right now, deader'n shit."

Once, when Phil was young, he fell from a tree.

The fall knocked the breath out of him and he lay there on the ground, unable to breathe and wondering if he would ever be able to breathe again.

Learning, just now, that he had just killed Sheriff Bixby affected Phil in the same way. He felt dizzy and for a moment was afraid that he would pass out. He grabbed hold of the bar to steady himself. His knees were weak and his breathing labored. He felt all the blood leaving his head.

"Are you sure he is dead?" Phil asked. "Absolutely dead?"

"He's dead all right."

"Is that true, Goodnight?" Muley asked. "Did you kill Sheriff Bixby?"

"I . . . I don't know," Phil answered. "If so, I didn't mean to kill him. I mean, he came into the jail as I was attempting to escape and, well, I just grabbed the nearest thing. It happened to be a chair."

"Hold it!" Pugh shouted from his table. "Don't say another word!"

Everyone in the saloon grew quiet and looked toward Pugh. Pushing his meal aside, Pugh got up and walked quickly across the open area that separated him from Phil. "Boy, don't you know nothin'? You don't answer any of these questions. . . . You don't say anything to anyone until you've had a chance to consult with your lawyer. Do you hear me?"

"My lawyer? And just what lawyer would that be? I don't think you are going to let me hire my lawyer back in Memphis, and I'm sure there are no members of the bar living in this town. Are there?"

"The court will appoint one for you," Pugh said.

"What court are you talking about?" Phil asked.

"My court," Pugh answered, smiling broadly and tapping himself on the chest.

"Hell, Angus, we don't need no trial. He done told us he killed Bixby," Weasel said. "I think we should just take the son of a bitch out front and hang 'im from the front porch."

"What?" Phil gasped.

"Nah, we ain't goin' to do that," Pugh replied. "Ever'one deserves a day in court. What we're goin' to do is give Mr. Goodnight here a fair trial." Pugh paused for a moment, before adding, "Then we'll hang him."

"Damn right!" someone said.

"And we ain't goin' to hang him from the porch," Pugh said. "We'll build us a gallows and have a proper hangin'."

"Sum'bitch, I ain't seen me what you'd call a proper hangin' since my cousin got strung up back in Fort Smith, Arkansas. And hell, that was fifteen years or so ago," another said.

Phil felt a hollowness in his stomach, a weakness in his knees, and a spinning in his head. He had to hold on to the bar to keep from falling.

"I believe you said something about a lawyer?" he asked.

"Yeah," Pugh said. "I'll give you a lawyer. Muley, since you 'n Goodnight have become such friends, I'm going to make you his lawyer."

"Muley is to be my lawyer?" Phil asked, weakly.

"Yeah, he ought to be damn good at it. He's always running his mouth off."

The others laughed.

"Weasel, you'll be the prosecutor."

"Yeah," Weasel said. "I'll prosecute the son of a bitch."

"This is a farce," Phil said. "They aren't lawyers, and you aren't a court."

"I told you, here, I am the court," Pugh said. "And Muley and Weasel are lawyers, simply because I said they were lawyers. Are you not satisfied with that arrangement?"

"No, I'm not satisfied," Phil answered emphatically. "How could you expect me to agree to such an arrangement? There's no way I can get a fair trial with this kind of an arrangement."

"Sure there is," Pugh said. "I will personally see to it."

"And just how are you going to see to it?" Phil asked.

"Easy," Pugh said with a smile. He looked at the two men he had just appointed. "Muley, are you going to do your best to defend Mr. Goodnight?"

"Well, yeah, Angus, you know I'm goin' to do that."

"And Weasel, are you going to do your best to prosecute him?"

"I'm goin' to prosecute him, right up until he gets his neck stretched," Weasel answered. He put his fist by the side of his neck, then jerked upward as if pulling on a rope. He dropped his head to one side, stuck out his tongue, and made a gagging sound. The others in the saloon laughed at his comic antics.

Pugh turned toward Phil. "See there? I have both their words that they are going to do the best they can."

"You will excuse me if I say that isn't very reassuring," Phil said.

"Oh, I almost forgot," Pugh said. He looked at the two "lawyers." "I want the two of you to do the very best you can. And in order to ensure that, Weasel, if you fail to prosecute, I intend to hang you in his place."

"Sure thing," Weasel said. "I reckon I better win my case then, hadn't I?"

Again, the others in the saloon laughed.

"And Muley, if you don't win your case, then we'll have a double hanging."

"What? What do you mean?" he asked, puzzled by Pugh's comment.

"If you don't get Mr. Goodnight off, I'll hang you right alongside him."

"What?" Muley shouted. Everyone else in the saloon gasped in amazement over Pugh's statement.

"Angus, you can't be serious about that," he said.

"I'm dead serious," Pugh replied. "That's the only way I know that I can guarantee a fair trial."

For a long moment, there was absolute quiet in the saloon.

Pugh broke the silence. "Besides, look at it this way. Everyone is looking for a hanging. This way nobody will be disappointed. Except for whoever winds up getting hanged," he added with a macabre laugh.

Nervously the others, with the noticeable exception of Phil, Muley, and Weasel, laughed as well.

"I gotta hand it to you, Pugh. You do make life in this here hellhole of a town interestin'," Ed Meeker said. "By the way, you can hold court right here in the saloon if you are of a mind to. And I won't charge you one penny of rent."

"Hell, the way you charge for drinks, you won't need to charge any rent," Pugh said. He looked toward a couple of the men who had done the Blodgett bank job with him. "You fellas take our prisoner down to the jail. And let's see if we can't keep him locked up this time."

"All right," one of the two men replied. "Come

on, *Mr.* Goodnight," he added, emphasizing the word "mister."

"Muley, Weasel, if I were you two, I wouldn't be standin' 'round here with your thumbs up your asses. I'd be studyin' on how I would present the case."

"Yeah," Muley said, his voice barely audible. "Yeah, I guess I had better get started."

"Me too," Weasel added.

Chapter Thirteen

Blodgett

"Sheriff, with your permission, Charley and I will handle the interrogation," John said.

"All right," Dobson replied. "But I intend to watch."

"Why do you want to watch? You don't think we're going to use a rope's end on him, do you?" Charley asked, with a little chuckle.

Dobson shook his head. "No, I never heard anything like that about either one of you. But I've heard that you do have a way of interrogating suspects, so I thought I might learn something from you."

"Then be our guest," John said.

Deputy Bobby Gilmore came into the office then, accompanied by Josh Watson.

"Mr. Watson, thank you for coming down," John said.

"Yes, well, I didn't have a lot of choice," Watson

replied petulantly. "Deputy Gilmore was quite insistent. What is all this about?"

"We'd just like to ask you a few questions, that's all," John said.

"As I recall, you questioned me at the bank," Watson said. He looked at Dobson. "I'm a busy man, Sheriff. Is this really necessary?"

"Please," John said, pointing to an armless, straight-backed chair. "Have a seat."

There was something ominous-looking about a single chair in the middle of the floor, and Watson licked his lips nervously, then took his case to Dobson one more time.

"Is this really necessary?" he asked again.

"If you cooperate, it will only take a few minutes," Sheriff Dobson said.

Watson let out a sigh of protest, letting it be known that he was much too busy for such a thing, then sat down.

John began by asking a few innocuous questions.

The questioning had been going on for half an hour and Josh Watson was becoming very agitated and very nervous.

"I know you got the job you wanted," John said. "What else did you get for setting up the bank robbery?"

"What?" Watson replied, shocked by the question. Until now, the questions had been general and non-accusatory. This was the first intimation that Watson himself might be a suspect. "Surely you don't suspect me?"

"You did rob the bank, didn't you?"

"I assure you, I don't know what you are talking about," Watson said. He was suddenly sweating profusely and his eyes darted about like those of a cornered rat.

"Do you want to take all the blame yourself?"

"The blame for what? I didn't do anything," Watson answered. "Phil Goodnight was the robber. Everyone knows. Ask Sheriff Dobson. He found the note on the floor with the combination numbers."

"No, in fact, you found the note, didn't you?" John said.

"I don't remember who found the note."

"Troy Jackson says you found it."

"Well, are you going to believe me or that nigger?"

"What reason would Jackson have to lie?" John asked. "He still has the same job he had before the robbery, and he's still getting paid the same."

"This isn't right," Watson said. He looked over at Sheriff Dobson, who was leaning against the wall with his arms crossed over his chest, watching the interrogation.

Like Dobson, Charley was also in the room, watching the interrogation. So far, Charley hadn't spoken, but Watson found the expression on Charley's face and in his eyes so frightening that he couldn't look at him. He looked back at Dobson.

"Sheriff, you know this isn't right. You said yourself that you believed Goodnight robbed the bank."

"That's because I thought the evidence pointed in that direction," Dobson said. "But the funny thing is, the evidence is now beginning to point toward you."

"What? What evidence?"

"Why didn't you try the lock when you came to the bank that morning?" John asked.

"I didn't need to. The door was already unlocked."

"How did you know that?"

"What? You're getting me confused," Watson said. "I don't know what you are talking about."

"Jackson says you didn't even try the lock, that you reached straight for the door knob, as if you knew the door was unlocked."

"It was unlocked."

"How did you know that?" John asked again.

"Please!" Watson said, putting his hands to his temples. "You are getting me very confused. Could I have a drink of water?"

"What about the back door? Why was it unlocked?"

"It wasn't unlocked."

"Sure it was. Jackson left by that door when he went to work over at the land office. You didn't unlock it for him, so it must've been unlocked."

"You are believing Jackson again," Watson said.

"And Deputy Gilmore," John added.

"What?"

John looked over at Dobson and nodded.

"Bobby?" Dobson called.

His deputy stuck his head in through the door. "Yes, Sheriff."

"You were with me in the bank on the morning we were investigating the robbery, weren't you?"

"Yes, sir."

"Did you see Troy Jackson go out the back door?"

"Yes, sir, you told me I could let him go."

"Did Watson unlock the door for him?"

"No, sir," the deputy said. "Watson was talking to you."

"Thank you," Dobson said.

"So," John said. "It appears the back door was unlocked. Did you unlock it for the robbers?"

"Phil Goodnight unlocked the front door," Watson insisted.

"Oh, I think you are right about that," John said. "You see, I think Goodnight saw something going on in the bank and came over to investigate. He let himself in through the front door, and that's when he saw you and the other bank robbers."

"No, that's not true."

"Hell, I'm getting tired of this!" Charley said in a loud voice. He pulled his pistol and cocked it. "Let's just shoot the son of a bitch and be done with it!"

"No! Please, no! Don't let him shoot me!" Watson screamed. He put his arms over his head.

"Better get him that water, John. I'm about to send him to hell and it's a cinch he won't get any there."

"All right! All right! I did it!" Watson shouted. "Please, don't let him shoot me!"

John smiled and nodded at Charley. The two men had worked this out between them before starting the interrogation.

John went over to the water dipper and drew a cup of water. He brought it back to Watson.

"Tell us about it," he said, gently.

"He took my job," Watson said. He drank deeply, then handed the cup back to John. "I was head teller of the bank. I should have been promoted to manager. They had no right to hire some stranger over me."

"I agree," John said. "From all I've heard, you had been doing a fine job."

"Yes! Yes, I had been," Watson said. He looked

at Dobson. "You know, Sheriff. You've come into the bank several times and I've helped you every time you've needed anything."

"That's true," Dobson said.

"It's a shame they hired someone else over you," John said.

"I'm glad you understand."

"I would probably have done the same thing if I had been in your shoes," John said. "So, what did you do with his body?" John asked.

"What?" Watson gasped, putting his hand to his mouth. John noticed that it was shaking. "What do you mean, his body?"

"Phil Goodnight's body. You did kill him, didn't you? I mean, when he came into the bank and saw you clearing out the vault."

"No, no, it wasn't like that!" Watson said desperately. "He didn't even see me. Besides, he isn't dead."

"Where is he?"

"They took him with them."

"They?"

"When I found out that someone else was going to get the job, I got the idea to rob the bank. Of course, I didn't know that Goodnight would come in on us while it was going on. I figured that just having the bank robbed on the first day he was here would be enough. It would make the job so hard for him that he couldn't handle it. And since I had been here long enough to know everything about the bank, I would be called on to help him. That way the board of directors would have to put me back in charge."

"But it didn't work out that way, did it?"

Watson shook his head. "No. Like you said, he unlocked the front door and came in while the robbery was going on. Who would've thought he would come into the bank at midnight?"

"You said they took him. Who is they? The people who helped you?"

Watson nodded. "My cousin."

"Your cousin?"

"He recently got out of prison, so I got in touch with him."

"Who is your cousin?"

"His name is Pugh. Angus Pugh."

"Angus Pugh?" Charley said. Charley and John exchanged a knowing glance. "Is Pugh the one who took Goodnight?"

"Yes," Watson answered.

"Where did they take him?"

"I don't know."

"You had better pray, Watson, that Phil Goodnight doesn't turn up dead. Because if he does, you will be charged with murder," John said.

"No! I told you, they took him. I don't have anything to do with him now. Whatever happens to him now isn't my fault."

"Yes, it is," John said. "If they murder him, it is still part of the same crime. And the law is very specific on that. If someone dies as the result of a felony commission, everyone involved with that crime will be guilty of murder. That includes you."

"But, I told you, I had nothing to do with that part of it."

"It won't be broken down. If you are guilty of part of it, you are guilty of all of it," John said.

Watson stood up. "Listen, I'm a very busy man. I don't have time to stay here and talk anymore. I have to get back to the bank; I've left paperwork undone. I shouldn't have come over here in the first place."

"Sit down, Mr. Watson," Charley said. Firmly, but not roughly, he pushed Watson back down in his chair.

"Sheriff, you saw that," Watson said, looking over at Sheriff Dobson. "This man is attempting to keep me here against my will."

Dobson sighed. "Get used to it, Watson. I imagine you are going to be held against your will for a very long time now. You won't be going back to the bank now or ever again."

"What? What are you talking about? Of course I'm going back to the bank."

"Josh Watson, I'm placing you under arrest for bank robbery and for complicity in the disappearance of Phil Goodnight. If Mr. Goodnight turns up dead, you will be tried for murder."

"Oh, my God," Watson gasped, putting his hand to his mouth. He began shaking uncontrollably. "You mean I might go to prison?"

"There is no might to it," Dobson replied. "You *are* going to prison."

Word that Josh Watson had been arrested for bank robbery spread quickly through the town of Blodgett. Concurrent with his arrest was the news that Phil Goodnight had been falsely accused. This sudden and unexpected turn of events was the talk of every corner, every store, and every dinner table that night. When the regulars gathered in the saloons the next day, the conversation continued.

"Hey, Paul, you know them two fellas that come in here the other day? The ones that come over to sit and gab with us? Turns out they was John Carmack and Charley Dawson," Smitty said.

"The hell you say," Paul replied.

"Yep. The two greatest lawmen ever to wear badges. They was sittin' right here at the table with us, and we didn't even know."

"Ain't that somethin' now? What were they doin' here in Blodgett?" a man the others called Dutch asked.

"Well, you heard that it was Josh Watson that robbed the bank, didn't you?"

"How could I not of heard that. Hell, it's all anyone's been talking about for the last two days," Dutch replied.

"Well, it was Carmack and Dawson what found all that out," Smitty said. "They went down to the bank and looked around, then sort of figured it all out. And when they started talkin' to Watson, why, he just broke down and tole 'em everything. Leastwise, that's what Deputy Gilmore said."

"Yeah, well, you know what? I could'a told you it was Watson all along," Paul said.

The others around the table laughed.

"You know'd all along that it was Watson, did you?" one of the others said.

"Damn right I know'd it," Paul insisted. "I never did like the son of a bitch anyway." Paul put his fingers to his eyes, demonstrating his point. "Didn't none of you ever notice how he always had that real sneaky look in his eyes?"

"Hey, Smitty, you reckon that's how Carmack 'n Dawson found out about him? 'Cause he had that sneaky look in his eyes?" Dutch asked, and again, those around the table laughed.

"You laugh, but it turns out I was right all along," Paul said. He pointed to Smitty. "And if you ask me, I don't know why your cousin ever hired him in the first place."

"Hell, Paul, he hired him because of that sneaky

look in his eyes. Ever'one knows bankers is sneaky bastards," Smitty replied.

More laughter followed Smitty's remark.

"What I don't understand is how come they was interested in this case anyway," Dutch said. "I mean, it don't seem all that important."

"Ha! I can tell you that," Smitty replied. He didn't go any further with his explanation, preferring to stretch it out as far as he could, enjoying the fact that he was the center of attention.

"Well, come on, Smitty, are you a'goin' to tell us, or ain't you?" Paul asked.

Smitty cleared his throat. "Well, accordin' to Deputy Gilmore, the reason they're goin' after Phil Goodnight is because John Carmack and Charley Dawson are his grandpas."

"What? You mean that little pip-squeak of a banker has grandpas like John Carmack and Charley Dawson?" Dutch asked.

"Accordin' to Bobby Gilmore, that's what brought them two over here," Smitty said.

"I'll be damned," Paul said.

"I'll tell you this," one of the others at the table said. "Whoever it is that's got a'hold of that Goodnight fella, ought to be thinkin' about lettin' him go. I sure as hell wouldn't want Carmack and Dawson to be houndin' my trail."

Buford Scruggs was standing alone at the far end of the bar, nursing a beer and listening to the conversation of Smitty, Paul, and the others. Scruggs stared into the top of his beer mug and, by doing so, managed to keep his face masked from the others in the saloon. He knew he had paper out on him. Whether or not any of it had reached Blodgett, he didn't know. But it was better to be safe than sorry.

" 'Bout ready for another one?" the bartender asked Scruggs.

Scruggs neither responded verbally nor looked up. Instead he just covered the top of his mug with his hand and shook his head no. Waiting until the bartender walked down to the other end to respond to another customer, Scruggs turned and left the saloon. Angus Pugh might be interested in knowing that his cousin was just arrested for bank robbery. He might be even more interested that the prisoner he was holding was the grandson of Sheriffs John Carmack and Charley Dawson.

In fact, he might even be interested enough to be thankful. And he might be thankful enough to express his appreciation with a reward.

Chapter Fourteen

Risco

The town of Risco had a powerful connection with its two most famous citizens. Even though John Carmack had his base of support, and Charley Dawson his, beneath it all the entire town was proud of both of them. When the citizens of Risco traveled to other parts of the country, they were always quick to point out that they were from the hometown of two of the best known lawmen in the country, and they took equal pride in John Carmack and Charley Dawson.

Most had collected newspaper accounts of the exploits of their local heroes, and though not everyone would admit it, several even had copies of the dime novels which featured John or Charley.

Although purporting to be "The True Account of The Heroic Exploits and Exciting Cases" of the two men, the stories were actually wildly outlandish plots with absolutely no connection to reality. Many bought the books in the belief that it benefited

John or Charley, though in fact the books were totally unauthorized stories and neither man received
a cent of compensation from the publication.

Most of the citizens of the town knew that John
and Charley shared a granddaughter. Since their
very public dinner the other night, the citizens of
the town had also learned that the granddaughter's
husband was a suspect in a bank robbery. John and
Charley had come out of retirement to search for
Goodnight, and their mission was the topic of conversation at breakfast tables in the town's cafes,
across shop counters, and in saloons.

"Do you think they found him?"

"If they are looking for him, they will find him."

"What if he's not guilty? What if someone else did
it and has just made it look like Goodnight did it?"

"If that is the case, then, woe betide the person
who is guilty of such deception."

There was almost an even split among the townspeople as to whether or not they thought Goodnight
was guilty as accused. But that issue was settled the
day before when, due to the miracle of telephone
and telegraph, the townspeople got word that Phil
Goodnight was not the bank robber. The wanted
posters were being called back in.

Everyone in town, including those who had actually thought Goodnight was guilty, breathed a
sigh of relief. They were glad that the two lawmen
would not have to face the stigma of having a bank
robber in the family, albeit a member of the family
by marriage only.

On the day that John and Charley returned to
Riscco, Carl May and Clyde Barnes of May and
Barnes Freight Company were down at the Horse-
shoe Corral, negotiating a fee for boarding their
teams. Because the corral was on the extreme edge

of town, the two freight men were the first two to see the returning lawmen.

"That's them," May said.

"What are they doing back here?"

"Let's find out."

May and Barnes didn't call out, but began following the two riders, keeping pace with them on the sidewalk as John and Charley rode slowly up the street. The children of the town were next to see them, and they gave up their games of baseball, hopscotch, and kick-the-can as they ran out into the street to follow the two riders. The children darted ahead, behind, and around the horseman. Some of the children held toy guns and they fired them at each other and at the two riders.

As John and Charley moved farther into town, they passed, in succession the blacksmith shop, the apothecary, the leather-goods store, the Golden Spur Saloon, Delgaddis's restaurant, the general store, the hotel, the newspaper office, and the dentist. As they passed each building, men and women hurried outside, then were drawn into the crowd following the riders. As a result, by the time John and Charley reached the sheriff's office, which was located on the far end of town, there were more than a hundred men, women, and children tagging along.

The whole thing took on the nature of a Fourth of July parade as men, women, and children talked, shouted, and laughed at being a part of the festivities.

"What'd you find out, Charley?" someone yelled. "Do you know who done it?"

"We know," Charley answered.

"Where's the Goodnight boy, Charley? Have you been able to locate him?" another called.

"Not yet, but we will find him. I promise you that, we will find him," Charley insisted.

"That's a boy, Charley. If anyone can find him, you can."

"What the hell, Charley, can't you tell your supporters to stay out of the way?" John asked, gruffly. "They do know you aren't running for sheriff anymore, don't they? Or haven't you told them?"

"They're all my men?" Charley asked.

"Yes, they are all yours," John insisted.

"Oh, you mean like Malcolm Peabody there?" Charley replied. He pointed to the newspaper man who was standing in front of the sheriff's office, writing in a small notepad. "As I recall, he's not only one of your men, he always managed to write editorials and news stories about you."

"Well, yes, he's here, and you just put your finger on why," John replied. "Everyone else is in the way, but Malcolm Peabody is the editor of the newspaper. He has a right to be here. Or haven't you heard of something called freedom of the press?"

"Freedom of the press, my eye," Charley said. "Malcolm Peabody's press was anything but free. You will never convince me that you weren't bribing our esteemed newspaper editor to print all those favorable stories about you."

"You had some pretty good stories written about you as well," John reminded him.

By now the two men were in front of the sheriff's office, and Charley looked over at John. Charley had a broad grin on his face.

"Yeah," he said. "But unlike you, I earned the good stories he wrote about me."

"Charley Dawson, you are as full of shit as a Christmas turkey," John said with a growl.

The two men dismounted then went inside. Sheriff Turley greeted them with a chuckle.

"If you boys had given me just a little advance word that you were going to lead a parade, I would've had Mr. Collins turn the band out for you."

"No thanks," John said with a growl. "Charley has a big enough following as it is."

"Oh, this is Charley's following, is it?" Sheriff Turley teased.

"It's not mine," Charley said. "I don't need a bunch of people telling me how great I am. I never was the glory hunter that John was. He was the one who shot Dingus Malloy."

"And you were the one who took out the Kincaid twins," Sheriff Turley reminded him. "The truth is, there is plenty of heroism to go around, and most people of the town think you two should share it, rather than continue to be enemies. After all, neither one of you are running for election anymore."

"You better believe I'm never going to run for office again," John said. "I've had enough campaigning to last me a lifetime."

"Yeah, well, at least John and I agree on that," Charley said. "Oh, by the way, you did get word to pull back the circulars on Phil Goodnight, didn't you?"

"Yes," Sheriff Turley said. "I'm glad for your sakes, and for the sake of your granddaughter, that he isn't guilty. Do you have any idea who is guilty?"

"You mean the new posters aren't out yet?" John asked.

"No," Turley answered.

"Tell him, Charley," John said. He walked over to the water bucket and took the dipper down, then scooped up a drink of water.

"Turns out the man we want is Angus Pugh," Charley said.

"Angus Pugh? Are you sure about that? I thought he was in prison."

John finished the water, then hung the dipper back on the hook. "We thought he was too," he said. "But he's served his full twenty years and is back out, starting all over again."

"What is there about a man like that, that he can't learn a lesson?"

"Some men are just born pure no-good, I reckon," Charley said.

"You think Pugh has your grandson-in-law?" Sheriff Turley asked.

"He's the one that took him from the bank," Charley said.

"This is a tough question to ask, and I wouldn't ask it if your granddaughter was standing here. But do you think Goodnight is still alive?"

"I think so," Charley said.

"I do too," John agreed.

"What makes you think that?"

"If they had wanted him dead, I think they would've killed him at the bank. They're keeping him alive for some reason," John said.

"Like what?" Turley asked.

"I'm not sure why," John said. "But it could be they plan to use him as a bargaining chip."

"What are you going to do now?"

"We're going over to the hotel to visit our granddaughter, and then we're going after Pugh," Charley said.

"Miss Lucy isn't at the hotel," Turley said.

"What?" both men asked as one.

"She hasn't left town, has she?" Charley asked.

"No, no, nothing like that. She's over at John's

house. She stayed with Ann while you two were gone."

"Good," Charley said, nodding. "I think it's good that she stayed with Ann."

"I'm glad you aren't jealous," John said.

"Jealous because Lucy is staying with Ann? Hell no. Ann's a good woman. I've never held it against her because she was married to the likes of you."

"You say you are going after Pugh?" Turley asked.

"Yes," John said.

"Do you have any idea where to start?"

"Yeah, we have a pretty good idea," Charley replied. "We think he went to Salcedo."

"Salcedo?" Turley responded. "Wait a minute, are you saying there really *is* a Salcedo? The place actually exists?"

"Damn right it exists," John said.

"I've heard of it, of course," Turley said. "A place where all the outlaws go, where there is no law. But I've always thought it was a myth. It's not on any map."

"No, it's not on any map," John agreed. "But it does exist."

"Do you know where it is?" Turley asked.

"Yeah," Charley said. "We know where it is."

At Ann's urging, John extended an invitation to Charley to eat with them, and to his surprise, Charley accepted the invitation, even bringing a bottle of wine when he showed up for dinner.

"Well I'll be damned, Charley," John said, looking at the wine bottle. "I do believe this is the first thing you've ever given me. You didn't poison it, did you?"

"John!" Ann said sharply.

"Oh, come on, Ann," John said. "You know I was just teasing."

"Well, it wasn't funny," Ann insisted. Then to Charley, "I apologize for John's rudeness."

"No apology needed," Charley replied. "I probably would've said the same thing."

"Oh, Grandpa, I'm so glad you came to dinner tonight," Lucy said. "It's wonderful having both of you." Moving over to Charley, she gave him a big, warm embrace.

"Have you heard anything from your mama and papa?" Charley asked.

"Yes. They both send their love, and they both say that if it is possible to find Phil and get him back alive, that the two of you can do it."

"We're going to try, darlin'," Charley said. "But don't be getting your hopes up too much."

"It's not hope, Grandpa, it's faith," Lucy said. "I just know that Phil is alive, and I just know that you two will find him."

"I'm going to take care of the wine," Ann said, starting toward the kitchen.

"I'll help get supper on the table," Lucy said, following her grandmother.

When Ann disappeared into the kitchen, John whispered to Charley. "Don't mention that we are going to Salcedo until I have a chance to break it to her, real gentle-like."

"I won't say a word," Charley promised.

Later at the dinner table, it was Ann who brought up the subject.

"I hear you are going to Salcedo," she said as she passed the potatoes.

John looked, accusingly, at Charley.

"Don't look at Charley. He's not the one who told me," Ann said.

"Well, uh, who did tell you?" John asked.

"The news is out, John, all over town. I heard it at the greengrocer's, and again at the butcher shop. Is it true? Are you going to Salcedo?"

"Yes," John said.

"Why?"

"Because we're pretty sure that's where Pugh went," John said.

"I don't like the idea of you going to that place," Ann said. "You do know, don't you, that more than half the men there will have a score to settle with you?"

"Of course I know. I mean, when you think about it, I probably sent half of them to prison," John chuckled. "And Charley sent the other half to prison, so they won't all be concentrating on me. Some of them will have a score to settle with him."

"It isn't funny," Ann said.

"Ann, if we're going to find Phil and bring him home safely, we are going to have to go there," Charley said, gently.

"I know," Ann replied. "But that doesn't keep me from worrying."

John reached out to put his hand in Ann's hair. "Don't worry about it, old girl. I'll have Charley with me."

Seeing John's moment of tenderness with Ann brought home to Charley how much he missed his own Sue. He felt a sudden, almost overwhelming sense of emptiness. Because she was perceptive, Ann read it in Charley's face. She reached over to put her hand on Charley's hand.

"And now that Sue is gone, I'll be worrying about both of you," she said.

"I'll look after him, Ann," Charley said. "I promise

you that. And though I won't admit it in public, I'll be glad to have him along, because I reckon he'll be looking out for me as well."

"I'll be praying for both of you," Ann said.

"As will I," Lucy added.

The Next Morning

As Ann had reported, everyone in Risco knew that John and Charley were going to Salcedo to hunt down Angus Pugh and bring back Phil Goodnight. They knew about it, and they talked about it.

"You mind it was the two of 'em sent ole Pugh to prison in the first place," May said to the others in the Golden Spur Saloon.

"Hell, May, you don't have to tell me," Pratt said. "I was standin' right here, watchin' the whole thing the night it happened. It was on election night of seventy-four, if memory serves me."

"Well, your memory ain't servin' you, 'cause it was in seventy-two," May said. "I remember it just as clear as if it were yesterday."

"Yeah, well, whenever it was, I'd almost be willin' to go along with 'em, just to see ole Pugh's face when he looks up and sees John Carmack and Charley Dawson comin' after him again," Pratt said.

"I don't suppose any of you boys have considered the fact that it's going to be two against practically an army of outlaws, have you?" Malcolm Peabody asked.

"Ha. You ain't talkin' about just any two men, though," Pratt said.

"No," Malcolm said. "I'm talking about two men

who are over sixty, going into a town that, two years ago, beat back an entire posse."

"The hell you say. They beat back an entire posse?"

Malcolm nodded. "A couple of outlaws held up a stagecoach near San Angelo. The sheriff put together a posse of eighteen men and trailed them all the way to Salcedo. But when they tried to go into town to make the arrest, they discovered that the whole town had just about been turned into a fort. There was a big gun battle, and the posse had three killed and three wounded. It was all they could do to get out alive."

"Damn! Yeah, now that you mention it, I do remember hearin' about that. Didn't know it was in Salcedo, though. I thought that happened at Commerce."

"Commerce was what went out over the wire services," Malcolm explained, "because there's really no such place as Salcedo."

"What do you mean, there's no such place as Salcedo?"

"It doesn't have a post office. Therefore, as far as the Census Bureau is concerned, it doesn't exist. It's not on any maps, either. The closest town to it is Commerce; that's why Commerce was the name used in the story."

"Why didn't you put Salcedo in the story that ran in your paper? You know about Salcedo."

"The story came over the wires as Commerce, so that's what I used," Malcom explained.

"Do you think John and Charley know about that posse being beaten back?" May asked. "Maybe somebody ought to tell them."

"I did tell them," Malcolm said. "I told them this morning."

"So what are they going to do?"

"What do you think they're going to do?" Malcolm asked. "They're going to Salcedo."

"Those are two brave men," Pratt said.

"Yeah," May agreed. "Brave, but foolish."

"It has been my observation that courage is often the result of a nexus between bravery and foolishness," Malcolm said.

Pratt laughed. "I don't know what you just said, but it sounded damn good."

The others laughed as well.

"What do you say, boys?" May asked, lifting his glass of beer. "To John Carmack and Charley Dawson?"

"To John Carmack and Charley Dawson," the others said, lifting their glasses to his.

Charley was back in his own house, getting ready to leave. He and John had agreed that they would leave just after lunch. Charley had a few things to prepare before they left, and he also wanted to give John some time to say goodbye to Ann. Neither he nor John had any false illusions about going into Salcedo after Pugh and Phil. They knew there was a very good chance they wouldn't be coming back.

Charley spread his bedroll, which consisted of a blanket, a piece of tarpaulin, and a rubberized poncho, out on the dining room table. He was about to start packing it when there was a quiet, coded knock at the back door. He smiled because he knew this could be only one person.

"Hello, Lillian," he said when he opened the door.

Despite her profession, Charley had always respected Lillian Culpepper. She kept a clean house, treated her girls fairly, and never cheated her customers. She still ran her house of pleasure, though there was now some movement in Austin to make prostitution illegal. When Charley asked Lillian what she would do if prostitution became illegal, Lillian said she would continue to provide a place of genteel entertainment for gentlemen, but stop short of illegality.

"That way, my girls won't be out of jobs," she explained.

It was well known that Lillian never went to bed with any of her customers, though she had done so several years before, when she was first getting her business established.

During his marriage, Charley had never cheated on Sue. It wasn't until a year after Sue's death that he and Lillian established a friendship that, gradually, developed into something more. Several people now knew of the relationship between Charley and Lillian, though no one spoke of it openly.

It was to maintain the façade of discretion that Lillian continued to come to the back door when she visited Charley at his home. She stepped inside rather quickly as soon as he opened the door, doing so to avoid being seen.

"Is it true, what everyone is saying?" Lillian asked in a worried voice.

"Is what true?" Charley asked, though he knew what she was asking.

"Are you and John actually going to Salcedo?"

"Yes," Charley said.

"Oh, Charley, do you think that's wise?"

Charley chuckled. "Wise?" he asked. He shook his head. "I doubt that it is very wise. But it's the only way we are going to get Phil back."

Charley turned and walked back into the dining room. Lillian followed him. There, laid out on the table, he had a change of socks, underwear, and a shirt. He gathered the various items up, put them in the bedroll, and started to roll it up. As he did so, he found that it was too lumpy to get into a tight roll.

"Here, wait, let me do that," Lillian said. Effortlessly, she folded the shirt neatly, then rolled up the socks and underwear. After that it was easy to make the roll.

With the bedroll taken care of, Charley began packing his saddlebags. In one he put a knife, jerky, and extra bullets, both rifle and pistol. As he was taking care of that saddlebag, Lillian packed the other with soap, a razor, shaving brush, and a toothbrush and powder.

"Do you have any idea of how long you will be gone?" Lillian asked.

"No."

"I will be worrying about you."

Charley smiled. "It's nice having someone to worry about me," he said.

"Yes, well, it might be nice if you are the worryee, but it isn't so nice if you happen to be the worrier," she said.

Charley put his arms around her then, and pulled her to him. He kissed her, and she kissed him back.

"Let's go to Delgaddis's restaurant for lunch," he said.

"No."

"Why not?"

"You know why not, Charley," she said. "You are a respected and admired man in this town. What do you think people would say if they saw you with the likes of someone like me?"

"They would say, 'Ole Charley hasn't lost his eye for women.' "

"No, they wouldn't say that," she said. "They would wonder if you had lost your mind. And you would lose their respect for consorting with a harlot."

"Lillian, do you think my friends don't know about you? They know, and they are pleased for me. If anyone thinks anything else of it, then I don't consider them my friends."

Lillian smiled coquettishly. "Anyway, why would you want to waste this time going to lunch when we could be doing something else? That is, if you aren't so old that you have lost interest."

Charley returned her smile. "I haven't lost interest," he said.

Taking him by the hand, Lillian led him toward the spare bedroom. Never during the entire time of their relationship had Charley and Lillian used the bed he once shared with Sue. It had not been a conscious thing, and it was never spoken of. It was just that way.

Chapter Fifteen

Salcedo

From his cell window, Phil could see the gallows going up in the middle of the street. Halfway through the morning on the day construction began, someone erected a sign.

> **On These Gallows**
> **Will Be Hung**
> **Phil Goodnight**
> **For the Murder of**
> **Sheriff Bixby.**

Phil was staring at the sign, trying to fight back the fear, when he heard the front door to the building open. Turning toward the door, he saw that it was Angus Pugh.

Bixby had not been replaced, so there was no sheriff, and no one who stayed in the building to watch him. Phil appreciated the fact that he didn't have someone watching him every minute, but it did have its drawbacks. He ate and drank only if someone happened to think to check on him. It was midafternoon, and he hadn't eaten all day.

"I brung you some grub," Pugh said. "A couple of biscuits and bacon."

"Thank you," Phil said. "I see that you are wasting no time in building the gallows."

"Yeah," Pugh replied. "The boys are doing a good job with it, don't you think? Hell, it looks as good as any gallows I've ever seen."

"So much for a fair trial," Phil said.

"Oh, you mean because we are already building the gallows?" Pugh asked, almost jovially. "That doesn't mean anything. I figured we would go ahead and build them. That way, if you're found guilty, why, we won't waste no time in hangin' you. We'll just bring you right out of the court and hang you that same day. I've seen lots of men waitin' for their appointment with the hangman. They all say the same thing. It's the waitin' that gets you. Believe me, you will appreciate the way I'm doing it."

"Yes, I'm already taking comfort in it," Phil said sarcastically.

Pugh laughed. "You know what, Goodnight? I like you. I hope Muley is able to get you off. That way, neither one of you will have to die."

"Were you serious in saying that, if Weasel doesn't get a conviction, you will kill him?"

"Yes," Pugh said.

"That's insane."

"A real smart fella that I met in prison once told me that there ain't that much of a line between insanity and genius," Pugh said. "By doing it this way, it guarantees you a fair trial. You do see that, don't you?"

"In an insane way, I suppose I do," Phil agreed.

Pugh laughed, and slapped his knee with his hand. "I'm glad you see it that way."

"But, either way, someone is going to die."

Pugh shrugged. "That's true," he said. "And you want to know something else that's true? If I had my choice of which one of them had to die, I'd rather it be Weasel. So you see, I've got two reasons for wanting you to win this case you got comin' up."

When Pugh returned to the saloon, a man who was standing at the far end of the bar started toward him.

"Better hold it right there, mister," Pugh said, holding out his left hand to stop the man while his right rested on the handle of his pistol.

"You're Angus Pugh, ain't you?" the man asked.

Smiling, the man took another step closer, sticking out his right hand to shake hands.

"I said, hold it right there."

"Why, Angus, don't you recognize me? I'm Buford Scruggs. Me'n you were in prison together. Onliest thing is, I got out 'bout ten years ago."

Pugh squinted at the man, then recognizing him, relaxed somewhat. "Yeah," he said. "Yeah, I recollect you now. You were workin' in the laundry."

"Yes, yes, that was me," Scruggs said, smiling broadly and nodding his head enthusiastically.

"You got out ten years ago? How is it you stayed out so long?"

"Well, I ain't exactly stayed out," Scruggs said. "I done me some time up in Kansas . . . four years . . . then I came back down here."

"What brought you to Salcedo?"

"I got me some news I thought you might want to hear," Scruggs said.

"What kind of news?"

Scruggs stroked his jaw. "Well, here's the thing, Angus. I'm a little down on my luck right now. What I was hopin' was, iffen I tole you the news, why, mayhaps you would think it was worth somethin'?"

"By worth something, you mean money?"

Scruggs nodded.

"You tell me the news first, then I'll let you know if it's worth any money."

Scruggs was trapped now, and he knew it. He had to tell Pugh what he knew. And if Pugh decided not to pay him anything, there was nothing Scruggs could do about it.

"Well, you goin' to tell me or what?" Pugh asked.

Scruggs sighed. "You know that banker fella you took from Blodgett?"

Pugh's eyes narrowed. "How'd you know about that?" he asked. "How'd you know it was me? We done it in the middle of the night, wasn't nobody who seen us that I know of."

"Yeah, there was one person that seen you. So now, ever'body knows you're the one that done it."

"Who was it? Who seen me?"

"Josh Watson," Scruggs said.

"What? Are you sure it was Watson?"

"Yep. He's done spilled his guts. He's tole the sheriff how it was you that robbed the bank and how it was you that took the banker fella away."

"Why, that son of a bitch," Pugh said. "He was in on it from the start."

Scruggs nodded. "Yeah they know about that too. Ole Watson, he's already in jail for it."

"Is that what you come here to tell me? That the sheriff knows it was me that robbed the bank?"

Scruggs shook his head. "No, there's more," he said.

"I'm listenin'."

"That young banker fella you took? Well, guess who he is?"

"Hell, I know who he is. His name is Phil Goodnight."

"There's more to it than that."

"Well, I ain't in no mood for no guessin' games. So if you got somethin' to tell me, just go ahead and spit it out."

"Phil Goodnight is the grandson of John Carmack," Scruggs said.

"The hell you say! Are you tellin' me the fella we got locked up here is John Carmack's grandson?"

"Yes."

"I'll be damned."

"And he's also the grandson of Charley Dawson," Scruggs added with a triumphant smirk.

"Dawson too?"

"Yep."

"How can that be? Ever'body knows them two men hate each other."

"Why hell, Angus, they don't have to like each other to have the same grandson. All that's got to happen is for Charley Dawson's son to like John Carmack's daughter."

"Yeah, I guess so," Pugh said. "Well, I'll be damned, what do you think about . . . Wait a minute! What kind of trick are you trying to pull on me?"

"Trick? What trick?"

"Iffen he was their grandson, he'd have one of their names, wouldn't he?"

Scruggs looked surprised.

"Well, wouldn't he?"

"I . . . I reckon he might at that," Scruggs agreed.

"So, what are you tryin' to do? Trick me out of some money?" Pugh pulled his gun. "I ought to shoot your miserable, cheatin' hide right here."

"No!" Scruggs shouted, holding both hands out in front of him. "I'm only tellin' you what I heard in Blodgett is all. They're sayin' that John Carmack and Charley Dawson are comin' after you."

"What do you mean they're comin' after me? Both them fellas has long ago hung up their guns. Ain't neither one of 'em sheriffin' now."

"Well, they put their guns back on because you took that banker fella with you."

"You're sayin' they're comin' after me 'cause that little scrawny fella I took from the bank in Blodgett is their grandson?"

"Yeah," Scruggs said. "Well, I ain't sayin' it. I'm just tellin' you what ever'one in Blodgett is sayin'."

"Hell, Angus, there's a way of findin' out if Goodnight is their grandson," one of the others in the saloon said.

"How's that?"

"Go ask him."

Pugh thought for a moment, then he put his gun back in his holster. "All right, I will," he said. He pointed at Scruggs. "But if he ain't their grandson, I expect you'd better be gettin' out of town. 'Cause if you don't, I'm goin' to shoot you."

When Pugh left the saloon, everyone in the saloon went with him. Others on the street, seeing a parade of sorts heading toward the jail, joined in.

"They about to hang Goodnight?" someone asked.

"I don't know. I mean, they ain't even had no trial yet, have they?"

"I don't think so. But if Pugh is aimin' to hang that fella, why, I intend to be there to watch it."

Phil was sitting on his bunk when the door opened, and Pugh and several others from the town came in. Shocked and frightened to see so many here, he stood up and backed into the corner of the cell.

"What is this?" he asked in a frightened voice. "A lynching?"

"I'm goin' to ask you a question," Pugh said, pointing at Phil. "And don't you be tellin' me no lies, boy, 'cause I ain't in no mood for lies. You got that, Scruggs? I ain't in no mood for lies."

Oddly, Pugh was looking not at Phil, but at the man standing beside him when he said that. The man that Pugh called Scruggs cringed under Pugh's stare, and Phil relaxed somewhat, sensing that he wasn't the one in immediate danger—it was Scruggs.

"What is the question?" Phil asked.

"You ever heard of John Carmack and Charley Dawson?" Pugh asked.

"Yes, of course I've heard of them."

"Who are they?"

"Why they're sheriffs," he said. "Or, more correctly, they are former sheriffs. As I'm sure you know, they are both retired now."

"Are they your—" Scruggs started, but Pugh interrupted him.

"I'm askin' the questions here," he said. He looked back at Phil. "What are them two fellas to you?" he asked. "Are they your grandpas?"

"What? No," Phil answered with a little laugh.

Pugh pointed his gun at Scruggs and pulled back the hammer. "I told you they wasn't his grandpas, you lyin' son of a bitch."

"Angus, no!" Scruggs shouted, throwing his arms up in front of him.

"Wait! I'm married to their granddaughter," Phil

said quickly, afraid that he was about to see some-one shot right in front of his eyes. "Maybe that is what Mr. Scruggs was referring to."

Pugh paused for a moment, still pointing his cocked pistol at Scruggs, who was cringing before him. Everyone else in the room was looking on in morbid curiosity, some actually hoping to see a shooting. Slowly, Pugh let the hammer down on his pistol, then he looked over at Phil.

"You say you are married to their granddaughter?"

"Yes."

"What is her name?"

"I fail to see how my wife's name would be any of your business," Phil said.

"I said, what is her name?" Pugh said, more forcefully this time.

"It's Lucy," Phil replied. "Lucy Goodnight."

"What was it before you was married?"

"Lucy Dawson," Phil said.

"See, I told you!" Scruggs said, relief evident in his voice.

"You didn't tell me nothin'," Pugh said. "This here ain't his grandson."

"But he's married to their granddaughter, which is why they're comin' after you," Scruggs said.

Pugh put his pistol back in his holster, and Scruggs began to breathe again. He was so re-lieved that Pugh didn't kill him, that he forgot all about pressing the issue of payment for informa-tion.

"Wait a minute," Phil said. "Did you say that my grandfathers-in-law were coming after Mr. Pugh?"

"Grandfathers-in-law, yeah, that's the word I was lookin' for," Scruggs said. He looked at Pugh. "That's the word I meant to say."

In truth, Scruggs had said that they were Phil's

grandfathers because that was the way it was being reported in Blodgett.

"It's impossible for them to be comin' for Mr. Pugh," Phil said.

"Why is that?" Pugh asked.

"Because, I told you, they are retired. And they are old. You can't expect a couple of old men like them to seriously entertain the idea of going after outlaws."

"He's right, Angus," one of the younger outlaws said. "I mean, I've heard of them old men. Who hasn't? But they gotta be what, now? Seventy? Eighty years old? You better watch out boys, them old men's liable to hit you with their walking canes," he teased.

The others laughed.

"Boy, they ain't no older than I am," Pugh said to the young outlaw. "You want to go up against me?"

"What? Why, no, Mr. Pugh, I didn't say anything like that," the young outlaw said in a frightened voice.

Phil noticed that the young man changed his form of address from Angus to Mr. Pugh.

"If you're tellin' the truth, that you really are married to their granddaughter, why I expect they are on their way right now."

"What would you pay me to go after them?" Scruggs asked.

"I won't pay you nothin' to go after them," Pugh replied. He looked at the others in the room. "But I'll pay you or anyone else five thousand dollars to kill both of them."

"Twenty-five hundred per man," the young outlaw who had commented on their age said. "That's pretty good pay. I may go after that myself."

Pugh looked at the man and shook his head.

"Twenty-five hundred dollars per head ain't what I said, Dingo. What I said was, I would pay five thousand dollars to have them both killed. I won't pay nothing just to get rid of one of them. It won't do me no good just to have one of them dead if the other'n is still alive. Whichever one of them stubborn sons of bitches that's left would just keep comin'."

Risco

"Ma'am, are you sure this is where you want to go?" the hack driver said when he stopped in front of Madam Lillian's House of Pleasure.

"Yes, quite sure," Lucy replied as she drew a coin from her purse to pay for the ride.

"This place is a, well, it's a, uh," the driver stammered, looking for a way to describe it.

"I know what kind of place it is," Lucy replied. "Would you mind waiting for me? I won't be long, and I shall require a ride back home."

"You mean you won't be staying?"

"Of course not."

The hack driver seemed to breathe a sigh of relief. "Yes, ma'am, I'll wait right here for you."

"Thank you."

Lucy stepped down from the hired hack and walked up the concrete sidewalk toward the house.

The house was large and well kept, with a fresh coat of paint. A wide porch wrapped around the front and one side of the house. Several swings hung by small chains from the ceiling of the porch, affording a view of the wide, gently rolling, and beautifully manicured lawn.

If one didn't know any better, one would never

guess that this was a house of prostitution because Madam Lillian's House of Pleasure looked like any beautiful home Lucy had ever seen back in Memphis.

When Lucy pulled on the bell cord, she heard a melodic ringing from inside. Getting no answer, she pulled again.

Finally the door was opened by a young black woman who was wearing a maid's outfit and carrying a feather duster. "We ain't open . . . ." she started to say, but paused in midsentence when she saw that it was a woman. "Yes, ma'am, can I he'p you?"

"I would like to speak with Miss Culpepper," Lucy said.

"Yes, ma'am, well, just go on up them stairs there," the maid said, pointing with the duster.

"Thank you."

Lucy walked to the bottom of the stairs, then hesitated for a moment. The maid had told her to go on up, but the upstairs seemed a more private part of the house, and she wondered at the propriety of intruding without being announced.

"Jus' go on," the maid said, when she saw that Lucy was hesitating. "It be all right."

Lucy nodded, then climbed the stairs.

When she reached the upper landing, she saw another black woman, also in maid's clothes. The maid looked around when she heard someone on the stairs.

"Oh, uh, the person downstairs said I could come on up," Lucy explained.

"Yes, ma'am, I reckon you be lookin' for Madam Lillian?"

"Madam Lillian? Oh, you mean Miss Culpepper. Yes, I'm looking for her."

The woman pointed to the end of the hall.

"That be her room down there. Just go knock on the door. But I don't think she be hirin' no new girls just now."

"Hiring?" Lucy replied. "Do you think I'm here looking for employment? Heaven's no, I'm married."

"So'm I, honey," another voice said, and looking around, Lucy gasped. The woman who spoke had just come from one of the rooms. It wasn't what she said that made Lucy gasp. It was what she was wearing.

She was wearing a pair of sandals.

And nothing else.

"Doney, are there any clean towels?" the naked woman asked, looking through the shelves on the closet.

"Ain't but one or two right now," Doney replied. "All the towels be hangin' outside on the clothes line. I 'spec's they'll be dry in another hour or so."

"Another hour?"

"Yes'm. 'Bout another hour is all, then I'll have lots of nice clean towels all ready for you."

"That's not good enough, Doney," the naked woman said. "Your job is to keep me in clean towels, my job is to spread my legs. Seems to me like it's a simple division of labor."

"Yes'm, Miz Haynes," Doney said. "I bring 'em to you just soon as they be dry."

"You do that," the woman said.

Lucy followed the entire conversation by sound only, for she had looked away the moment she saw the woman was naked. She was still averting her eyes.

"My name is Charlotte Haynes," the naked woman said to Lucy. "What is yours?"

"Lucy Goodnight," Lucy replied, still not looking at Charlotte.

"Damn, honey, ain't you ever looked in a mirror before?" Charlotte.

"I . . . I beg your pardon?" Lucy replied, not understanding the reference.

"You're actin' like you've never seen a naked woman before. All you'd have to do is look in a mirror."

"Yes, well, I, uh, don't believe I've ever seen anyone so . . . uninhibited before," Lucy said.

Charlotte laughed. "Uninhibited? I'm not sure what that word means, but it sure sounds educated. Yes, ma'am, Madam Lillian is going to like having the likes of you around."

"I told you, I haven't come seeking employment."

"Look at me when you talk to me," Charlotte said. "It makes me nervous, you looking away like that."

"I'm sorry," Lucy said. "It's just that, well, it's sort of difficult to look directly at someone who isn't wearing any clothes."

"Ha!" Charlotte said. "The men sure don't seem to have any trouble with it."

"Are you really married?"

"I sure am, honey," Charlotte replied. " 'Course, I haven't seen him in about five years, and I have no idea where he is. If you aren't here for a job, what do you want with Madam Lillian?"

"Yes," another woman said. She had just stepped through the door Doney had indicated was the door to Madam Lillian's room. "If you aren't looking for a job, what do you want with me?" Though attractive, the woman was considerably older.

"You are Miss Culpepper?"

"I am."

"Miss Culpepper, my name is Lucy Goodnight. You don't know me, but I'm—"

"Oh, but I do know who you are, honey," Lillian said quickly, interrupting Lucy in midsentence. "Come into my room," she invited.

"Thank you."

Lucy stepped inside Lillian's room, though it could more appropriately be called a suite, for it consisted of a bedroom and a sitting room. The room was beautifully furnished and carpeted. Rich red velour curtains hung over the windows, and the wallpaper was crimson, overlaid with a raised gold pattern.

"Please, have a seat," Lillian offered.

"Thank you," Lucy replied, accepting the older woman's offer.

"Lucy, what are you doing here? I certainly hope nobody saw you coming. It could be ruinous to your reputation."

"Oh, heavens," Lucy said. "How could visiting a friend be ruinous to my reputation?"

"Visiting a friend?"

"Well, I hope we are friends," Lucy said. "I know about you and Grandpa Carmack. So I just naturally assumed that we would be friends."

"How do know about Charley and me? Did he tell you?"

"No, my grandmother told me."

"Ann Carmack," Lillian said. It was a comment, not a question.

"Yes, ma'am."

"No doubt with a warning for you to stay away from me."

Lucy shook her head. "No ma'am, it was nothing like that at all. Quite the contrary, in fact. Grandma Dawson speaks very highly of you."

"Ha! That's hard to believe," Lillian replied. "I mean, given that I run a whorehouse."

"No, she really does speak well of you. And she explained that, out here, your profession does not bear the same stigma it would be back home."

"Well, that's nice of her to say," Lillian said. "But I'm not sure your grandfather would approve of you being here."

"My grandfather is part of the reason I am here," Lucy said.

Lillian gasped and put her hand to her chest. She got a horrified look on her face.

"God in Heaven!" she said. "Has something happened to Charley?"

"Oh, no, nothing of the sort!" Lucy said quickly. She put her hand out to touch Lillian's arm. "I'm sorry if I frightened you. Please forgive me."

Lillian breathed a sigh of relief, then she smiled. "Oh, heavens, dear, no forgiveness is needed. But I must confess that you did frighten me," she said. "Just what did you mean when you said you were here because of your grandfather?"

Lucy reached into her reticule, then withdrew a letter and handed it to Lillian. "This is for you, from my grandmother," she said.

With some trepidation, Lillian took the letter, then began reading.

Dear Miss Culpepper,
Or would you think it too bold of me to call you Lillian? I hope not, because I think friends should feel free to address each other by their Christian names.
I would like to thank you for bringing some hap-

piness back into Charley Dawson's life. I know how distressed he was when Sue died. Sue was a good woman and a wonderful wife for him, and he was so lonely without her that I worried for fear he would die of a broken heart.

Since you have come into his life, though, his entire attitude has changed. You have put a gleam in his eyes and brought a buoyancy to his step. Those of us who care about him have noticed this change, and, though John is a very private man and has not spoken directly of you, we know that you are the reason for this change.

And yes, I do care about John, though that may seem strange to you as John and my husband spent so many years as political adversaries. You should know, however, that despite their political differences, the two men have always maintained a tremendous respect for each other, and I know that just beneath the surface of that respect is admiration.

Mutual respect and respect is the basis of what could develop into a real friendship, and that has long been my hope and my prayer. Now that prayer may be answered.

As I'm sure you know, Charley and my husband, John, are united in a common goal, having set out to find our granddaughter's husband, Phil Goodnight. Mr. Goodnight was captured by Angus Pugh during a bank robbery. In what can only be a coincidence arranged by God, his captor, Angus Pugh, is the same man John and Charley arrested and sent to prison on the one time they did work in concert. Now, they are working together again.

I know that you are as worried about Charley as I am about John, and to that end, I would like to invite you to have dinner with Lucy and me this evening. We could commiserate with each other and perhaps thereby pour a soothing balm on our anxious souls.

I am sure that you are surprised by this invitation, and perhaps even a little hesitant to respond favorably. But be assured that this is a sincere invitation. You may send your response with Lucy. Please say that you will come.

Hopefully yours,
Ann Carmack

Chapter Sixteen

On The Trail

The sound of the shot reverberated through the canyon so that neither John nor Charley could tell where it came from. Instinctively, they dismounted as one, snaking their rifles from the saddle sheaths. They slapped their horses on the rump to get them out of danger, and the horses galloped through the canyon, the hoofbeats clattering on the rocks as they did so.

The two lawmen squeezed together into a nearby crevice, then started searching the top of the wall on the opposite side of the canyon.

"You see anything?" John asked.

"No," Charley answered.

They waited a long moment, but saw nothing, nor did they hear another gunshot.

"Let's fire a few shots," Charley suggested. "Maybe he'll answer us."

"Good idea," John replied. The two men fired

three shots each, aiming toward the top of the canyon wall. Afterward, Charley held up his hand in a signal to stop. The echoes of their own shots rolled back to them, but nothing else.

"Well, that didn't work," John said.

"You have any ideas?"

"Yeah," John said. "I don't like it worth a damn, but I think it will work."

"What is it?"

"One of us needs to show himself, and hope to draw fire," John said. "If we get shot at, the other can keep his eyes open to see where it comes from."

"One of us?" Charley asked.

"Yeah, one of us."

"Which one?"

John was quiet for a long moment, then, with a sigh, he responded. "I could do it, I suppose."

"Good idea," Charley said.

John looked at Charley. "That's it? All you are going to say is good idea?"

"What do you want me to say?"

"You might say, 'No, John, I'll show myself, and you look for the shots.'"

"Hell, that's crazy," Charley replied. "I'm not going to say something like that."

"What do you mean, crazy? When I suggested that I was going to do it, you said it was a good idea. I didn't misunderstand you, did I?"

"No, that's what I said, all right. I said it was a good idea."

"Well, why is it a good idea for me to do it, but not for you?"

"Because it was your idea," Charley said. "Now, are you going to get out there, or do I have to push you out?"

"Yes, but you're younger than I am," John said. "That means you could move faster. You'd have a better chance."

"I'm younger?"

"Yes."

"Then that means I've still got my life in front of me. You're old and way past your prime."

"Wait a minute, Charley Dawson. I'm only one year older than you are, and you know it."

"Which means I'm only one year younger, and not that much faster," Charley said. "Now, are you going to talk this idea to death or do it? Because if you are going to do it, do it. Otherwise, shut up about it."

John took a deep breath, then ran out toward the middle of the canyon. He stood there for a long moment, feeling a prickly sensation on the back of his neck. Then he felt the wind of a bullet, just missing him. It made a whizzing sound, followed by the sound of the bullet slamming against rock, then whining off down the canyon. That was followed almost immediately by the concussive report of a rifle, a single boom at first, but joined by merging echoes.

"John, get back!" Charley shouted. "I've got him spotted!"

John ran back to the crevice, getting behind the rock just as a second bullet came whizzing in, this one so close that it sent rock chips stinging into his face.

John slid down to the ground with his back against the face of the rock. He was breathing hard.

"You did a good job, partner," Charley said.

"Some partnership," John replied. "I stand out there and get shot at, and you stay safe in here and look. You did see him, didn't you?"

"Yeah, I think so."

John looked up sharply. "What do you mean, you think so? I about get my head shot off and the best you can come up with is you think you saw where the shot came from?"

"I'm pretty sure I saw it."

John stood up again, then started looking toward the top of the canyon wall.

"Where is he?"

"You see that long red scar there?" Charley said, pointing to the rock wall.

"Yes."

"Look just above it, then come to the right a little ways."

John studied the wall, shielding his eyes against the sun. That was when he saw it, a black, flat-crowned hat, barely lifting above the crest, making it visible in silhouette.

"Yeah, I see him," John said. "The question is, how are we going to get him?"

"One of us is going to have to climb up there," Charley said.

"One of us?" John replied.

"That's the only way."

"How is 'one of us' going to do that? That's a sheer wall."

"I think, right down there, someone could get enough foot- and handholds to make it to the top," Charley said, pointing down to their right.

"Good idea. I'll cover you."

"Yeah, I was afraid you might say that," Charley said.

"I've already done my 'one of us.' Besides, I'm better with a long gun."

"All right," Charley said, reluctantly. "You start

shooting now, and keep him back so he won't see me running across the floor. Once I get over to that wall, the only way he would be able to see me is by leaning over. And if he does that, he will expose himself and you will get a shot at him."

John raised the rifle to his shoulder, then looked over at Charley. "You say when," he said.

Charley laid his own rifle down, then took a deep breath. "Now!" he said.

John began firing, squeezing off a round, jacking another shell in, and firing again, all in rapid succession. Looking up toward the top of the opposite wall, Charley could see that the bullets were hitting right at the edge, and doing a good job of keeping whoever was up there back.

Charley dashed across the open area, then reached the base of the wall. He looked back at John and gave him a wave. John nodded, but made no other sign of acknowledgement, lest whoever was on top would see him and figure out that someone was trying to climb the wall.

It was very hard going. Charley had been at it for about half an hour and he could still see John, quite clearly, hunkered down in the crevice on the other side of the canyon. He hoped that whoever was shooting at them didn't move down to this end of the of the wall, because if he did, he would have a clear, unrestricted shot at John.

Charley was now clinging to the side of the cliff, moving only when he could find the tiniest handhold or the smallest crevice for his foot. Behind him was nothing but air, and if he missed a hand- or a foothold, it would mean a drop of more than three hundred feet to the rocks below. Thinking about it made him dizzy, and he had to force the idea from his mind.

Sweat was pouring into his eyes. It was funny— just half an hour ago he had been cool, and now he was as hot as on the hottest summer day.

Progress had just gotten more difficult. For the last several minutes, he had been trying to negotiate his way by a rather substantial rock outcropping and had almost reached an impasse. He was about four-fifths of the way around the large rock, but now found himself unable to proceed because he had been unable to find another foothold.

Reluctantly, Charley decided to start back. He hated giving up after climbing this high, but the alternative was to fall to a certain death from this rock.

Charley reached for the handhold he had surrendered a couple of minutes earlier, the first step in retracing his path. He had a good handhold, then he moved his foot across. This time the small slate outcropping that had supported his weight before failed, and with a sickening sensation in his stomach, he felt himself falling.

Desperately, Charley threw himself against the side. He started sliding down the wall of the cliff, the ragged rocks scraping and tearing at his flesh. He flailed against the wall with his hands, and after a drop of some fifteen feet, found a sturdy juniper tree. The tree supported his weight, and he hung there for a long, terrifying moment, looking down between his feet at the canyon floor far below. He saw the slate outcropping that had broken under his weight, still in free fall. When it finally hit the ground, he saw a puff of dust then, a second later, heard the sound of its impact.

Charley knew that could have been him, and might still be him, if he couldn't do something to improve his position, and do it very quickly.

Charley looked to his right. About four feet away from him there was a narrow shelf. If he could gain that shelf, he would be all right. He took a deep breath, then swung his feet to the right and up. He caught the ledge with the heel of his boot, then, slowly, managed to push away from the juniper tree until his knees were also on the ledge. After gaining purchase, he worked himself up slowly until, at last, he was on the ledge.

He stayed there, on his hands and knees for a long moment, breathing hard, and taking stock of where he was and what his next move should be.

From his position on the canyon floor, John had watched Charley's ordeal. He couldn't help but admire how Charley was able to climb what looked like a sheer wall. He was sure that men half Charley's age would not be able to do what Charley was doing.

Because he was watching Charley closely, he realized when Charley got into trouble. He saw the rock overhang and knew that Charley couldn't go over it, but would have to find some way around it. He held his breath as Charley started a lateral movement along the wall, then gasped when he saw Charley fall.

"Charley, no!" he said as he saw the body plummeting down. "Yes!" he said, thankfully, when Charley grabbed the juniper tree.

John was beginning to feel the strain in his own body as he contorted and worked with Charley, willing him to find a better position. Not until he saw Charley pull himself up on what appeared to be a ledge of some sort did John breathe easily.

"Damn," he said under his breath. "I never thought I'd care this much about what happened to some son of a bitch that's been my political enemy all these years."

As Charley examined the ledge, he saw signs of it having been a trail at one time. Possibly it was an ancient path that existed until erosion took part of it away. Charley followed it until it gradually widened enough for him to actually get up off his knees and stand erect.

With his circumstances much improved, the nauseating fear that had overtaken him earlier was gone, and he was able to walk upright, strolling along the trail almost as easily as if he were walking down the sidewalks of Risco.

A few minutes later, Charley heard someone moving around, and he knew he was very close. He drew his pistol and approached very quietly.

"What about it, Pancho, do you think they're still down there?" a voice asked. There was a moment of silence, then the same voice said, "Well, I tell you what. I ain't seen 'em in quite a while, but they're still there.

"How do I know they're still there? 'Cause they sent their horses runnin' off, remember? And them horses ain't come back." This was still the same voice.

Nobody was replying to the speaker, and Charley

wondered if whoever it was was talking to himself, or possibly to a horse. He knew that men who spent a lot of time alone often talked to themselves just to hear a voice. It then became such an ingrained habit with them that even when somebody else was around, they continued to do it, totally oblivious of whatever reaction their monologue might engender.

"I'd say that maybe they've worked their way out around the other side. Only there ain't no other side. That's how come I chose this place to ambush them."

Charley crept closer.

"I tell you what, Pancho, when that Apache cut out your tongue, he sure didn't do me no favor," the voice said. "One of these days I'm goin' to get spooked by your bein' so quiet all the time, 'n I'm just goin' to have to shoot you."

Pancho? He's talking to Pancho Montoya, Charley thought.

Charley knew about the outlaw who had run afoul of the Apache when he was barely sixteen. The Apache had cut his tongue out, then let him go. Charley never knew if having his tongue cut out had been the cause of Pancho going bad, or, if his tongue had been cut out because he had already gone bad. He figured Pancho was probably already bad. He had to do something to get the Apache that angry with him.

Charley continued to move slowly, quietly, toward the sound of the voice.

"Ole Pugh said he's givin' a five thousand dollar reward to anyone who kills Carmack and Dawson," the voice said. "I aim to have me some fun with that money, and you better believe there ain't one whore or one bartender in Salcedo that's goin' to get one red cent of that money. No sir. I'm goin' out to California. They say you can live like a king in California, iffen you got the money."

Charley eased his way closer until he was behind a small rock outcropping. He had his gun in his hand as he looked over the top of the rock. From there he could see two men. One of the men was Pancho Montoya, a small, wiry-looking Mexican. The other man had red hair. Charley didn't recognize him. Both were lying on the ground, staring over the edge of the cliff into the canyon below.

As Charley moved to improve his position, his foot scraped against the rock. When it did so, it made a small sound.

"What was that?" the redheaded man asked. Both he and Pancho stood up and began looking around.

Charley picked up a stone and threw it. When it hit, both the redhead and the Mexican turned toward the sound. That gave Charley the opportunity to step out from behind the rock. He moved into the open, with his gun in his hand.

"Drop your guns," he commanded.

The two men turned toward him, their guns still in their hands.

"What the hell? How did you get up here?" the redhead asked. "There ain't no way a mountain goat could come up the side of this cliff, let alone an old man like you."

"Where is Goodnight?" Charley asked.

"Where is who? Phil Goodnight, you say? I never heard of such a fella," the redhead said. Then he smiled. "Ah, that explains it. You got the wrong man. You're looking for Phil Goodnight, and I'm Red Patterson. Why don't we just call it quits here? You go your way, I'll go mine."

"I didn't say his first name," Charley said.

"What?"

"I said Goodnight. You said Phil Goodnight."

Patterson smiled. "Well, now, I reckon you caught me in a lie at that," Patterson said. "As a matter of fact, I do know about him. He would be the fella that's married to your granddaughter, wouldn't he?"

"Is he in Salcedo?"

"Well, I reckon he is," Patterson replied. "That is, iffen he's still alive."

"Why wouldn't he be alive? Has he been shot?"

"No, he ain't been shot. But he's likely to be hanged."

"Hanged?" Charley responded in surprise. "What are you talking about, hanged?"

"It seems this Goodnight fella murdered Sheriff Bixby. Now, we're what you call a wide-open town, but we don't allow murder in Salcedo, especially someone murderin' our sheriff. So Pugh is plannin' on hangin' him. 'Course, it's goin' to be all legal and proper, seein' as how Pugh is goin' to have a trial and all. I'll lead you to him, if you'd like."

"What I would like is for you to drop your guns," Charley said.

Patterson shook his head. "No, I don't think I want to do that," he replied. He looked over toward the Mexican who was standing alongside him. "Don't you be droppin' your gun neither, Pancho. Let's just kill this old bag of bones and get it over with."

"You forget, I'm holding a gun on you," Charley said.

Patterson laughed. "You're holding a gun on us? There's two of us, in case you ain't counted.

And both of us have already got guns in our hands. So while you're shootin' at one of us, the other'n will be shootin' you. And I gotta tell you, now, I think you're too old and too slow. When the smoke clears away, you'll be lyin' there dead."

"I don't think so," Charley said, and now he smiled. His smile was one of extreme self-confidence, and it had the effect of chilling Patterson to the bone.

Patterson's smile left his face, and his eyes grew flat.

"Now, Pancho!" he shouted, trying to bring his own gun around.

Charley's first shot caught Patterson right between the eyes, and he fell backwards.

Pancho turned and ran from Charley.

"Hold it right there, Pancho!" Charley called. He aimed at Pancho, but couldn't bring himself to shoot the fleeing Mexican in the back.

Pancho twisted around and fired back over his shoulder toward Charley. The bullet came closer than Charley would have thought, and all compunctions about shooting Pancho left. He cocked his pistol for another shot, but the shot wasn't needed.

Pancho tripped on a rock, then pitched out over the precipice. One moment he was there, and the next he was gone.

Pancho had no tongue, and thus was unable to speak. But that didn't keep him from screaming, and the scream he emitted as he plunged to his death was something bloodcurdling.

Down on the ground, beneath the mesa, John had heard the two shots being fired. Raising his rifle to his shoulder, he sighted toward the top of the mesa, ready to shoot if the opportunity presented itself. Because of that, he was in perfect position to see Pancho fall.

He watched the figure falling, hearing the terrible cry as he plunged several hundred feet down from the top. The plummeting body hit with a sickening splat, spraying blood as it bounced off the rocks, then lay still and broken.

John waited another moment; then he saw a figure against the sky. Because he was in silhouette, John couldn't tell who it was, and he raised his rifle to shoot. Just before he pulled the trigger, though, the man waved and he knew it must be Charley.

John waved back; then Charley disappeared. John hurried out toward the fallen body to see if he was still alive. It didn't take a very close examination to see that he wasn't.

"Yes, I remember Red Patterson," John said that evening as he tended to his cooking. "I had a run-in with him about fifteen years or so ago. He held up a freight wagon and got ten years in prison for it."

"I figured he might probably have had a record," Charley said. "But I didn't recall ever having any dealings with him."

John had cooked up a concoction of beans, jerky, and peppers, and he took it from the fire and spooned half of it out onto a tin plate. He handed the plate to Charley, while he would eat out of the skillet.

"Damn," Charley said, taking a bite. "This is good. I didn't know you could cook like this."

"I couldn't always," John said. "But after Sue died, it was either learn to cook or go hungry."

"Ann was just real sorry when Sue died," Charley said. "Of course, I was too, but Ann seemed particularly upset by it. The funny thing was, all the time you'n me was fightin' against one another, Ann and Sue were good friends."

"Yeah, I know," John said. "Sue told me once that they got to be real good friends during the war."

"It's a shame we had to be such horses' asses all those years," Charley said. "Because of us, they didn't get to enjoy each other's company as much as they would've liked."

"I know," John admitted. He looked into the Dutch oven and took out a couple of biscuits. He tossed one to Charley.

"Damn, biscuits too? You're some kind of traveling partner, John Carmack."

John smiled. "Well, you're not too bad yourself," he said. "You went up the side of that cliff like it was nothin'. I owe you that."

"I reckon you paid your debt when you ran out into the open to draw their fire," Charley said.

John chuckled. "Yeah," he said. "That was kind of brave of me, wasn't it?"

Charley laughed. "Well, now let's not get carried away with it. I mean, you aren't going to get any medals for it, or anything."

John took a bite of his biscuit, then asked, "Did you say they were talking about a reward Pugh has out on us?"

"Well, Patterson was talking about it. If you remember, Pancho Montoya couldn't talk. I believe Patterson said it was five thousand dollars," Charley replied.

"I wonder how Pugh knew we were comin' for him?" John asked.

"We made a little noise back in Blodgett, if you recall," Charley said. "Probably someone who saw us there got word through to Pugh that we were comin' after him."

"Yeah, well, they would have had to go to Salcedo. It's not like they could send him a telegram or anything," John said.

"That's true. I just hope we don't get there too late."

"You're talking about the murder trial Patterson said Pugh is having for Lucy's husband?"

"Yes," Charley answered.

"Do you believe him?"

"Yeah, I do. It's just the kind of crazy thing someone like Angus Pugh would do."

"Emmett Bixby," John said. "He was the sorriest excuse for a lawman I ever knew. He got run out of every county there ever was. It's no wonder he wound up in Salcedo. I'll say this, if Phil did kill him, he did the world a favor."

"If he killed him," Charley said. "From what little Lucy told us about him, he doesn't seem like a likely candidate to kill anyone."

"I don't know," John said. "You put someone in desperate straights, they're likely to find gumption they never knew they had."

"That's true," Charley said. He chuckled. "And I can't see our Lucy marrying anyone who didn't have a little backbone in 'em."

"Yes, that's pretty much what I'm thinking, too."

"Which means we can't waste any time in getting there," Charley said. "I'd hate to let Lucy down now."

"We aren't going to let her down, partner," John said, sticking his hand out across the fire.

Charley looked at his hand for a moment, then smiled and took it. For the first time in many years, John and Charley shared a hearty handshake.

Chapter Seventeen

Risco

When Ann answered the door, she saw Lillian Culpepper standing on her front porch. Lillian was wearing a dark blue dress, its high neck closed with a small ivory brooch. Her face was devoid of makeup, and her hair was pulled back into a bun. In dress and demeanor she could have been the matriarch of the finest family in Risco.

"Good evening, Mrs. Carmack," Lillian said. "I must be crazy, accepting your kind and generous invitation. I have no right to make your neighbors talk."

"Nonsense, you aren't crazy, you are gracious to accept it. Let the neighbors talk all they want, it doesn't bother me. Please come in, won't you? And, do call me Ann."

"All right . . . Ann," Lillian said, her hesitancy in doing so setting Ann's name apart from the rest of the sentence.

"I do hope you like baked ham. Clara does such a marvelous job with ham."

Clara was Ann's maid. Lillian saw a plump black woman bustling about in the dining room.

"Won't you have a seat until dinner is ready?" Ann invited. "Would you like something to drink? Coffee or tea?"

"Coffee, thank you," Lillian said.

"Lucy, dear, would you do the honor?" Ann invited.

"Yes, ma'am," Lucy replied.

A silver service set was on a small table, and Lucy poured the coffee, then served the two older women before pouring a cup for herself.

"So, how long have you and Charley been seeing each other?" Ann asked.

"We were not seeing each other before his wife died," Lillian said defensively.

"Oh, I'm sorry, I didn't mean to imply that you were," Ann apologized quickly. "I was just curious as to how you met, is all."

Lillian smiled. "When you are in a business like mine, you meet lawmen," she said. "Most of the time they are just lawmen and nothing more. But I noticed John, I mean really noticed him for the first time, when he dealt with the Kincaid twins."

"Oh, yes, how well I remember that incident," Ann said. "Even John was impressed by Charley's bravery that day."

"I tell you, I had never seen anything so terrifying or wonderful in my life than the way he stood up to those two evil men."

"I know about that," Lucy said. "My mom and dad have the newspaper article about it."

"It was wonderful, but terribly sad. Those awful

men killed poor Monroe. They shot him in the back." Lillian's eyes teared.

"Who was Monroe?" Lucy asked.

"Monroe was such a dear, dear man. He had been with me since I was a child, and stayed with us, even after the slaves were freed. Then we lost our farm. After that, my mother died and I came west. Monroe offered to come with me, to look out for me. I don't think I would have made it without him."

"I understand he was quite the piano player," Ann said.

"Yes, he was," Lillian replied. "I wish it had been possible for him to play somewhere other than in my house. The citizens of Risco who never got to hear him were poorer because of it."

"Miz Ann, the dinner be ready now," Clara said, stepping into the living room.

"Thank you," Ann replied. "Ladies?" she invited. "Shall we have our supper?"

"Oh, it all looks so good," Lillian said as they sat at the table. She picked up a roll and took a bite, but put it back down quickly when she saw Ann bow her head for a blessing.

"Ladies," Ann said, looking up at the other two. "We are three, joined by the common dangers shared by our men. Let us not only give thanks for the food, but pray for their safety."

Ann blessed the food, gave thanks for friendship, and finally invoked the Lord's protection for Phil, John, and Charley.

"Amen," she said.

"Amen," Lucy added, joined, a second later, by Lillian.

After dinner, the ladies adjourned to the parlor

where, shyly, Lucy asked if she might give Lillian something.

"It's a drawing I made of my Grandpa Dawson," she said, handing the drawing to her. "I thought you might like to have it."

Lillian looked at the drawing, then drew a quick breath. "You did this?" she asked.

"Yes, ma'am. I hope you like it."

"Like it? I love it! You have captured him beautifully." She started to hand the drawing back to Lucy.

"No," Lucy said. "I want you to have it."

Lillian looked at Lucy in surprise, then at the drawing. Her eyes welled with tears.

"This," she said, "is the most beautiful thing anyone has ever done for me. I thank you, child. From the bottom of my heart, I thank you."

Salcedo

Dingo and Ernie came into the jail about mid-morning to get Phil.

"Hey, Ernie, look over there in Bixby's desk and see if you can find any handcuffs to put on our prisoner," Dingo said.

Ernie went through the drawers, opening them and slamming them shut one at a time until the search was completed.

"Ain't none here," he said.

"Pugh told us to come get the prisoner and take him down to the trial. Now, how are we goin' to do that without handcuffs?"

"I don't know," Ernie answered. "I just know there ain't none here."

"You couldn't find your ass with both hands,"

Dingo said disgustedly. He walked over to the desk and began his own search.

Like Ernie before him, Dingo pulled open drawers and began searching through them.

"I would hate to walk into the courthouse with our prisoner not in handcuffs," Dingo said, giving up the search.

"Courthouse? What courthouse?" Ernie asked. "We ain't got no courthouse in Salcedo."

"I'm talking about the saloon, dummy," Dingo said. "Didn't you hear Pugh say that the saloon was goin' to be the courthouse?"

"Well, why didn't you say the saloon, then?" Ernie asked.

"Because, damnit, it ain't a saloon while there's a trial goin' on in it," Dingo insisted. "It turns into a courthouse."

"I wouldn't know about nothin' like that. Onliest time I was ever in a trial was when I was sent to prison for burglary. And then it was in a real courthouse. It wasn't in no saloon."

All the time they were talking, Dingo was continuing his search through the drawers. Now he slammed the last one shut in disgust.

"No handcuffs," he said.

"I told you there weren't any," Ernie said.

Dingo stroked his chin for a moment while he thought about what to do. Then he pulled his gun.

"All right, we'll just have to do it this way," he said. "You take your gun out and keep it pointed at him. I will too. If he starts to run, we'll both shoot him."

"All right."

"You got that, prisoner?" Dingo asked Phil. "If you start to run, we'll both shoot you."

"I don't intend to run," Phil promised.

Dingo opened the cell door, then, with his pistol, motioned for Phil to come out. Warily, and with his hands raised, Phil did so.

"You can put your hands down," Dingo said. "I don't reckon you got any guns on you."

"Thanks," Phil said, lowering his hands.

Once outside, Phil blinked in the bright morning sun. It was the first time he had been outside in several days, and the brightness hurt his eyes.

"It gets to you, doesn't it?" Ernie asked with a chuckle.

"I beg your pardon?" Phil replied.

"The sun shinin' in your eyes like that. I remember the time I did seven days in the hole. When I come out, the sun hurt like someone was stickin' red-hot pokers in my eyes."

They walked by the gallows and as they did so, the handle was pulled and the trap door swung open with a loud thump. Phil jumped.

"Ha, ha!" Ernie laughed. "Dingo, did you see the way this feller jumped when ole Beckwith tested the trap?"

"You worried about fallin' through that trap door, are you?" Dingo asked, joining Ernie in laughter. "Well, you don't need to be worryin' none about that. You ain't goin' to fall all the way through, if you get my meanin'."

Ernie put his fist beside his own neck, then jerked up as if it were a hangman's knot.

"Schreek," he said, making what he thought was the sound of a neck being broken.

Dingo laughed at Ernie's antics.

Phil was the center of attention as Dingo and Ernie walked him down the main street of Salcedo from the jailhouse to the saloon. There were several people gathered outside the buildings looking on, as well as men and women hanging through open windows.

Three heavily made-up women, their breasts bare and legs exposed, were standing in front of the saloon. When Dingo and Ernie took Phil inside, the three women followed them in. They sat in chairs next to the woman Pugh had called Mabel. When they arrived in Salcedo. Mabel was considerably less exposed than the other three women were.

All of the saloon tables had been moved out of the way and were stacked up under the stairs that led up to the second floor. The chairs had remained, though, and were now aligned in several rows. Phil saw that the chairs were nearly all occupied. Ed Meeker, the saloon keeper, was sitting on one of the bar stools, a bar towel draped across one shoulder.

Centered at the front of the room was one rectangularly shaped table. Between the first row of chairs and the rectangular table, but sitting off to the side, were two smaller round tables.

Muley was sitting at the table to the left, while Weasel was at the table to the right. Muley had an empty chair beside him. There was also an empty chair sitting behind the square table that was in front of the room.

The rows of chairs were arranged to allow a center aisle, and Dingo and Ernie escorted Phil down that aisle to Muley's table. There, they shoved him down in the empty chair.

"Sit there," Dingo said, gruffly.

Before majoring in business, Phil had considered becoming a lawyer, and he had actually studied law for two of his four years of college. He was surprised and impressed that, in a rather bizarre way, this saloon really did resemble a courtroom.

"I have to confess, you've made this look like a real courtroom," Phil whispered to Muley.

"Hell yeah, it's real," Muley replied. "If they's one thing nearly all of us have seen, it's a court-room."

"I don't suppose there is any chance that you are a real lawyer?" Phil said.

Muley laughed. "Well, I ain't exactly what you'd call a lawyer," he said. "And neither is Weasel. But I reckon we've both been around enough to know what's goin' on."

"That's, uh, encouraging," Phil said. "But as my life is on the line here, I would be more comfort-able with a real lawyer. Would there be such a per-son in town?"

Muley laughed. "We've got lots of outlaws in this town," he said. "But we got to draw the line some-where. We don't let no lawyers in here."

"Ever'body stand up!" Dingo suddenly shouted.

Phil heard an unseen voice say something, though the voice was so mumbled and quiet that he couldn't make out what was being said.

"I mean all rise!" Dingo corrected himself.

There was a scrape of chairs as everyone stood. All conversation halted, and for a moment, the room was unusually quiet.

"Hear ye, hear ye, hear ye!" Dingo shouted. "This here court is now in session. Angus Pugh is the judge."

Pugh came from somewhere by the bar. He stood just behind his table for a long moment, and when some in the room sat down, he glared at them.

"There don't nobody sit down until I say you can sit down," he said with a growl.

Those who had sat prematurely hopped up quickly.

Pugh waited until all were standing again, then he sat down. Using the handle of his revolver, he slammed his pistol against the table.

"Be seated," he ordered.

As one, the gallery took their seats.

Pugh was wearing glasses, something Phil had not seen before. Pugh took his glasses off, polished them vigorously, then put them on, fitting them very carefully over one ear at a time.

The result was striking. Without the glasses, Pugh was a very frightening looking man. With the glasses, however, he could almost be someone's kindly old grandfather.

Pugh examined the room, his gaze falling on the three topless women who had just come in.

"Mabel, you know better'n to let them women come in a courtroom like that," he said, pointing to them. "Now you tell them to get them titties covered up. I will not have bare titties in my courtroom."

"Your courtroom?" one of the men called. "Come on, Angus, this ain't a courtroom. This here is a saloon. Let them titties show!"

The comment was greeted with loud laughter, the laughter only subsiding after repeated raps on the table with the handle of his pistol.

"Coleman, you are hereby fined fifty dollars for contempt of court," Pugh said, pointing to the offender.

There was a universal gasp throughout the courtroom.

"What?" Coleman shouted in protest. "Where

the hell do you get off tellin' me I gotta pay a fine? It ain't like you're a real judge!"

Pugh banged his gun on the table again. "By God, I'm as real a judge as you're likely to see. You are now being fined one hundred dollars," he said. "And if you say anything else, I'll have you thrown in jail. Do you want to try me, Mister?"

Coleman started to speak again, but he held his tongue.

"Very well," Pugh said. "Baliff, publish the case."

"What's that?" Dingo asked.

"Tell the court what this here trial is about," Pugh said.

"Oh, yeah," Dingo said. Dingo stepped up to the front of the court. "This here case that we've come for, is the town of Salcedo, agin' this here fella, Phil Goodnight. And what we're sayin' he done was, he murdered Sheriff Bixby."

After delivering his spiel, Dingo stepped back behind Pugh's desk.

"Prosecution, is your case ready?" Pugh asked.

"Yeah, Angus, I'm all set to go," Weasel called back.

"Weasel, you are fined fifty dollars," Pugh said, banging his gun on the table.

"What? What for?" Weasel asked.

"For not showing proper respect for this court. You will refer to me as 'Your Honor.' "

"Your Honor? What the hell, Angus? For what do we have to call you Your Honor?"

"One hundred dollars," Pugh said, banging his gun on the table.

"Look here, Angus . . . uh, Your Honor," someone in the gallery said. "Where's all this fine money goin'?"

"We'll use it to buy drinks when the court is over," Angus said.

There was a general round of approval for Angus's pronouncement.

"Yeah," someone shouted. "Hey, Weasel, call His honor 'Angus' again."

"I'm sorry, Your Honor," Weasel said, realizing that, with the support of everyone in the town, Angus's fines could and would be enforced.

"That's more like it." Pugh said. He looked over at the defendant's table. "What about you, Muley? Is defense ready with its case?"

"Defense is ready, Your Honor," Muley replied, standing and showing the proper decorum.

"Very well, prosecutor, you may begin your prosecutin'," Pugh said.

"Please the court?" Phil called.

Pugh glared at him. "What? What does that mean?" he asked.

"I'm asking permission to address the court, Your Honor." Phil asked.

Pugh smiled broadly and looked at Muley and Weasel. "Now, I like this fella. See how polite he is? Maybe you two could learn somethin' from him." He looked back at Phil. "Yeah, go ahead. If you've got somethin' to say, spill it out."

"Don't I get to have a jury?"

"Sure you do. Fact is, you got about the biggest jury of all. That's 'cause ever'one in here is goin' to be part of the jury," Pugh answered. "After the trial, we're goin' to all have a vote, and the majority rules. Now that's fair, ain't it?"

"No, Your Honor, it isn't fair," Phil replied. "And I object."

"You can't object. You ain't the lawyer."

"Object, Muley," Phil whispered to his lawyer.

"Why should I object?" Muley asked. "It seems fair to me."

"No, it isn't fair. This is a capital trial. And in such trials it's not decided by a majority vote. It has to be unanimous."

"What is unanimous?"

"That means everyone has to agree that I am guilty. And don't forget, your fate is intertwined with mine. According to Pugh, if I hang, you hang."

"Damn! You're right," Muley said. "Angus, I object," he shouted.

Pugh glared at him.

"Call him Your Honor," Phil whispered.

"Uh, Your Honor, I mean. I object."

"What are you objectin' to?"

"When you have a trial to hang somebody, it ain't just the majority, ever'one has to say he's guilty," Muley said. "What you're doin' here ain't right."

"Overruled," Weasel shouted.

"You dumb bastard, you can't overrule my objection," Muley said.

"Who are you callin' a dumb bastard?" Weasel retorted.

"You! I'm callin' you a dumb bastard, you dumb bastard. Only Ang . . . uh, only His Honor can overrule an objection."

"I can, too, overrule it," Weasel insisted. "I done heard my lawyer do it lots of times."

"No you can't overrule his objection," Pugh said, pointing at Weasel. "Now, sit down or I'll throw you in jail."

Meekly, Weasel sat down.

Pugh stroked his chin as he thought about the

objection. "Look here," he finally said. "There's nearly fifty people in here. Are you telling me that ever'one of 'em has to vote to hang the prisoner?"

Muley looked at Phil, and Phil nodded yes.

"Uh, yeah, that's what I'm saying," Phil said. "That is, if you really intend for this trial to be fair."

"Hell, it's impossible to get ever'one in here to agree to the same thing. So we're just going to let the majority rule."

"Your Honor, may we approach?" Phil said.

"Approach what?" Pugh replied.

"May we approach the bench?" Phil said. "Uh, that means, can we come up and talk to you? Privately?"

"Yeah, yeah, sure come ahead," Pugh said, motioning them forward with a wave of his hand.

Phil got up, then looked at Muley. "Come with me, Muley. Remember you have a stake in this as well."

"Yeah, you're right," Muley said. He got up and approached the bench with Phil.

Phil looked over at Weasel, who was, at that moment, picking his nose.

"Your Honor, prosecution has the right to approach as well," Phil said.

"Weasel, get up here," Pugh said. When Weasel joined them, Pugh looked at Phil. "All right, what is it you want?"

"I would like two things, Your Honor," Phil said. "I would like you to impanel a jury of twelve, and grant us the right of voir dire. I would also like—"

"Wait. You want the right to do what?" Pugh asked, confused by the term.

"Voir dire," Phil said. "It means we can question the potential members of the jury to make sure they are fair and impartial. And I would also like to sever Muley as lead council, and have you appoint me as council of record."

"Council of record?"

"I want to defend myself."

"Yeah, I want that too," Muley said, grateful that Phil may have just given him a way to avoid hanging with his client.

"Are you a lawyer?" Pugh asked.

"Not exactly," Phil said. "But I have read for the law."

"And you agree with this, Muley?" Pugh asked.

"Hell, yes, I agree," Muley said enthusiastically.

"Well, hell, I don't agree," Weasel said. "I don't think it's fair at all."

"Why not?" Pugh asked.

"You heard what he just said, didn't you? He's read for the law. I ain't. That means he's smarter than I am."

Pugh laughed. "Hell, Weasel, ever'body I know is smarter than you."

"Yeah, well, the thing is, if I lose, you're a'plannin' on hangin' me. Ain't that what you said?"

"That's what I said," Pugh agreed.

"Well, if Muley ain't the lawyer on the other side, if I win, ain't nobody goin' to hang but Goodnight. Muley's gettin' a free ride."

"You've got a point," Pugh said.

"So, Muley has to stay on as his lawyer, right?" Weasel asked, pleased that it seemed to be going in his favor.

"Muley," Pugh said.

"Yeah?"

Pugh glared at him.

"Uh, I mean, what you want, Your Honor?"

"Weasel is right. I set this here trial up like this

so as to make it fair. But if he's a'fixin' to hang, and you ain't, then that's not fair. So, I'm going to keep it the way it was. If you lose, you hang. If you win, Weasel hangs. Now, do you still want Goodnight to defend himself?"

"Wait a minute, that ain't right," Muley said. "If Goodnight is the lawyer and he loses, then he's the one who ought to hang."

"He will hang," Pugh said. "And so will you. Now, who do you want to be the . . . what was it you called it, Goodnight? The council of record?"

"Yes, Your Honor," Phil replied. "Uh, may I have a moment with Muley?"

"Sure, go ahead."

Phil walked back toward the defense council's table, motioning for Muley to come with him. Weasel came along as well, still picking his nose.

"Your Honor, privilege of council," Phil said. "This is a private consultation. Please inform prosecution to return to his own table."

"I thought I could listen in on everything," Weasel said.

"Get your ass back over there, Weasel," Pugh said, and the gallery laughed.

"Muley," Phil said. "I will value your input, but I really believe I can defend myself better than you can. And, don't forget, by defending myself, I am also defending you."

"Yeah," Muley said. "Yeah, I guess that's right. You would be defending both of us, wouldn't you?"

"So, what do you say?"

"Did you really read for the law?"

"I did."

"All right. You do it then."

"Thank you."

Phil turned back toward the bench. "Your Honor, Muley has agreed to the change. With your permission, he will still be part of the defense team, but I will be lead council."

"All right. Let the record show that Phil Goodnight is now lead council for the defense."

"What record is that? We ain't got nobody taking notes," Weasel said.

"It's just something you say," Pugh replied. "It means Goodnight is defending himself."

"But Muley still has to hang if they lose, right?" Weasel asked, anxiously.

"Yes."

"Then it's all right by me," Weasel said with a broad smile.

"You ain't got any say-so in it," Pugh said. "So it doesn't matter whether it's all right with you or not."

"And now, Your Honor," Phil continued. "I ask for a ruling on impaneling a jury, and allowing voir dire."

Pugh looked out over the gallery. "You men in the first two rows," he said. "Move your chairs over here."

The men complied.

"Now," Pugh said, looking over at Phil. "How does this voir dire work?"

"Both the prosecution and I get to question each juror," Phil said. "And if we can find cause why they shouldn't serve on the jury, you will replace them with someone else."

"Yeah," Pugh said. "Yeah, I think I remember seeing that done in some of my trials. All right, Mr. Goodnight. Commence your voir dire."

Risco

After Charlotte Haynes found the note from Lillian, she knocked on the door to her employer's suite. As she waited for Lillian, she went over in her mind all the events of the last few days.

Had she done anything that would cause Lillian to want to see her? She was a little bossy around the other girls, sometimes, she knew that. But it was generally just to get them to do what they should be doing anyway, like keep their rooms clean and pick up after themselves in the parlor. The House of Pleasure did employ maids, but that was no excuse for sloth and laziness.

When Lillian opened the door, there was a big smile on her face. That was a good sign, and Charlotte relaxed a little.

"Charlotte, won't you come in, please?" Lillian invited.

Charlotte went inside then saw, to her surprise, that the table had been set with fine china and crystal.

"I thought we might have our lunch together," Lillian said. "That is, if you don't mind eating with me."

"Thank you, I would be honored to have lunch with you," Charlotte said, still not certain where this was going. She looked around the room. "You have such a lovely suite," she said. "I always love coming in here."

"How would you like for this suite to be yours?" Lillian asked.

"I beg your pardon?"

"I'm getting old and tired," Lillian said. "Too

old and too tired to keep going in this business. I think it's time for me to quit. How would you like to buy the House of Pleasure?"

"Oh," Charlotte said. "Oh, I don't know. I confess that I have thought about starting a place of my own someday. There is no way I could afford this place, though."

"Sure you can," Lillian said. "We'll work something out."

Chapter Eighteen

On The Trail

It was dark and quiet. A coyote howled, and an owl hooted. There was the scratch of hooves on the ground and the creak of riders in saddle leather.

When Mort Tully saw the flickering flames of a small campfire, he held his hand up to stop the others. He had rounded up eight more riders, promising them five hundred dollars each of they were successful in finding and killing both John Carmack and Charley Dawson. That left his share as one thousand dollars, but he figured that, being the leader, it was money he deserved.

They had been on the trail for two days and nights, but the campfire offered the promise of success.

"You think it's them, Mort?" Pardeen asked. Pardeen was riding closest to Tully.

"Yeah, I don't know who else it could be," Tully answered.

"Watch out!" someone else said in a short, angry voice. "You damn near ran me over."

"Keep it quiet," Tully hissed. "You want them to hear us?"

"Hell, what if they do? There's nine of us, two of them," Pardeen said.

"Maybe you ain't heard of who those two are," Tully said.

"Oh, yeah, I've heard of 'em. I've heard all about them," Pardeen said. "But they are really old. Hell, they could be my grandpas. Besides, they must be slowin' down in their old age. I mean, if they were as good as you keep tellin' us they are, do you think they'd be burnin' a campfire like that for all to see?"

"Nevertheless, keep quiet," Tully said. "There ain't no sense in blowin' trumpets to let 'em know we're here."

"I reckon they're goin' to find out we're here soon enough," Pardeen said. "Soon as we start shootin' their sorry old asses." He giggled.

"All right, men, here's what we're goin' to do," Tully said. "When I give the word, I want everyone to shoot toward the campfire. Like as not, they're sittin' right next to it, and if we shoot it up real good, we'll probably get 'em both. But don't shoot until we get a little closer, and I give the word. Have all of you got that?"

"Yeah, yeah, we've got it," Pardeen said, and the others agreed.

John and Charley had heard the riders approaching nearly ten minutes ago and had made preparations for them. They waited patiently.

"The campfire will draw them in," John said.

"When they get close enough for you to pick out a target, start shooting. If you start shooting before I do, I'll open up as well. If I start before you, you open up."

"All right," Charley agreed.

The two men went to their positions then, John going about fifteen yards behind and to the right of the fire, while Charley went the same distance behind and to the left. Old hands at this game, they chose their positions carefully so they would have overlapping fields of fire without harming each other.

John took his rifle, then got into position and waited. In the dim, orange glow of the fire, John looked over at Charley. Charley preferred a pistol to a rifle, and John could see him holding a Colt up, waiting for the approaching riders to present a target.

The men who were after them were still too far away and it was too dark to make them out well enough for a shot, or even to determine exactly how many there were. Then, finally, they drew close enough. John saw the men raise their weapons and point at the campfire.

"Fire!" one of the riders barked.

With the muzzle flash from their guns, John had a target. He squeezed off a round, firing just to the right and slightly below one of the flashes. He heard a grunt of pain.

"They got me!" someone yelled.

"Damn! Where the hell are they?"

John's firing was a signal to Charley to open fire as well, and he began shooting.

"What the hell? They've ambushed us! We've got to get the hell out of here!"

John heard the sound of hoofbeats as the outlaws turned their horses and began beating a retreat. John and Charley fired three or four more times, but they were just shooting in the dark with no idea as to where their targets were. It didn't really matter. The idea now was simply to run them off, and they had done that.

"Charley, are you all right?" John called.

"Yeah. You?"

"I'm fine," John said. The two men came out from their firing positions and met just outside the little golden bubble of light that was cast by the fire.

"Think they will be back?" Charley asked.

"Oh, I think we can count on it," John said. "I just don't think it will be tonight."

"I don't either. Let's see who's out there."

With guns at the ready, the two men walked out into the dark to check on the men they had shot. There were three lying on the ground: two were dead, and one was dying.

"You got 'ny water?" the dying man asked.

"Yeah, right here," John said, offering the wounded man his canteen. It was a sign of John's experience that he had taken the canteen with him when he went out to check on the wounded. He knew about the terrible thirst dying men often experienced, and though a doctor had once told him that water wasn't good for someone with a belly wound, John figured there would be no harm in making the last few moments of life as comfortable as possible.

"What's your name?" John asked, as he gave the man water.

"Riddle. George Riddle," the man asked. He drank thirstily. "Thanks."

"You know these other two over here?" Charley asked.

"I don't know. I didn't see who it was that got hit, and it's too dark for me to see them now," Riddle answered. "How many of us did you get?"

"Looks like three," John said. "Unless one or two of 'em rode away wounded."

"Sum'bitch," Riddle said, his voice strained with pain. "This wasn't s'posed to happen. This was s'posed to be easy money." He gasped a few times. "Easy money," he said again, then, with a life-surrendering sigh, he died.

The Next Morning

The sun was high overhead, a brilliant, white orb fixed in the bright, blue sky in such a position as to take away all the spots of shade where the cattle would normally congregate. With the shade denied them, the cows had all moved down to mill around the stream of water that made this area a ranch instead of a stretch of barren desert. Some of the cows had come to water, while others were there just to be nearer to the band of green grass that followed the stream on its zigzagging path across the otherwise brown floor of the valley.

Both John and Charley knew the ranch, the Bar-X, and its owner, Emile Lewis.

The Bar-X was the closest ranch to Salcedo, and the only ranch within the area of the outlaw town that didn't seem to suffer heavily from cattle rustling. Emile Lewis claimed that the outlaws left him alone because he allowed them to cut a few steers out of his herd from time to time for food.

Neither John nor Charley believed that, though. Back in the early days of ranching, Emile Lewis developed the reputation of throwing a long loop to build his herd, and both John and Charley had always suspected that Lewis now ran stolen cattle that he bought at rock-bottom prices from the outlaws.

It was never anything that they were personally involved with, though, because his ranch was out of their immediate jurisdiction, and none of the ranchers in Tywappity county had ever made an accusation toward Lewis. That left them no reason to investigate the rancher. Even so, they were convinced that Lewis was in cahoots with the outlaws.

Because of their suspicions, they avoided the main house as they passed by Lewis's ranch on their way to Salcedo. At the moment, they were at least a mile away, riding alongside a barbed wire that marked the southern boundary of the Bar-X. Just ahead of them, and on the other side of the fence, was a line shack that sat empty and baking under the hot, summer sun.

"Hold up for a moment, will you, Charley?" John called.

Charley was riding in front and he stopped, then twisted around in the saddle. "What is it?"

"Guess." John swung down from his horse, then began unbuttoning his pants.

Chuckling, Charley turned his around to face John. "Damn, you've watered the lilies every hour on the hour," he said. "Is that what I've got to look forward to when I'm as old as you are?"

John chuckled. "When you are as old as I am? Oh, you mean next year? Well, it could be," he said. "It could be."

While John relieved himself, Charley studied the line shack, making certain it was empty. That was when he saw the five riders. From the way they were riding, he didn't think they had seen him.

"John," Charley called quietly.

"I'm about finished," John replied.

"John," Charley said again.

"Hold your horses, Charley," John said. "This ain't somethin' you can rush, you know."

"I'm not talkin' about that," Charley said. Leaning over his horse's neck, he pointed. "Look over there, beyond the line shack, through the porch. Do you see them?"

John buttoned his trousers then looked up. "Five riders? Yeah, I see them."

"Are they riders for Lewis, do you think?" Charley asked.

"You got your spyglass," John said. "Take a look."

Charley pulled his telescope from the saddle. Then, crossing his leg and hooking a knee on the saddle horn to brace himself, he raised the glass to his eye and looked.

"I'll be damned," he said. "You know who the guy in the lead is?"

"Can't tell from here," John said.

"It's Mort Tully."

"Mort Tully? Are you sure? Isn't he that guy you arrested for murder and rape?"

"That's him."

"I thought he was supposed to hang."

"He was supposed to, but he escaped prison before they could carry out the sentence, remember?" Charley said.

"Yeah, now that you mention it, I do remember it. You know what? You should've shot the son of a bitch when you had the chance."

"If I had known what was going to happen, I would have," Charley said.

"Who's with him?"

"Nobody else that I recognize," Charley said. He snapped the telescope shut, then put it back in the saddle holster. "But whoever they are, you can bet they are up to no good."

John and Charley continued to look toward the five riders. "You think they were the guys who tried to hit us last night?

"Well, seein' as how Mort Tully is with them, I'd bet ten dollars on it," Charley replied.

"He's the one ridin' in front?" John asked.

"Yes."

John snaked his rifle from the saddle sheath, then leaned on the fence post and aimed at Tully. He aimed, but he didn't cock his rifle. Although he would kill when killing was needed, he wasn't the kind of man who could dry-gulch his quarry, even someone like Mort Tully. He raised up from the rifle and was surprised to hear a quiet chuckle.

"I didn't think you could do it," Charley said.

"Well, hell, can you?" John asked.

"No."

"So, what do we do next?"

"Well, we could—" Charley started to answer, but his answer was interrupted by an angry buzz, then the sound of a heavy bullet tearing into flesh. A fountain of blood squirted up from the neck of Charley's horse, and the animal went down on its front knees, then collapsed onto its right side. It was almost a full second after the strike of the bullet before the heavy boom of a distant rifle reached their ears.

The fall pinned Charley's leg under his horse. Charley also dropped his pistol on the way down, and now it lay just out of reach of his grasping fingers.

"Charley! Are you hit?" John called.

"No, but I'm pinned under the horse. Get me out of here!" Charley shouted.

John hurried to help extricate Charley, but it wasn't easy to do. Though the side of the horse was resilient enough not to crush Charley's leg, the way Charley was trapped made it very difficult to pull his leg free.

There was another rifle shot, and this time the bullet dug into the saddle, sending up a little puff of dust just inches from Charley's face.

"Son of a bitch! Who is shooting?" John asked. He looked up and saw that this shot, like the first, had come from the opposite side from where they had seen the riders.

"Damn, we've got 'em on both sides of us," he said. He started working to get Charley's leg free.

Luke Pardeen had gone out from the rest of the riders, looking for the two lawmen. He was the one who spotted them, and saw that they had seen Tully and the others but hadn't seen him. That gave him a free shot at them, and he took it.

He was disgusted with himself that he hadn't killed the one he shot at, but he had at least hit the horse, and now he saw that one of them was pinned down and the other was trying to help him get free. That not only kept them both busy, but also it kept them from seeing him, giving him the opening he was looking for. He slapped his legs against the side of his horse, urging it forward.

"Ha!" he shouted in triumph. "I've got both you sons of bitches now!"

* * *

Because John was working hard trying to get Charley free, his attention was diverted. As a result, he didn't see the rider bearing down on them.

Charley was also trying to extricate his leg, but he happened to look up just in time to see that the shooter was almost right upon them. The problem was, Charley had no weapon, his pistol having slipped from his grasp when his horse went down.

"John! Look out!" Charley warned.

Responding to Charley's warning, John looked up just as the rider was getting into position to make the kill. John's rifle was lying on the ground beside him, and quickly, he jacked a shell into the chamber.

"Goodbye, boys," Pardeen shouted, smiling broadly as he raised his pistol and took careful aim. The smile left his face when he saw the end of John's rifle suddenly come up from behind the horse. The rifle spit a finger of flame and the .44-40 bullet rifle hit Pardeen just under the chin, then exited the back of his head along with a pink spray of blood and bone. Pardeen fell from the saddle but the horse's momentum carried the animal forward, and he had to leap over John, Charley, and Charley's dead mount to keep from crashing into them.

"They got Pardeen!" the lawmen heard someone shout and, looking around, they saw that the riders they had noticed earlier had been attracted by the shooting and were now bearing down upon them.

At that moment, with a mighty effort, Charley managed to get his leg free. He picked up his pistol and stood up.

"Here they come," John said, dropping to one knee in front of Charley.

"John, give me your pistol!" Charley shouted. John handed his handgun back to Charley, who then stood with a gun in each hand and a grimace on his face as he faced the charging outlaws.

There they stood, blazing away as the five riders charged them. Two of the charging outlaws went down under the hail of bullets. The other three, including Mort Tully, turned their horses and fled.

John and Charley held their position for a long moment, wisps of smoke drifting up from the barrels of their guns.

Not until the riders were small in the distance and still retreating did the two lawmen relax their vigil.

"Looks like they are skedaddling pretty good," John said.

"Yeah," Charley agreed. He holstered his pistol, then handed John's gun back to him. Turning, he looked down at his horse. The animal lay on the ground beside him, his large, brown eyes opaque in death.

Charley knelt beside his dead mount, looked at it for a long moment, then sighed.

"He was a good horse," Charley said, patting the animal on his neck. "I hate to lose him this way."

"You had him what? Ten, twelve years?" John asked.

"Fifteen," Charley said.

"I'm sorry. I know what it's like to lose a good horse."

"Looks like I'm going to need another one," Charley said.

"Well, there should be three wandering around here now," John said. He swung into the saddle of his own horse. "I'll round them all up, then bring them back so you can take your choice."

"I'll get my saddle and gear," Charley said as he began working.

Risco

Don Norton had owned the Golden Spur Saloon for all thirty years of its existence. It was he who changed the lights in the saloon from kerosene lanterns to gaslights and then to electricity as each new innovation occurred. He had even put indoor bathrooms in the saloon, one for women and one for men. There was also a telephone behind the bar.

But Norton had come to Risco from St. Louis, and he had always planned to go back some day. The only way he would be able to do it, though, would be by selling his saloon. And now that long-awaited day had come, because today he would be meeting with the buyer.

"Mr. Norton?" his bartender said, knocking on the door of his office. "The buyer is here."

"I'm ready," Norton said.

While Pete went to escort the buyer back to his office, Norton poured two glasses of wine. When Pete came in a moment later, Norton smiled and held one glass out toward the person who was making his dream come true.

"Miss Culpepper," Norton said. "It's nice to see you."

"Heavens, Don, it's been Lillian for many years," Lillian said, taking the glass of wine. "I see no reason to change now."

"I suppose not," Norton said. "By the way, did you have a lawyer look over all of the papers the bank prepared? Are you satisfied with everything?"

"I am more than satisfied," Lillian replied. She looked around the office. "I think I shall enjoy running the Golden Spur Saloon."

"Well, it isn't quite as luxurious as your, uh, old business," Norton said. "But it has certainly served me well over the years."

"You haven't told Charley about our arrangement?" Lillian said.

"No, I haven't breathed a word to him," Norton said.

Lillian smiled. "Good. I want it to be a surprise to him. I wonder what he will think when he learns that I have bought the Golden Spur? I know it is his favorite establishment."

"Knowing Charley, Lillian, I am sure he will be very pleased."

The smile left Lillian's face. "I just hope he gets home safely," she said. "I've been worried about him ever since he left."

"Listen," Norton said. "Charley is as tough as a walnut."

"So everyone says. But I'm afraid everyone is remembering the Charley of twenty years ago. He has gotten older, you know. Heavens, we all have," she added.

"He is older," Norton agreed. "But don't forget, he is with John Carmack, and John is as tough as Charley is. Now, you put those two together, and they are at least as good, and maybe better, than either one of them was alone twenty years ago."

The worry left Lillian's face. "That is true, isn't it?" she said.

Norton held his glass out toward Lillian. "To

Lillian Culpepper, the new owner of the Golden Spur," he said.

"And to the safe return of Charley, John, and Phil," Lillian added.

"Hear, hear," Norton agreed.

Chapter Nineteen

Salcedo

Weasel began questioning the jurors, but it was obvious that he didn't really know what he was doing. He asked one of them if he had ever been in jail.

"Why hell yes, I've been in jail. You know that, Weasel, me'n you both spent time for stealin' from that feed store back in San Angelo."

The gallery laughed.

After questioning a few more of the jurors, Weasel sat down.

"Well?" Pugh asked.

"Well what?" Weasel replied.

"Do you want to replace anyone?"

"No, they all seem like good men to me," Weasel said.

The jury smiled in satisfaction.

"Say, Goodnight," Muley whispered before Phil stood. "Can you really get rid of someone offen the jury?"

"Yes."

"Well, then you ought to get ole Harvey off. Me'n that son of a bitch ain't gotten along since we were in prison together. It would be just like that bastard to vote you guilty, just so's he could see me get hanged."

"Which one is Harvey?"

"It's that real ugly bastard," Muley said.

Phil looked at the jury and almost laughed. There was nobody on the jury he wouldn't classify as an "ugly bastard."

"Which ugly bastard is that?" Phil asked.

"Second one from the left," Muley said.

Phil nodded. "Okay, I'll take care of it. Thanks for the information."

Harvey was the first person Phil approached. "Could I have your name, sir?" he asked.

"Harvey Taylor."

"Mr. Taylor, do you know my co-counsel?"

"Your what?"

"I'm talking about Muley. Do you know him?"

"Yeah, I know him."

"What do you think about him?"

"I think he's a sorry piece of shit, and if he's the best you can come up with for a lawyer, then I feel sorry for you."

Phil turned toward Pugh. "Your Honor, I wish to strike this juror for cause. He is prejudiced toward my attorney."

"Get up, Harvey," Pugh said.

"What? Wait a minute. I was sittin' on the front row. You said ever'one in the front row could be on the jury."

"Get up," Pugh ordered again.

Reluctantly, Harvey left his seat.

"You," Pugh said, pointing to one of the others in the audience. "You take his place."

Phil continued questioning people. He had listened to the questions Weasel asked, so he knew who had served time, and, for the most part, what they had served time for.

"Have you ever killed anyone?" he asked someone.

Before he answered, the juror looked up toward Pugh. "Hey, what is this? Do I have to answer his questions?"

"Answer the questions, Arnie," Pugh said.

Arnie glared at Phil for a long moment before he answered. "Yeah," he said. "I've killed a few in my time."

"You don't look old enough to have been in the war," Phil said. "So, when you say you have killed, you aren't talking about killing in war, are you?"

"No."

"Why did you kill?"

"Because the sons of bitches needed killin'," Arnie answered.

"You want to replace Arnie?" Pugh asked.

"No, Your Honor," Phil said. "Arnie will do just fine."

During his voir dire, Phil learned that no fewer than seven of the twelve jurors had killed someone. He did not request the replacement of any of those seven.

He did get rid of three more, though, including Beckwith, who had worked on building the gallows that now stood in the street. A second admitted that he had made a bet on the outcome of the trial, and the third said that he owed Muley forty dollars.

"What'd you get rid of him for?" Muley asked when Phil returned to the defense table. "Hell, he owes me a favor."

"No," Phil replied. "He owes you forty dollars, which he won't owe you if you are hanged."

"What?" Muley said. "Damn, you're right." Muley turned and pointed to the juror Phil had just struck. "You son of a bitch!" he shouted. "You would like that, wouldn't you?"

"What?" the struck juror replied. "What are you talking about?"

"You know damn well what I'm talking about, you no-account bastard!" Muley said.

There was an immediate reaction to Muley's unexpected reaction, and everyone began yelling at once. Pugh had to pound on the table several times to restore order.

"All right," he finally said when the court was quiet once more. "The court will take a fifteen-minute recess so's ever'one can go take a piss."

"What about the bar, Angus? Can I open the bar during this time?" Ed Meeker asked.

"Hell yeah, you can open the bar," Pugh said. "And bring me a beer."

During the recess the liquor flowed. Jurors and gallery discussed the upcoming case together, and Weasel disappeared with one of the women Pugh had ordered to cover herself. Finally Pugh declared that it was too late to go on tonight, and he announced, with the slap of his pistol against the table, that the trial would continue the next day.

Dingo and Ernie took Phil back to jail, this time proudly and importantly, having placed him in a pair of handcuffs they had found at the saloon.

They didn't exactly find them there. They learned from a patron that one of the whores had a pair of handcuffs in her cubicle, and they confiscated them.

"What would a whore be a'wantin' with a pair of handcuffs in the first place?" Ernie asked, as they escorted Phil back down the street to the jail.

"Beats the hell out of me," Dingo replied. "When I asked Mabel about it, all she done was smile and say that some folks likes it that way."

"Likes it what way?" Ernie asked.

"That's what I asked too," Dingo said. "All she said was, if I ain't ever tried it, come see her sometime an' she would show me."

Mercifully the handcuffs were removed when they put Phil back in the cell. They closed the door, locked it, then, remembering his previous escape, put the keys in one of the desk drawers rather than hanging them on the hook.

"What do you say we go back down there and get us a beer?" Ernie asked.

Dingo was still holding the handcuffs in his hand. "You go have the beer," he said, examining the handcuffs. "I aim to go have Mabel show me just what it is she does with these here handcuffs."

Ernie and Dingo had been gone for nearly an hour. The sun was down, and the shadows inside the unlighted jail lengthened until the room finally became very dark. Phil was worried about Lucy. He wished he could get word to her.

He knew that she knew where he had been taken from the bank because he knew that her grandfathers were coming after him. He was also satisfied that it was now known that he had nothing to do with the robbery in Blodgett, though he was certain that Lucy never would have believed that of him anyway.

He hoped she was all right, wherever she was.

As it grew even darker, Phil lay on the bed with his hands laced behind his head. He stared into the dark void overhead, unable now even to see the ceiling of his cell. He thought of the turn of events that had gotten him here.

Phil's father was a lawyer and he had wanted Phil to follow him into the business. It was for that reason that Phil had begun his schooling by studying the law. Midway through school, however, he realized that he didn't really want to be a lawyer. He discovered a flair for numbers and started studying business accounting. Accounting led to an interest in banking.

After graduation, Phil's father arranged for a position for his son at a prestigious bank in Memphis, but there, he would be no more than a teller. One of his professors knew of the bank in Blodgett, and arranged for Phil to go there, not as a teller, but as bank manager.

Phil had known Lucy for many years, his father having been Greg Dawson's lawyer. Somewhere during the time of that relationship, Lucy turned from a pesty little girl to a friend, then from a friend to a fiancée. Phil asked Lucy what she thought about his accepting the position in Blodgett, and she thought it would be exciting, mentioning that it would be close to her illustrious grandfathers.

Phil and Lucy were married in one of the largest weddings of Memphis's social season. After the wedding, they took a riverboat down to New Orleans for their honeymoon, then went by train from New Orleans to Blodgett, where he was all set to take over the bank.

That had all seemed so rosy, so exciting, so promising. And now it was all gone. At this moment, that life was a part of his memories only. Reality was here and now, and the reality was he was a prisoner of a band of outlaws. Indeed, as improbable as it might seem, this was an entire town of outlaws and those who consorted with outlaws.

Phil reached over and wrapped his hand around one of the steel bars, as if to convince himself that this was no mere nightmare. He was a prisoner in a town from hell, in a trial that was more bizarre than anything he could imagine.

"Hey, Goodnight, you in here?" someone called from the darkness. Phil recognized it as Muley's voice.

"Now, where else would I be, Muley?" Phil replied.

Muley chuckled. "Yeah, I reckon that's right," he said. "Wait a minute, I'll light a lantern so we can see."

Phil sat up on his bunk, then heard the scratch of a match. He saw Muley cup a small flame in his hand, then hold it to a lantern, and a moment later the room was filled with brightness. Muley brought the lantern over and set it down next to the jail cell.

"Are you hungry? I brought you a couple of pieces of fried chicken," he said, handing a folded package through the bars.

"Thanks," Phil said, taking the food.

"Goodnight, you think you can win this here case?" Muley asked.

"Yes, I can win it," Phil answered, as he took a bite of the chicken. "Of course, that doesn't mean that the jury will award me the win. Or, even if they do, that Pugh won't decide to hang me anyway."

"Yeah, I sort'a been thinkin' that too," Muley said. "Damn, that don't seem right. I mean, if you win, and we hang anyhow."

"If we win, you are probably safe," Phil said. "I'll probably be the only one that hangs."

"What about Weasel?"

"Oh, I think my hanging will be enough to satisfy everyone," Phil said. "I doubt that he will carry through on his threat to hang either you or Weasel."

"Damn," Muley said, breathing a sigh of relief. "I'm sure tickled to hear that."

"I thought you might be," Phil said flatly.

"Oh, hey, listen, I don't mean I want to see you hang," Muley said quickly. "Truth to tell, I've sort'a took a likin' to you. When they hang you, I prob'ly won't even stay around to watch it."

"That's gratifying," Phil said.

"Yeah," Muley said, not picking up on Phil's sarcasm. "I mean, who wants to stand around and see his friend get his neck stretched?"

"Indeed," Phil said.

Muley was quiet for a long moment. "I tell you the truth, Goodnight, iffen I had it all to do over again, why, I wouldn't of never took part in that bank robbery where we snatched you up like we done."

"How many banks have you robbed?" Phil asked.

"That's the onliest one," Muley replied. "Afore that, onliest thing I ever done was, me'n and a friend rustled some beeves from a cattle drive. Then we took the cows into the next town and sold them." He chuckled. "We had us a good time there for 'bout three days, drinkin' and gamblin' and eatin'. You ever eat somethin' called a lobster? It's some kind of a big bug, but it sure is good."

Phil smiled. "Yes, I've eaten lobster."

"We sported with the women too, but we stayed there too long 'cause the trail boss came into town and found them cows before they were shipped on. Well, of course, the man that bought the cows know'd we was the ones sold 'em to him, so he got the sheriff after us." Muley was quiet for a moment. "The sheriff, he come right into that whore's room after me without so much as a by-your-leave. Well, I got took to court, didn't have me no smart lawyer neither, and next thing you know I was doin' me ten years in the prison. That's where I met Harvey," he added. "That's the one you took off the jury."

"Yes, I remember. What happened between you and Harvey?"

"Me'n Harvey tried to escape once. We would'a made it all the way iffen I had killed one of the guards like he told me to."

"You didn't kill him?"

"No," Muley said. "So we got caught and put back in prison. We done thirty days in the hole, too. Truth to tell, Goodnight, I ain't never killed nobody. Don't know as I have the stomach for it. But I'd just as soon you not tell anyone that."

"Your secret is safe with me."

"Listen, the reason I come over here was, one of them women that was in the courtroom today said she'd come pay a visit to you tonight if you wanted her to," Muley said. "If you want, I can fix it up for you. And it won't cost you nothin'."

"No, thank you."

"You sure? She ain't really all that bad a'lookin'."

"I'm married," Phil said.

"Yeah, well, I know that. But some folks, even iffen they are married, won't turn down a good lookin' woman if they get a chance."

"I'm sure that's the case," Phil said. "But I am only recently married, and I intend to remain faithful to my wife."

Muley thought about it for a moment, then

chuckled. "I reckon I can understand that," he said. "Most 'special since the woman you're married to is kin to Carmack and Dawson. Them is two tough hombres. I sure wouldn't want them to get mad at me 'cause I done somethin' like run around with another woman when I was married to their granddaughter."

"I'm glad you see my point of view," Phil said. Finishing his chicken, he wrapped the bones up in the paper the chicken had come in. "Thank you, that was quite good. Or maybe I was just very hungry."

"I'll take them bones," Muley said. "There's an ole dog stays down under the porch in front of the general store all the time. I'll give them to him."

"Muley, for an outlaw, you have a good heart," Phil said.

"Yeah, well, like I said before, don't go tellin' things like that to folks around here. I mean, that ain't the kind of thing you talk about in a town like Salcedo."

"I understand," Phil said.

Muley got up and stretched. "You want I should leave the lantern in your cell with you? That way you'll have light."

"Yes, thank you," Phil replied.

Muley tried to pass the lantern through the bars, but it was too big. "Can't do it," he said.

"The key's over there in the desk drawer," Phil said, hopefully.

Muley started toward the desk, then halted. He stood there for a moment, then turned back to Phil with a smile on his face.

"No," he said. "I know what you're tryin' to do, and I better not. Tell you what, I'll just leave the lantern sittin' on the floor right outside your cell.

That way you'll have light, but you can reach through to turn it off when you're ready."

"Thanks," Phil said, disappointed that Muley wouldn't open the cell door. Though as he thought about it, unless he would be able to talk Muley into just letting him go, there would be little advantage to opening the door. He certainly would not be able to overpower him.

They forgot to bring Phil breakfast while he was in jail, so he sat at his table eating from a can of beans that Muley provided for him as Weasel finally presented his opening statement.

"We aim to prove this here banker fella is guilty of murderin' Sheriff Bixby," Weasel said. "All of you know that we don't care much for lawmen here in Salcedo. So whenever we got us one that was to our likin', what happened? Why, this here son of a bitch come along and murdered him," he said, pointing at Phil. "So, what I want you fellas to do is find him guilty of murder in the first degree, so's we can all go outside and string him up on that fine gallows we done built. That's all I got to say for now," he concluded.

Phil got up to make his opening statement. He looked into the faces of all the jurors and, though he had done the best he could do through his voir dire, realized that there were included in this jury men who had killed, robbed, and committed all other sorts of crimes. Most, if not all, had served time in prison.

And it was to these men that Phil would have to plead his case.

"I don't know for sure that I killed Sheriff Bixby," Phil began. "But I may have."

Before he could go any further, there was an immediate reaction from Weasel.

"Did you hear that, Angus? Uh, I mean, judge? Did you hear what he just said? He just said he killed Bixby."

"I heard him," Pugh said.

"Well, hell, Angus, Your Honor. If he's done confessed to murderin' him, why are we even goin' on with this here trial?"

"Weasel's got a point, Goodnight," Pugh said. "If you've already confessed to murderin' Bixby, why should we continue with this trial?"

"Oh, but Your Honor, I did not confess to murdering Sheriff Bixby," Phil said, holding up his finger to make the point.

"The hell you say," Angus replied. "I heard you with my own ears. Ever'one in this court heard you say that."

"Yeah, we heard it," someone from the gallery said, and his comment was seconded by dozens of other affirmatives.

"No, Your Honor. What I said was, I *might have killed* him. That I might have killed him is indisputable, since I had already admitted that to you. But I am being charged with murder, and although all murders are killings, not all killings are murders. I request that you allow the trial to continue, so I can prove my point."

Pugh thought about it for a moment, then nodded. "All right, go ahead," he said.

"Thank you."

Phil turned back toward the jury, all of whom had followed the discussion with interest.

"As I was saying," Phil continued. "It might very well be that I killed Sheriff Bixby, but if I did kill him, I did not murder him. For, if I did kill him, then that killing was an act of justifiable homicide.

"You, Mr. Garner," Phil said, pointing to someone on the second row. He knew Garner's personal history—in fact, he knew every juror's personal history, not only from voir dire but also to the degree that Muley knew their histories. "I believe you admitted to me during voir dire that two years ago, you were involved in a killing incident in Abilene, Kansas. Is that right?"

"Yeah," Garner said, nodding his head. "I killed a fella in Abiline, name of Jensen."

"Why did you kill him?"

"Because the son of a bitch needed killin'," Garner said and, when the audience laughed, he looked at them with a broad, self-satisfied smile.

"Other than the fact that you say he needed killing," Phil said, "Let us reconstruct what actually happened that day. You were playing cards, I believe you said, and Jensen accused you of cheating. He drew a gun on you, and you shot him dead. Is that correct?"

"That's right. But it was Jensen who was the one cheating, not me," Garner said. "He was the one cheating, but the son of a bitch accused me of doin' it. Then he drew his gun."

"And you killed him?"

"Damn right, I killed him."

Phil quit speaking to Garner, and began addressing the rest of the jury.

"Mr. Garner shot Mr. Jensen, but he was not guilty of murder. In fact, he wasn't even brought to trial because there were enough witnesses present to testify that Mr. Garner did, indeed, shoot Mr. Jensen in self-defense. In fact, if the case had been brought to trial, and if you were serving on the jury, I have no doubt but that each and every one of you would have voted for acquittal."

Phil paused for a moment, and was gratified to see that, to a man, Garner included, everyone nodded their head yes.

"Self-defense is a form of justifiable homicide. And if a homicide is justifiable, then it is not murder."

Again, the jury shook their head yes, which was exactly the reaction Phil wanted.

"Now, here is an interesting aspect of the law as it refers to self-defense," Phil continued. "You do not have to actually be facing a drawn gun, in order to be able to plead self-defense. It is enough that you *believe* yourself to be in imminent mortal danger.

"On the day of my confrontation with Sheriff Bixby, I believed myself to be in imminent, mortal danger. I took steps to defend myself. It was not my intention to kill him, it was only my intention to stop him from killing me. That, gentlemen of the jury, is justifiable homicide. Now, here is one more thing. And this is the rub of our wonderful judicial system. The advantage is *always* to the accused. What that means is you don't have to be one hundred percent convinced that what I did was justifiable homicide. All you have to have is just the faintest idea that what I am telling you *might* be true. Because, you see, if any of you believe that what I am telling you has even the remotest chance of being true, then that means you are harboring some shadow of a doubt as to my guilt." Phil paused in his presentation, then walked back over to the table. He addressed his next statement directly to Angus Pugh.

"When this trial is completed, before you retire to consider the verdict, His Honor, Judge Angus Pugh will give you his instructions. Those instructions will remind you that in every court of law in America. . . ." Phil paused, and took in the saloon with a wave of his hand. "And Your Honor, gentlemen of the jury, and distinguished counselors, you have made this a court of law," he continued. "In every court of law in America, the judge will tell you that in order to find someone guilty, you must be convinced, beyond the merest shadow of a doubt, that he is guilty. If you have any idea that I might"—he held up his finger—"just *might* be telling the truth, you will have to acquit me.

"Thank you."

"Whooeee damn!" Muley said as Phil sat down. "This son of a bitch is good! I wish I'd had him on my side when I rustled me them cows!"

The gallery laughed.

Chapter Twenty

Weasel was cross-examining Corey Peters.

"When did you first learn that Bixby was dead?"

"When I seen him dead."

"And what did you do then?"

"I come back to the saloon with Tully."

"You were here when Tully told everyone that Bixby was dead?"

"Yeah, I was."

"And did you tell anyone that Bixby was dead?"

"I didn't have to tell nobody. Ole Tully was doin' a pretty good job of tellin' ever'one his own self."

"But you did see Bixby dead?"

"Yeah, I seen him lyin' there on the floor, dead, just like Tully said."

Phil, who was taking notes, looked up at that comment.

"All right, you can sit down now," Weasel said. Peters started to get up, but Phil called out.

"Wait. I have the right to cross-examine," he said.

"Yeah, that's right," Angus said. "Okay, ask him your questions."

"Mr. Peters, whenever the prosecutor asked you if you had seen Bixby dead, your answer was," Phil walked back over to the table and picked up the tablet on which he had been taking notes. " 'Yeah, I seen him lyin' there on the floor, dead, just like Tully said.' Is that right? Is that what you said?"

"Yeah."

"What do you mean by that, Mr. Peters?"

Peters looked confused. "What do I mean by what?"

"By the fact that he was dead, just like Tully said. Couldn't you tell that he was dead?"

"Well, yeah, I could tell. Hell, anyone could tell."

"Then why did Tully have to tell you?"

"Well, 'cause he seen Bixby first. See, I was front of the leather-goods store. I had just come out of Cindy Lou's crib . . . Well, you bein' a stranger here'n all, you might not know that she keeps her crib down behind the leather-goods shop."

"A crib?"

"Yeah, you know. It's like a little house where she does her business."

"I see. Then Cindy Lou would be a . . ." Phil paused, looking for an acceptable word, but Peters supplied it for him.

"A whore," Peters said. "Cindy Lou is a whore."

"And I'm a damn good one too, honey," a woman's voice called out from the back of the room. Everyone laughed.

"Go ahead," Phil invited. "You said you were standing in front of the leather-goods store when Tully came out of the sheriff's office?"

"Yeah," Peters said. "Tully saw me there and told me that Bixby was dead."

"Mr. Peters, do you think it possible that Tully might have killed Bixby?"

Phil waited for Weasel to make an objection, but none came.

"Wait a minute. I thought you killed him," Peters replied. "Ain't that what you done told the jury?"

"I told the jury that I *might* have killed him," Phil said. "I did hit him with the chair. But what if all I did was just knock him down, and I didn't kill him? What if Tully found him on the floor? Is it possible that Tully might have gone into the jail, saw Bixby lying on the floor, not yet dead, but, for reasons of his own that we may know nothing of, took advantage of the situation and killed Bixby?"

"Ha! I see where you're goin' at with this. He could kill ole Bixby and folks would blame you," Peters said.

"Yes," Phil replied. "Do you know anything about the past relationship of these two men that would make you believe Tully could do something like that?"

"Yeah, well, Tully and Bixby hated each other. Ever'one knows that."

"Since you didn't see what happened, since nobody saw what happened, then it is possible that Bixby was still alive when Tully found him, but Tully finished him off. Isn't it?"

"Well, yeah," Peters said. "I reckon that's possible."

Phil looked up at Pugh. "No further questions, Your Honor."

The remaining witnesses called by Weasel testified as to how good a sheriff Bixby was for a town like Salcedo. Phil had no questions for them. Then it came time for him to put on his own witnesses.

"Defense calls Angus Pugh to the stand," Phil began.

"Wait a minute, you can't call the judge, can you?" Pugh asked.

"It depends on you, Your Honor. You are the judge; you set the rules of this court. If you say I can call you, I can. If you say I can't call you, then I can't. You are in charge."

"Yeah," Pugh said. "Yeah, I am in charge." He stroked his chin for a moment, then nodded. "All right, but I ain't movin' over into no witness chair. You got 'ny questions for me, you're goin' to have to ask me while I'm sittin' here."

"Very well," Phil answered. "Your Honor, when was the first time you ever saw me?"

"I don't exactly recollect what day it was," Pugh replied. "It was about six or seven days ago, I reckon."

"And where was that?"

"Well, that would'a been in Blodgett."

"That would be Blodgett, Texas?"

"Yeah."

"Would you tell the court exactly where, in Blodgett, you saw me?"

"It was in the bank," Pugh said. "I was makin' a withdrawal at the time." He smiled, and the others in the courtroom laughed.

"What was I doing in the bank?"

"You had just come in," Pugh said. "That surprised the hell out of all of us, especially my cousin. I mean it was the middle of the night. You had no business bein' there."

"When I came into the bank, was I struck?"

"Do you mean did someone hit you over the head? Yeah, Weasel done it," Angus said, nodding toward Weasel.

"After you had completed your . . . business . . . in the bank, did you then leave Blodgett?" Phil set the word *business* apart from the rest of the sentence.

"Yeah, we left."

"Did I stay behind?"

"No, you come with us."

"How did I come, if I was unconscious on the floor?"

"Well, hell, we picked you up and throw'd you across a horse. We had to borrow the horse too," he added, with another broad smile. Again, the gallery laughed.

"Then, you would say that I did not come of my own volition, wouldn't you?"

"Your own what?"

"I did not volunteer to come with you."

"No. We just brought you."

"So, what you are telling this court is that I was brought to this town against my wishes and, once here, illegally confined by Sheriff Bixby."

"Yeah."

"If that had happened to you, Mr. Pugh, would you have made an effort to get away?"

"Damn right I would."

"And if someone attempted to restrain you, would you have used whatever force you deemed necessary to make your escape?"

"Yeah," Pugh agreed.

"Thank you, Your Honor. No further questions."

With his examination of Pugh completed, Phil took the stand himself.

"I'm going to ask myself if I killed Sheriff Bixby,"

he told the jury. "And the answer is, I don't know if I killed him or not. I was attempting to escape when he came into the jail and saw me. He started to draw his gun, but before he could do so, I picked up a chair and hit him. He went down on the floor, and I ran.

"At the time, I didn't think I had killed him. I thought I had just knocked him down. It was not until Mort Tully came into the saloon and announced that I had killed him that I even considered that possibility. Did I kill Sheriff Bixby? I may never know. You may never know. But I do believe that there is a strong possibility that Mort Tully came into the jail after I left and, seeing Bixby unconscious or stunned on the floor, took advantage of that opportunity to finish the job."

Rising from the witness chair, Phil said, "I now call Mr. Corey Peters back to the stand."

Corey returned to the chair. By now he was actually enjoying being a part of the drama that was unfolding before the whole town.

"Mr. Peters, you said that Mort Tully and Sheriff Bixby didn't like each other, didn't you?"

"That's what I said."

"Do you know why they didn't like each other?"

Phil was taking a chance with this question, because in a real court of law Peter's answer would be thrown out as hearsay. But such a distinction would require a knowledgeable attorney, and Weasel was anything but that. Therefore there was no objection to the question.

"Tully and Sheriff Bixby got into a fight over one of the whores," Peters said.

"Do you know what the fight was about?"

"No. But you can ask Kitty. She's sittin' right back there."

"Thank you," Phil said. "You may step down and defense calls Kitty."

Kitty was one of the bare-breasted women who had come into the courtroom. Now, in response to Pugh's order from the bench, she and the other others had their breasts covered. As she took the chair in front of the courtroom, however, it was obvious by her provocative demeanor and the way she was dressed and made up that she was a soiled dove.

"Miss, uh, Kitty," Phil began. "You heard the witness say that you were the cause of a fight between Sheriff Bixby and Mort Tully. Is that true?"

"Yes, sir, it's true," Kitty answered.

"Were both of them vying for your attention?"

"Does that mean did both of them want me to spread my legs for them?"

"Uh, yes," Phil answered.

Kitty shook her head. "No. If that was all there was to it, wouldn't be no problem. Hell, ever'body in town knows I'll spread my legs for anyone."

The gallery laughed.

"Then in what way were you the cause of the disagreement?" Phil asked.

"I went to Bixby to complain about Tully," Kitty said. "Tully, he's not like other men. What he wants to do is hurt me."

"Hurt you?"

Kitty nodded. "Yes. He liked to hurt all the girls. You can ask any of them."

"How would he hurt you?"

"Well, in lots of ways. Like, one way is he put his cigar here," Kitty said, reaching for the top of her dress. She turned toward Angus. "Angus, uh, I mean, Your Honor, can I show him my titty where Tully burnt me with his cigar?"

"Yeah, judge, we want to see," someone in the gallery shouted.

Pugh nodded. "Go ahead."

Kitty bared her breast, showing an ugly scar near the nipple. "He tried to burn the nipple too. He said he wanted to burn it off, but I pulled away," she explained.

"How did Sheriff Bixby respond to your complaint?" Phil asked.

"What he did was, he tole Tully that if Tully did it again, to me or to any of the girls, he'd kill 'im. They yelled at each other a lot, and I thought they were goin' to start shootin' right there, but nothin' happened."

"Did Tully ever attempt to hurt you again?"

"Hell, I wouldn't let the son of a bitch bed me anymore after that," Kitty said. "Neither would none of the other girls."

"Thank you, you have been a big help," Phil said. "You may step down now."

With examination and cross-examination completed, it was ready for the closing statements. Prosecution was supposed to get the last word, but when Angus asked Weasel to speak first, Phil didn't correct him.

Weasel got up and walked over to the stand in front of the jury.

"You've all heard a lot of good men, men that you all know, tellin' you what a good man Sheriff Bixby was. We are, all of us, thieves, murderers, and robbers. We're the kind of men that can't live in an ordinary town, so we've all come together here in Salcedo. But even in a town like Salcedo, we need someone to sort of keep things straight, and that's what Bixby did for us.

"And the best thing was, Bixby was a real sheriff.

He had actually done some sheriffin' in other towns, but he come here to be our sheriff. But this-here galoot killed him. Now I ask you, where are we goin' to get another man like Bixby? The answer is, we ain't goin' to.

"Goodnight told us that maybe he killed Bixby, but now he comes along an' he says, 'Lookie here, maybe I didn't do it. Maybe Tully done it.' That's easy for him to say, 'cause Tully ain't here to say different. But remember, when Tully came into the saloon that night, what he said then was, this here fella killed the Sheriff." Weasel pointed accusingly at Phil.

"And they's one more thing we should think about." He pointed toward the street. "Beckwith got us a gallows built outside. It's a good lookin' gallows too an' I think we all owe Beckwith here our thanks for doin' such a good job."

Beckwith beamed under the praise.

"Now it seems to me a shame to go to all the trouble to build them gallows, and then not hang the son of a bitch they were built for. So I say, we find 'im guilty, and then we hang his sorry ass."

Weasel sat down.

"Gentlemen of the jury," Phil began. He paused for a moment. "You may think that the appellation, gentlemen, is misplaced here, especially in light of the fact that Weasel called you all thieves, murderers, and robbers. But I say it is not misplaced because at this pivotal moment in your lives, you are fulfilling one of the most sacred duties any American can do. You are constituted as a jury, a deliberative body with the authority to decide the fate of another human being.

"That authority lifts you above your personal history. You are no longer thieves, murderers, and robbers. You are, as of this one, critical moment, citizens of America, equal to any other citizen in the country. You are gentlemen of the jury, free to act as guided by your conscience, and not by your misspent past.

"I have told you that the law says to convict, you must be convinced, beyond the slightest shadow of a doubt, that I committed murder, because murder is the charge for which I am being tried.

"In view of this requirement I ask you to consider the following two things during your deliberation.

"Number one, is it possible that I didn't even kill Sheriff Bixby? I have confessed to striking him with the chair. I have even confessed that he went down. But in truth, when Tully came to the saloon to report that I had killed the sheriff, that was the first time that I even considered that the blow might have been fatal. I was genuinely surprised and mortified.

"We have also heard that Mort Tully did not get along with Bixby, and we know that Tully was the first one to find Bixby. Is it possible that Bixby was still alive when Tully found him? Is it possible that Tully saw this as an opportunity to settle old scores, and so he killed Bixby making it look as if I did it?

"I wouldn't be able to refute it. When I fled from the jail, I assumed Bixby was still alive.

"But I also ask you to consider this. Suppose, when I hit Sheriff Bixby over the head with that chair, that I actually did kill him. I did not plan to kill Bixby. My plan was to escape from what was, in fact, illegal confinement. I perceived that my life was in danger, and remember, the *perception* that your life is in danger is as valid an argument for justifiable homicide as was Mr. Garner's situation when he was assaulted by Mr. Jensen, with gun in hand. If I did kill Sheriff Bixby then, it was in self-defense.

"And number two," Phil held his finger up and, leaning slightly toward the jury, began waving his finger back and forth, "You don't have to believe one hundred percent of either of those two scenarios. All you have to believe is one-tenth of one percent of the possibility that it could have happened either of the ways I just told you. And if that is so, then you have enough of a doubt as to my guilt to legally acquit me. I thank you, gentlemen, for allowing me the opportunity to plead my case before you."

To Phil's surprise, there was applause when he sat down.

"Ed," Pugh called to the bartender. "This here bar is open. These folks can drink while me'n the jury meets in the back room to decide this case."

Phil looked up in surprise when he heard Pugh include himself in the jury deliberation.

"Your Honor, you aren't allowed to meet with the jury while they are deliberating," Phil called.

"Who said I can't?" Pugh replied.

"Those are the rules," Phil explained.

"I thought you said I made the rules."

"Well, yes, in as far as courtroom procedure. But you can't interfere with the jury's decision."

"Well, I'm changin' the rules," Pugh replied. He looked over at the jury. "Come on boys, we got us some decidin' to do."

"This ain't good," Muley said quietly. "You did some powerful talkin' an' Pugh's afraid you talked them boys into lettin' you go."

"Won't he honor the decision of the jury?" Phil asked.

"Sure," Muley said. "As long as they decide the way he wants 'em to."

"Come on, prisoner," Dingo said, stepping up to the defense table then. "It's back to jail with you."

"Can't he wait here until the jury has made up its mind?" Muley asked. "We may have some more consultin' to do."

Dingo laughed. "Oh, don't you be worryin' none about that, Muley. You'll be gettin all the consultin' done you need. Pugh told us to put you in jail, too."

"What?" Muley asked in alarm. "What for?"

"Pugh didn't say what for. He just said to do it, and that's what I aim to do," Dingo said.

"I tell you what, that boy pure-dee can talk," Garner said. Garner was in the back room of the saloon where the jurors were meeting to decide the case. "Hell, I'm goin' to say he's not guilty."

"Me too," one of the other jurors said. "Hell, I wouldn't be surprised if Tully did kill Bixby."

"Yeah," Garner said. "Besides which, even if Goodnight did it, why, it wasn't no different from me killin' Jensen. It was, what did he call it?"

"Justifiable homicide," one of the other jurors said.

"Yeah," Garner said. "Justifiable homicide."

"I say he's guilty, and he's going to hang," Pugh said resolutely.

"Wait a minute, Angus," Garner said. "You heard what Goodnight said. If they's just a chance that what all he was tellin' us is true . . . just a little bit of a chance, then we have to say he is not guilty."

"Where do you think you are?" Pugh asked sternly. "This isn't a court in Austin, or Denver, or

St. Louis. This here court is in Salcedo, and we make the rules in Salcedo. And in Salcedo, we get to do things a little different. Hell, if we let somebody like Goodnight get away with murder 'cause of somethin' like doubt, next thing you know we'll have people shootin' each other down in the street for no reason at all.

"He called you gentlemen, but you and I both know better. You ain't no gentleman, and neither am I. We're exactly what Weasel said we was. We are thieves, murderers, and robbers. And if we don't have some kind of control over things, who knows where it will lead? We have to find this fella guilty, and we have to hang him. It's the only way we can keep control of things."

"All rise," Dingo said when the court was reconvened.

Phil, Muley, and everyone else in the saloon responded as Pugh came back in.

"Sit down," Pugh said.

There was a scraping of chairs as everyone took their seats.

"Me'n the jury have decided," Pugh said without introduction. "Mr. Goodnight, you're guilty, and tomorrow mornin' at dawn, we're goin' to hang you."

"What?" Muley shouted.

"What are you worried about, Muley?" Pugh said. "I've decided not to hang you."

"I ain't talkin' about me!" Muley said. "I'm sayin' Goodnight ain't guilty, and anyone who says he is, is an ignorant son of a bitch!"

"I'm saying he's guilty," Pugh said. "Does that mean you are talking about me?"

"I'm especially talking about you," Muley said angrily.

"Muley, sit down, and be quiet," Phil warned.

"Better listen to your friend there," Pugh said.

"Pugh, you are a dumb, evil bastard, do you know that? Somebody should'a put a bullet in your brain a long time ago."

Pugh smiled, a slow, evil smile. "Muley, you just talked yourself into a hangin'," he said. "Dingo, take 'em both to jail. We'll hang 'em first thing in the mornin'."

Chapter Twenty-One

It was dark when Mort Tully and the two riders with him returned to Salcedo. Dismounting in front of the saloon, they went inside and stepped straight up to the bar.

"Whiskey," Tully said, holding up three fingers. "And leave the bottle."

Meeker put three glasses out, then set a bottle on the bar, but he held on to it until Tully produced the money. Tully paid, poured himself a glass, drank it, and poured himself a second before he passed the bottle to the two men with him. Then, holding the whiskey glass in his hand, he turned his back to the bar and looked out over the saloon. Pugh was sitting at a table in his usual position, toward the back of the saloon. Tully glared at him.

"Where's Pardeen and the others?" Pugh asked.

"Dead," Tully said. "All of 'em, dead."

"Wait a minute," Toby Riddle said. "My brother was with you. Where's George?"

Tully tossed the whiskey down, then refilled his

glass before he answered. "He's dead, too," he said.

"What happened?" Riddle asked.

"Them two lawmen? Carmack and Dawson? They aren't men," Tully said. "They are devils."

"There were nine of you that left here," Pugh said. "Are you telling me that nine of you couldn't handle two old men?"

"I notice you didn't go after 'em yourself," Tully said.

"Yeah, well, after tomorrow it won't matter anyway," Pugh said. "We're hangin' Goodnight. With him dead, there won't be any reason for Carmack and Dawson to come sniffin' around anymore."

"You're hangin' Goodnight?" Tully asked.

"Yes," Pugh replied. "For murder. I mean, after all, he did kill Bixby, didn't he?"

With Pugh's question, everyone stared at Tully. He had lifted the glass halfway to his lips but, becoming aware that everyone was looking at him, lowered the glass with an expression of wariness on his face.

"What's ever'one lookin' at me for?" he asked.

"Goodnight said you killed Bixby," Pugh said.

The wariness was replaced by a flicker of concern. He blinked a few times, then licked his lips.

"Did you kill Bixby?" Pugh asked.

Tully took the drink, then wiped his mouth with the back of his hand before he answered.

"No," he said. "No, I didn't kill Bixby. Goodnight did it, just like I said he did."

Pugh said nothing, but his long, hard stare so unnerved Tully that his hand began to shake.

"Yeah," Pugh finally said. "I thought it was prob'ly something like that. Tell you what. How would you like to be the hangman tomorrow? You can pull the lever."

"Yeah," Tully said. "Yeah, I'll pull the lever."

"I thought you might like that," Pugh said. "By the way, you'll be hangin' Goodnight and Muley."

"Yeah, okay," Tully said. "Sure, I'll be glad to do it."

Tully turned back to the bar and the rest of the patrons in the saloon went back to their own conversations. Toby Riddle, with tears in his eyes, picked up a guitar and began playing a sad, mournful song.

"Toby, play somethin' a little more cheerful," someone said.

"Leave 'im alone," Kitty said. "Can't you see he's mournin' his brother?"

Pugh continued to stare at Tully's back. "Dingo," he said, quietly.

"Yeah, Angus?"

"Tomorrow, soon as Tully gets through hangin' Muley and Goodnight, I want you to kill the son of a bitch."

"You want me to kill Tully?"

"Yeah," Pugh said. "Goodnight was right. Tully killed Bixby."

The night creatures called to each other as John and Charley stood looking toward Salcedo. A cloud passed over the moon and moved away, bathing in silver the little town that rose up like a ghost before them. A couple of dozen buildings, some of which were lit up, fronted the main street. The biggest and most brightly lit building was the lone cantina at the far end of town.

Inside the saloon someone was playing a guitar, and John and Charley could hear the music all the way out in the hills. The player was good, and the music spilled out in a steady beat with two or three poignant minor chords at the end of each phrase. An overall single-string melody worked its way in and out of the chords like a thread of gold woven through the finest cloth.

John liked that kind of music, mournful, lonesome music, the kind of melody a man could let run through his mind during long, quiet rides. He looked over toward Charley to see how he was taking it and saw that Charley seemed to be enjoying it as well.

Too bad he and Charley had been such bitter political enemies all these years. During the last few days he had discovered that he and Charley were quite a bit alike. It seemed a shame now that they wasted a lifetime of friendship.

"What do you think?" Charley asked. "Walk into town? Or ride?"

"Let's lead our horses in," John suggested.

"Good idea. We're less likely to be noticed that way, I think," Charley agreed.

The two men checked their pistols. They were loaded and slipped easily from their sheaths. From the insight of years on the trail, nurtured by the need to live by their wits, they knew that their best insurance was a ready gun.

As the two men started into town, they caught the smell of beans and spicy beef from one of the houses.

A dog barked.

A woman laughed.

Normally, when John or Charley would enter a town, they would stay in the middle of the street to avoid ambush from the shadows. But this was an entirely different situation. This time the dark, instead of being their enemy, was their ally. They moved through the shadows, staying out of sight until they reached the jailhouse.

"No lights in the jail," John said quietly. "Doesn't look like there's anyone in there."

"We won't know until we check it out," Charley said. Charley walked over to the barred window. "Goodnight?" he called, quietly.

John, with pistol in hand, kept a watch on the street.

"Phil Goodnight," Charley called again. "Are you in there?"

A face appeared in the window. "Who are you?"

Charley chuckled. "Damn, you look just like the picture Lucy drew of you," he said.

"You are Lucy's grandfather?" Phil asked.

"I'm one of them," Charley answered. "Anybody in there guarding the store? Or are you alone?"

"I'm not alone," Phil said. "But there's nobody watching over us."

"We'll be right there," Charley said.

Charley and John hurried around to the front of the jail. Again, with John keeping watch, Charley opened the door and stepped inside. "Where are you?" he asked.

"Over here," Phil answered.

Charley lit a match and, in the match's glow, saw a lantern. He lit the lantern but kept it low. Looking toward the back of the building, he saw two men standing in the cell, their hands wrapped around the bars.

"You know where the key is?"

"In the desk drawer," Phil answered.

"John, is it still clear out there?"

"Yeah," John's voice sounded from outside.

Charley jerked the drawer open and found the key. Walking over to the cell, he pulled his pistol and pointed it at the man in jail with Phil. "You, get back," he said.

"No!" Phil said quickly. "He goes with us."

"Look here, son, John and I didn't come through hell and high water to turn out every jail bum we might come across. We're here because of you. Well, Lucy more than you."

"But you don't understand," Phil said. "This is Muley. He stood up for me. That's why he's in here. They're planning to hang both of us in the morning."

"What's your real name, Muley?" Charley asked.

"Slater. Gary Slater."

"I've never heard of you," Charley said. "John," he called. "You ever run across anyone named Gary Slater? Calls himself Muley?"

"No," John called back. "What's keeping you in there?"

Charley opened the cell door. "All right, if neither of us has ever heard of you, then we've got no beef with you. Come on out."

"Thanks, Sheriff," Muley said, exiting the cell with Phil.

"We're going to have to get you a horse somewhere," Charles said. "You can ride, can't you?"

"Yes, sir."

"I know where we can get a couple of horses," Muley offered.

"All right, let's get them and get out of here."

"What about the money?" Phil asked.

"Money? What money?"

"The money that was stolen from the bank in

Blodgett," Phil said. "Grandpa . . . uh . . . which grandpa are you?"

"I'm Charley Dawson. John Carmack is out front."

"Grandpa Dawson, I'm not leaving here without the money that was stolen from the Blodgett bank."

"Hey, Grandpa Carmack, get in here," Charley called.

John backed in through the door, gun in hand, still looking out toward the street.

"What is it?" John asked.

"Meet your grandson-in-law," Charley said.

John nodded. "Good to meet you, boy. Now, what's the holdup? Let's get out of here."

"Tell him," Charley said.

"I'm not leaving without the money that was taken from the bank in Blodgett," Phil said.

John looked at Charley. "You think this little shit is serious?" he asked.

"He's serious, all right," Muley said. "I ain't never seen me a more serious man."

"Who the hell is this?" John asked.

"Muley, meet Grandpa Carmack," Charley said.

Muley smiled and stuck out his hand. "Glad to meet you, Grandpa Carmack."

"Grandpa?" John said.

Charley laughed.

"He's going with us," Phil explained.

"For someone who is getting rescued, you sure have a hell of a lot of conditions," John said. "First the money, then him."

"I'm sorry," Phil said.

"Where is this money you're talking about?"

"It's in the bank across the street," Phil answered.

"In the bank?"

"Yes."

John sighed. "All right," he said. "Let's go get it."

Charley turned to Muley. "I believe you said something about getting us a couple of horses?"

"Yes, sir."

"Get 'em."

"I'll be right back."

"Can we trust him?" John asked.

"Yes," Phil said.

"I hope so," John said. John reached into his saddlebag and took out several sticks of dynamite.

"Damn, John, how many do you think it's going to take?" Charley asked.

"I'm pretty sure they don't have the best safe in the country," he said. "One stick should do it. The others are to get things a little confused."

They crossed the street to the bank. Charley picked the front door lock with his pocketknife and swung it open.

"If the door is any indication, the vault will be easy," Charley said.

"I'll get it ready," John said, "but I won't blow it until Muley gets back with the horses."

"Here he comes now," Phil said with a sense of relief.

"Get mounted," John ordered. "The horse could get skittish when this stick blows. And if you aren't already mounted, you might not be able to get on."

"Yes, sir," Phil replied.

Taking a candle with him, John went back into the bank to find the vault.

* * *

The blast shook the windows and brought all conversation in the saloon to a halt.

"What the hell was that?" someone asked.

Everyone looked at each other in surprise. Ernie was nearest the door and he walked over to have a look.

"See anything, Ernie?" Ed Meeker called.

"No, I . . . Wait a minute. Looks like there might be some men in front of the bank."

"In front of the bank?"

"Son of a bitch!" Dingo said. "Someone is robbing our bank!"

With Dingo's pronouncement, several men started toward the front door. There were so many of them, though, that they crowded up at the door and couldn't get out easily. They saw winks of light and muzzle flashes, followed by two shots. One muzzle flash was from an upstairs window in the hotel right across from the bank, and the other came from the street in front of the bank.

Mort Tully's room was on the second floor of the hotel that was right across the street from the bank. Awakened by the blast, he hurried to the window and looked outside. He realized at once what was happening and saw, also, who it was.

"Well, Christmas has come early," he said to himself. "You dumb shits have given me another chance."

Pulling his rifle from beneath his bed, he cocked it, then aimed at the man coming out of the bank, carrying a sack.

He didn't know whether it was Carmack or Dawson, but he didn't really care. By the glint of the badge on the man's vest, he knew it was one or the other.

"Sheriff! Up there!" Muley shouted, pointing to Tully.

Muley's shout gave John just enough time to jump back inside, and the slug from Tully's rifle dug into the wooden floor of the bank.

Charley answered Tully's shot with one of his own, and Tully fell forward from the window and hit the porch overhang. He slid down, then tumbled to the street, raising a cloud of dust as he hit. He lay there, face down and unmoving.

"Grandpa!" Phil shouted, pointing toward the other end of the street. By now, several people had come out of the saloon.

Charley shot toward them, intending more to run them back inside than to kill any of them. His shooting had the desired effect, for they all ran back inside.

John mounted his own horse, then lit the fuse on a second stick of dynamite and threw it as far down the street as he could.

Ernie and several others, now with pistols in hand, came back out onto the porch in front of the saloon. That's when they saw sparks tumbling toward them through the night air.

"What the hell?" Ernie said. "What's that?" He pointed to the sputtering sparks.

The stick of dynamite went off then, this time so close that it broke windows on both sides of the street. It also threw up dirt and detritus from the street, including a generous amount of horse apples. The ones nearest the front suddenly found themselves covered with a veneer of manure.

"Son of a bitch!" Ernie shouted, wiping feces from his face and spitting distastefully.

"What the hell's going on here?" Pugh shouted.

Pugh's question was answered with another blast of dynamite. This time, everyone dived under the tables.

"Answer me!" Pugh demanded. "What's going on?"

"The bank's being robbed," Ernie said.

Tacora Canyon, Sunrise The Next Morning

John and Charley lay on top of the canyon wall, looking toward the approach to the canyon. From the flare of dust in the early morning sunlight, quite a posse had been assembled.

John chuckled.

"What's so funny?" Charley asked.

"I've led many a posse in my day, but this is the first time I've ever been chased by one."

Charley laughed as well. "Yeah, me too," he said. "You know, sometimes I used to feel sorry for the poor sons of bitches we were chasing. I'd wonder how it felt."

"Yeah, well, we're the poor sons of bitches now," John said. "How does it feel?"

"Not particularly good," Charley admitted. He looked behind him, where Phil and Muley were holding on to the horses. Because they were back from the edge of the canyon wall, they were out of sight to anyone approaching from below. "It would help some if Phil could ride a little faster."

"I agree. But you've got to hand it to the little shit. He does have gumption."

"He does at that," Charley said. "Lucy could've done worse."

"They're getting closer," John said.

Charley jacked a shell into his rifle and looked toward the approaching riders. "John, anybody ever get away from you when you were leading those posses?"

"Not a one," John said.

"I never lost one either," Charley said.

"At the moment, Charley, I don't find that all that encouraging," John said.

"Neither do I," Charley said, taking aim.

There was a reason John and Charley had chosen this specific location. Here, at the western approach to the canyon, there was a very narrow constriction, a needle's eye draw that would force the riders into single file. The restricted draw continued for about forty yards before it opened onto a much wider canyon floor.

John and Charley sighted down their rifles at their targets.

"Give me the word when the last one clears the entrance," Charley said.

"Have you got your target?" John asked.

"I've got it."

"All right, now!" John said.

Both men fired at the same time, but the crack of their rifles was drowned out immediately by the roar of dynamite. Heavy explosions at the entrance and exit of the narrow draw brought rocks cascading down to block each end, effectively sealing Pugh and his outlaws inside.

The outlaws' horses whinnied and reared in fear and confusion, unseating a couple of the riders.

Pugh, in the lead, started screaming in rage and firing his pistol at the top of the canyon walls, even though he had no target.

"Pugh!" John called down to him. The echo repeated the name: *Pugh, Pugh, Pugh.*

"Where are you?" Pugh replied. "Show yourself, you son of a bitch!" *Of a bitch, bitch, bitch.*

"Pugh, do you see that hole in wall?" John called.

Pugh looked around. Behind him, at ground level, was a small, hollowed-out place, almost like a fox's den.

"Yeah, I see it," Pugh said.

"I want you and all your men to put your guns in that hole."

"To hell with that," Pugh said. "I'm not puttin' my gun anywhere."

"Are you ready?" John asked Charley, speaking quietly.

"I think so," Charley said. "Remember I'm not as good with a long gun as you are."

"You can do it," John said. "You take the left side, I've got the right."

"Carmack, Dawson, can you hear me?" Pugh shouted. "Where are you? What's going on?"

"On three," John said quietly. "One . . . two . . . three."

At the count of three, both men squeezed the triggers. The two rifle shots were so close to each other that they sounded like one shot.

Blood splattered out from either side of Pugh's head as the rifle bullets cut through both of his ear lobes. Dropping his pistol, Pugh slapped his hands over his shredded ear lobes.

"Ahh!" Pugh cried out in pain.

"Pugh," John said. "That could just as easily

have been your eyes. Now, you and all your men, put your guns in that hole like I told you to."

"You've got our money!" Pugh shouted. "We're not going anywhere without our money!"

John fired again, this time shredding one of Dingo's ear lobes. Like Angus before him, Dingo cried out in pain, and slapped his hand to his ears. Now the others began milling about nervously, looking up toward the top of the canyon wall, trying to figure out where the shooting was coming from.

"Put your guns in that hole!" John ordered. "Or we're going to start chipping away at your parts."

Dingo was the first to obey, taking off his pistol belt and throwing belt, holster, and gun into the hole. The others followed suit, including someone who picked up Pugh's dropped pistol and threw it into the hole as well.

"Rifles, too," Charley called down to them.

Without further protest, the men snaked all the rifles from the saddle sheaths including Pugh's rifle. A moment later, not one man was armed.

Not until then did John and Charley stand, showing themselves to the outlaws below.

"You boys better move back to that far corner over there," John called down to them, pointing back toward the entrance.

"What? What are you talking about?" Pugh yelled up at him angrily. "Where do you get off giving all those orders?"

"You can stay there if you want," John said. "But I wouldn't want to be where you are now when the next charge goes off."

"What next charge?" Pugh asked.

"The charge that's going to bury your guns under about ten tons of rock," John said. He raised his rifle to his shoulder and aimed at a cache of dynamite he had planted just over the top of the hole where the outlaws had thrown their guns.

"Shit! We better get out of here!" Dingo shouted, and he led the charge back to the front of the draw.

John fired, and once more the canyon echoed and re-echoed with the roar of a dynamite explosion. This blast used the last four sticks of dynamite, and the effect was to bring half the wall cascading down, burying the guns under tons of shale rock.

When the smoke and dust of the blast cleared away, the outlaws, who had gone to the ground and covered their heads with their arms, looked around. Slowly, coughing from the acrid smell of powder and rock dust, they began brushing themselves off and checking for wounds.

By now, Phil and Muley had joined John and Charley, and all four men were standing on top of the canyon wall, looking down upon the dazed and confused outlaws.

"Any of you boys badly hurt?" Muley called down.

"Muley?" Weasel shouted. "Muley, you're with them? What are you doing siding with them lawmen against your own pards?"

"You mean my own pards who were going to hang me?" Muley replied.

"Muley, you ain't never comin' back to Salcedo, do you know that?" Weasel shouted. "You ain't never goin' to be able to come back to Salcedo."

"I don't care," Muley called back down to them. "I don't intend to ride the outlaw trail no more. I'm goin' straight."

"I should'a hanged both of you yesterday, right after the trial," Pugh said angrily. "You got us trapped in here like rats in a cage. What happens now? Do you start shooting?"

"What happens now is up to you," John said. "If all of you work together, you can probably dig up your guns in about two days."

"Two days?"

"Or, if all of you work together, you can dig your way back through the entry there, in about two hours. Whichever you chose to do is fine with us."

John and the others turned away from the top of the wall and, within a few steps, could no longer be seen by those on the ground.

"Wait!" Pugh called. "Come back here! Come back here, you son of a bitch! You can't leave us like this! Come back here!" The last word echoed and re-echoed through the canyon, and John, Charley, Phil, and Muley rode away.

Austin, Texas, 1930

The governor of Texas stood behind the podium in the Great Hall of the Texas State Capitol Building.

"Ladies and gentlemen, I am pleased to accept, upon the behalf of the great state of Texas, a painting done by one of America's premier artists, Mrs. Lucy Goodnight. This fine daughter of Texas is one of the treasures of our state, having recently been inducted by the American Art Institute into their Hall of Fame.

"The painting she has given to the state is particularly significant, not only because it is one of the finest examples of Mrs. Goodnight's work, but because it represents an exciting moment in our state's wonderful and storied past. The painting, entitled, *Confrontation at Tacora Canyon,* depicts an incident featuring two of our most famous law-men: John Carmack and Charles Dawson. It is particularly significant because those two legendary, bigger-than-life men were Mrs. Goodnight's grandfathers.

"And now, here to unveil the painting, is Mrs. Lucy Goodnight."

Lucy walked briskly over to the draped painting, and the governor put a cord in her hand.

"Now," the governor said. "As this moment belongs to this beautiful lady of Texas, I'm going to step out of the way."

The governor's comment was greeted with polite laughter and a scattering of applause.

"Thank you, Governor," Lucy said.

"Speech," someone shouted.

"Yes, give us a few words, Lucy," another called. "Tell us something about your famous grandfathers."

Smiling, Lucy shook her head. "The governor promised me that I wouldn't have to speak. And, as to my famous grandfathers, I hope this painting will speak for me. After the ceremony, please feel free to come up and study it."

Lucy pulled the cord and the cover fell from the large painting. There were several oohs and aahs from the crowd over the scope and sweep of the painting, and the brilliant colors of the shale, sandstone, and sky. In addition to the breathtaking scenery, it also showed action—two ruggedly handsome men with rifles to their shoulders, a finger of flame coming from the end of the rifles, and a little spray of red mist flying from each of the shredded earlobes of one of several evil-looking men gathered on the canyon floor.

The audience moved close to examine the painting in great detail. Lucy stood to one side, just watching the crowd's reaction. She thought of her grandfathers and hoped that they would have approved of her treatment of this famous incident.

"You have my respect and admiration, ma'am. You have captured the incident exactly as it happened," a voice said.

Looking toward the sound of the voice, Lucy saw a tall, rather gangly young man examining the painting.

"I'm honored that you would think so," she said.

"I've long been an admirer of yours," the young man said. "And I've always wanted to meet you." He stuck his hand out. "My name is Johnson, Lyndon Baines Johnson. I teach school in Houston, but made a special trip here, just to be here for the unveiling."

"You flatter me, Mr. Johnson," Lucy said. She smiled. "But I'm curious, what makes you think I have captured it so accurately? There are many who say this whole incident is just legend."

"Oh, it's no legend," Johnson said.

"How do you know?"

"When I was a boy in grammar school, the janitor who worked there told me this story firsthand."

"First-hand?"

"Yes, ma'am, word for word," Johnson said, pulling on his ear lobes. "My oh my, shootin' off both earlobes must've hurt. Especially if he had ears like mine."

Lucy chuckled at the young man's self-deprecating remark.

"Excuse me, Mr. Johnson, but for the janitor to tell you something as first hand, that means he had to be there."

"Oh, but he was there," Johnson insisted.

"He was?"

"Yes, ma'am."

"I'm curious. What was his name?"

"Mr. Slater," Johnson replied. "Gary Slater."

"Muley!" Lucy said, laughing. "You're talking about Muley!"

"You know, I think some people did call him that from time to time. Of course, I always just called him Mr. Slater. He was a wonderful storyteller, and he could really make a body feel good about himself. 'Lyndon,' he used to say to me. 'A boy with your gift of gab needs to get into politics.' I couldn't have been more than nine or ten then, but that one little comment has sort of stuck with me, and you know, I'm thinking about doing just that."

"Getting into politics, you mean?"

"Yes, ma'am."

"Interesting, isn't it, how a tiny nudge at an early point in your life can be an overpowering push at a much later time?" Lucy said.

"Yes," Johnson answered. "It's like the beat of a bird's wing over a South Pacific Island, generating the trade wind in the Atlantic Ocean that brought Christopher Columbus's ships to our shore."

Lucy laughed out loud. "Muley was right, Mr. Johnson. You *should* get into politics. With the gift of gab, there's no telling how far you will go."

THE LAST GUNFIGHTER SERIES BY
WILLIAM W. JOHNSTONE

Coming In October 2003, *The Burning*